This book is a work of invention. As in all honest fiction, my characters are composites of interesting people I have known first hand and in literature. While elements of the back story are similar to events in my life, the book's characters are my creations. As such they are intentionally unlike actual participants in those same events.

For Annie

Table of Contents

Acknowledgements

Each spark of creativity might have died a charred ember without the air of encouragement. I am grateful to many friends for oxygen. Special thanks go to Laurie Webb for her editorial genius. Laurie is the Escoffier of plot thickening. I also extend my humble appreciation to buddies in Vermont, Florida, and Utah who gave feedback as the project accumulated its vile characters and red herrings. Last, but foremost I want to thank Ann Brown for her tireless faith in me as a writer.

1.

Ice jam

Canaan, Vermont, Friday morning, mid-January, 1982

"One, two . . . bang! bang! That's one way to shut up a bitch!" Monty spoke to himself as his ears continued to ring from the screaming and gunshots. Set against his height and muscular upper body, the 20-gauge double-barrelled shotgun in his gloved hands looked like a giant's toy. He hesitated before re-racking the gun below the other two and letting his gray eyes adjust to the snow-enhanced sunlight splashing through the east-facing window. He surveyed the furniture and blue paisley wallpaper. There were clues to this bedroom's other uses in its filing cabinet, bookshelves, and fly-tying ensemble complete with table, vice, glue, black twine, and menagerie of feathers. But Monty could care less. He glanced back at the warm living room and listened nervously for any change in pattern. Other than his inward ringing, the house was reassuringly still. Monty felt his shoulder and neck muscles loosen slightly.

The most odious task was complete. There would be hard physical work ahead and many tracks to cover, but now there would be no rush, no resistance. He knew it was time to return to the numbers…the old man's step-by-step plan could work, but his next moves needed to be exceedingly careful or this killing would be for nothing. Well, maybe not for nothing. Apart from the old man's schemes,

Monty did see some personal advantage to this murder. Either way, the tedious task ahead would result in a completely convincing pattern of clues. He could smell the acrid gun smoke that his insulated white coveralls had helped carry upward from the basement. Its aroma had trailed him through the kitchen and living room into the smaller corner bedroom where the gun was normally stored. The smell intensified after he thumbed the gun's toplever, opened the action, and pocketed the spent yellow cartridges. He chuckled as he gently closed the action and mounted the gun in its rack. *And where there's smoke* . . . he let the phrase dangle in his mind for a satisfying moment. With the old man's plan, he knew that the fire that was certain to follow would be the gun owner's problem and not his own.

The following morning

The fur ruff on Reilly Bostwick's parka tickled his neck as he scraped frost from the bedroom window. The outdoor thermometer read fifteen below. *Could be worse*, he thought. Just before leaving the room, he carefully lifted the brown barrel 12-gauge shotgun from its rack and pocketed six cartridges. His felt-lined boots echoed his walk across the living room and kitchen, then beat a deeper tune on his frigid back porch. Reilly strapped on his snowshoes and awkwardly walked the shoveled path before climbing the snowbank, ready for his morning hike.

He stepped into the deep snow and paused, studying the gentle hillside with meditating eyes. He stooped to scoop a sample of the loose powder. As he put the snow in his mouth, he slowly closed his eyes. He liked to begin each solo hunt or hike with a unique rite of season. He paused to take stock of his senses and more fully appreciate the patterns within nature's tapestry. The Vermont woods had gradually become his chapel of choice. Although he sometimes described himself as a "Home Baptist," this was a ruse. He couldn't put his deeper thoughts into words even for his friends. These ceremonies remained secret. Lately, Reilly had found a measure of wholeness within nature's unfeeling beauty. He stood with anticipation, waiting for the last errant thought to scamper from his mind. When he felt centered, he opened his eyes, stepped forward, and let his sensory world blossom.

Reilly's eyes sketched in blue, brown, green, gray and white . . . mostly white. His mind's canvas framed the geometric lines of shadows amidst the asymmetry of glacial boulders and the echoing shapes of balsam needles, branches, and trees. These sensations expanded with the smell of cedar, the song of chickadees, and the taste of snow.

He preferred to make his own path, edging parallel to his and Amy's toboggan trail. He welcomed the physical challenge of deep snow. His snowshoes squeaked at the bottom of each uncertain step. In the deep fluff, no surface was firm and the clues to stability were confused: more like balancing on a loose wire than walking a trail. With each step, Reilly sunk a foot or more. He had to lift his legs high to move forward and higher yet to cross drifts and adjust to the upward slope of the hill. Without his wood-and-leather Tubbs, he would have been leg-bound and hip-high in three feet of loosely packed powder. The sky was sliding to overcast, but it was still bright enough to print his eyes with the afterimage of boulders and trees just passed. Occasionally he would misstep, list to one side, and fall in a twisted lurch. *This is authentic North Country fun*, he mused. Reilly liked metaphors, and moving ahead in this border village was a snowshoeing experience. It entailed much energy and more than a little thrashing. He smiled as he trudged slowly into the shadows of spruce trees at the edge of the woods.

He climbed onto the toboggan trail and looked ahead to the three slopes he and his eight-year-old daughter loved to slide. He remembered the fresh smell of Amy's blond hair and how it blew in his face as they careened down the steepest slope. He recalled her scream as they rolled off the toboggan at the twist in the trail that would have sent them airborne through the trees. How they laughed at each other's snow covered faces. Any excuse to regress to childhood was good enough for Reilly, particularly if it cheered up Amy. Trained in biology, he had read that humans are the only primates that play as adults. Reilly thought this droll and took any opportunity to reaffirm his species identity. Life had been too serious lately for them both. Amy was struggling with a difficult year, cut off from her mother and unhappy at school. Sledding was one activity that had not lost its thrill. Reilly pledged himself to find more shared times of delight. Amy's recent friendship with that wild redhead Lottie

Clayton was a superb bonus to his newly discovered love for her mother, Adele. Reilly turned slowly and surveyed the hill ahead. The toboggan trail was a series of connected up-slopes and plateaus that ascend the hillside like a giant set of steps. The surrounding fir trees dominated the winter hill now that the hardwoods had relinquished their autumnal glory.

The north wind puffed fine snow against Reilly's face. As the slope grew steeper, he became breathless and stopped just short of the high trail. Reilly's heart calmed while he looked back to the wood smoke rising from his home below. Pivoting his snowshoes slightly, he saw the valley of Canaan. To the north, the southernmost edge of Canada was a few miles distant. Reilly tightened his parka collar to the wind and rubbed his gloved hands. He knew the day was far too cold for a January rabbit hunt, but aside from his ritual, he needed exercise to dispel the stress of job and home. He agreed with Jefferson: you see more on a walk when you carry a gun. His rabbit gun was an antique hammer double by Thomas Newton. He wondered if Jefferson had ever applied this idea to snowshoes and three feet of fluff.

Reilly could feel his body heat slowly rise and flow through the hood of his parka. The moist updraft fogged his sunglasses but protected his alert Scottish face and clear green eyes from the stinging cold. He touched gloved hand to face as the frost on his reddish brown beard began to melt. *Does facial hair actually insulate? Well,* he thought, *even if it doesn't, it pleases Adele ....besides, it solves the other problem.*

Reilly was thin, yet his 5'11" frame was surprisingly strong and quick for someone with a sedentary job like teaching. This, too, led people to underestimate his age. As he rested and cooled, he thought about his appearance and the protection that a beard offered. He alternately winced and smiled at a quick succession of memories. He remembered being mistaken for a student his first day of high school teaching. There were years of repeating challenges for every six-pack purchased, and then the worst embarrassment: the crappy luck of being carded at Brattleboro's first X-rated movie just after three of his high school students had entered without IDs. He had been twenty-nine at the time, and his friends were merciless. Even now, he knew that without his beard, he would be pegged as twenty-five or younger.

Soon, Reilly's eyes could again feel the heavy, frigid air. The sweat on his forehead was gone, and his sunglasses had cleared. He turned slowly toward the briar bushes next to a small stand of cedars. It was time to observe the morning news written in snow. The tracks near the top of the hill told a story of coyotes, snowshoe hare, and partridge. A partridge had left a snow angel with fine feathers marking the exultation of its rise that morning. The bunny tracks were diffuse and playful, the coyote tracks few but purposeful. There appeared to be 100 rabbits and one eastern coyote, but that was an illusion. Reilly loved to question Amy "How many tracks does a rabbit make?" or "How many moos are there in a cow?" It had been six months since he had recovered Amy in England, where her mother had abducted her. Now he remained deeply concerned about her happiness and safety. Do I know where she is? How do I know for sure? This weekend, Amy was assuredly safe; her only risk was being spoiled by her grandmother in Richmond, Vermont. Knowing this fact helped lessen his anxiety and fear of loss.

The rabbits needed no life insurance that day. Reilly passed up two shots as the wind started filling in tracks. The sky darkened as snow clouds moved overhead. As Reilly reached the crest of the hill, he halted suddenly. The toboggan trail that should have started at the top of the steepest run now ran on to the plateau ahead. Where he had expected to see a snowy furrow from previous hunts, there extended a fresh, ribbon-like trail. Reilly looked fifty yards ahead and was surprised to see someone sitting on a log and facing away. That log with its embedded cant-dog hook was Reilly's favorite resting spot. It was parallel to the trail next to an enormous stump. Reilly was puzzled; he never found others on the back hill, even in summer. He yelled a greeting, but the figure didn't move. As he trudged closer, he could see a woman's blond hair. She wore neither hat nor gloves. His curiosity gave way to dread when he saw the pale parchment color of her extended left hand. She was frozen on the snow-covered log. The snow was disturbed in front of her, but no tracks were visible. Reilly moaned as he recognized the familiar body form and the snowflake pattern on the powder-blue ski parka he had given Klarissa years before. Reilly moved around her and was horrified to see that close-range shotgun blasts had transformed her face into a congealed bloody pulp. He muttered, "Oh my God . . . ."

Reilly felt crushed by this unearthly tableau. Here was his dead ex-wife displayed with her left hand on the stump and her right hand around the rusted cant-dog projecting from within the log. Reilly used to consider that hook a bookmark to the time when it had embedded in the growing tree. It had inspired his informal name for the hill, but now this relic tool was merely a bizarre detail in a surreal scene.

In shock, Reilly staggered backward from the body. His snow-shoes tangled. As he fell, the snow engulfed him. He landed sitting low, looking at Klarissa's body. Suddenly, he was sweating and his breath was shallow. Beyond, he could see the placid valley that, a few moments before, had been his reality. Reilly couldn't muster the will to move. He averted his eyes, groping for something living and familiar. He knew there was personal menace in this death beyond the raw, severed affections it evoked. This was a lucid view of evil. He suddenly felt like the sole keeper of the world's worst secret. What should he do? Klarissa was beyond earthly help. It was time to divulge, to share the grief, to start an unstoppable process. He knew this was a death intended to spin other lives beyond control. And Amy.... What of Amy? How would she be able to stand this misery beyond misery?

While drawing a deep breath, Reilly used a sapling to regain his footing and face away from the body. He staggered to the trail's downslope and compulsively looked back. He was shaking uncontrollably as he turned to trudge down the stormy hill.

A dirty pathway in the snow marked the prints of the town constable, the outpost Vermont state trooper, and the state medical examiner's staff. In the background, Reilly heard the police snowmobile make another trip. The snow was picking up, and the body remained on the hill. The detective's flood of questions had stopped for now. Reilly's cavernous, snow-walled driveway held several police vehicles. Until a few minutes before, the traffic had seemed endless in and out of his basement entrance and up and down the wooden stairs to the kitchen. He felt thankful that Amy was far away. Just the day before, his greatest fear had been that Klarissa would try to kidnap her again. Now he didn't know what to feel beyond a sincere horror and sadness at Klarissa's death. He knew Amy was about to experience another emotional cyclone. Ironically, this one, too, involved her mother. Behind everything he felt was Reilly's knowledge, shared with the gathered constabulary, that he had had the motive, the weapon, and the opportunity for this murder and that these suspicions wouldn't depart with Klarissa's body.

Reilly sat with his head down on the kitchen table for close to an hour. His wandering mind recalled his last glance of Klarissa alive, in England after he had regained custody of Amy. He had just left the London court and had taken the train to Winchester. Amy was climbing into the taxi with her haphazardly packed suitcase. From the time of her abduction until ten minutes before, she hadn't known which parent she would live with or which country she would call home. Klarissa had stood at the door in a lattice arch of flowers surrounding the entrance of the stately brick townhouse and waved goodbye to her daughter with tear-stained cheeks. Beyond those tears, Reilly had thought he could still see arrogance, determination, and anger that meant Amy's future was still not settled.

Reilly's temporary clarity slowly gave way to stunned nausea. His face was white with fear, and he shuddered. He felt an immense internal ice jam blocking the flow of his life with no dynamite or hope of spring . . . wild, random in effect, yet caused, and somehow intended. He felt the water rise as the frigid air made ice and a yet-larger dam. Reilly wondered if he could regain the courage that had helped save him in London. With Klarissa's and his well-known confrontations, Reilly was vulnerable to his most-dreaded fears. Caught in this perfect trap, could he again save Amy?

Misquamicut, Rhode Island

Adele Clayton had no idea why she needed to be cold . . . maybe to numb the sadness. Her wide-set blue eyes revisited the deserted Rhode Island beach, and she shivered as the sea breeze ruffled her soft chestnut hair. Perhaps she had chosen the light jeans and old chamois shirt for this discomfort, if she had chosen at all. The sugary pretense of the family gathering had started to smother her. Despite her dad and uncle Josh's easy authenticity, she knew her uncle's cancer battle was almost over. The other adults' sensitivity to the children glazed the conversation with a cloying optimism that Adele had felt compelled to escape. The penetrating cold allowed her to cry alone. She slowly turned and climbed the sand-scoured front steps of her parents' beach house and slipped inside as the phone in the near bedroom started to ring.

It was late in the afternoon when Reilly's call sounded an alarm from the opposite edge of New England. Adele took the phone from her mother. She braced herself, picking up on the fear in Reilly's voice.

"Oh, honey! That's awful! You must be horribly upset." Adele immediately understood the implications of his discovery.

With the pulse in his neck throbbing, Reilly exclaimed, "Adele, I don't know what this means! It's too crazy! What can I possibly tell Amy? This might destroy her!"

Hearing his panic, Adele changed tack. "Reilly, stay calm. Tell me exactly what's going on. We are coming home tonight....I'll be there to help you in the morning." Adele searched frantically around her mom's desk and found a pen and pad of paper.

Reilly reluctantly described the morbid scene and how he was being offered up as the prime suspect by some macabre sleight of hand. As he explained his discovery, Reilly's leadened words spoke crisis. Somehow, this man and his child who had so recently found an unexpected place in her heart had been caught in a whirlpool of ice water and knives. Despite her sadness, she immediately understood the risk and urgency. Yet she also knew that this call to action would give her some relief, or at least escape, from her uncle's unsolvable problem. As they talked, Adele felt strengthened by Reilly's absolute trust. This in turn allowed her to think quickly and clearly. She understood that her new love was asking her to sort through the rubble of his personal history and to rally his talented band of friends. They both knew that this was a cry for help that would test her gifts to the extreme.

"Reilly, this is a terrible shock . . . . but you can't be sure it's Klarissa. If it is, you'll mourn her . . . *and then maybe we'll want to find an attorney and start our own investigation,....for* the moment, however, you only need to protect yourself and Amy."

Adele scribbled notes as she talked. "You don't want Amy to believe her mother has been killed and then find that she hasn't been."

"No, that would be...unthinkable. . . . Could you help me protect Amy for a few days? She needs to be away from anyone who might talk about this murder."

"Of course, but remember, if this isn't Klarissa, everything could be fine. The whole crisis could blow over before she learns about it."

"Look, I pray that Klarissa isn't dead, but I know what I saw. The goddamn detective is pushing me hard like I'm a suspect. And what about our custody battles and the kidnapping? Wait 'til he learns about that. The police will say I hated Klarissa and killed her for revenge or maybe to stop another abduction. Damn it! Someone plans to put me in jail, where I won't be able to help Amy."

"Maybe," said Adele, "but hold the conclusions. Police usually suspect the person who finds the body. If it isn't Klarissa, they'll move on."

"We can wish, but shouldn't we prepare for the worst? At least if we hide Amy with friends, we'll have time to make plans."

"Listen, I agree we need a temporary shelter for Amy . . . which means she can't be in school for a few days. What if you asked your mother to drive back with her? Our friends will know the right place. Even better . . . I could pull Lottie from school to keep her company. Maybe your mother can stay and look after both of them. We'd have to make up a good cover story, but I think that'll work."

Adele's rapid-fire suggestions helped Reilly focus. "Yes . . . that would buy time. I'll call my mom. Maybe you could call Nancy to find a place for them to stay."

Nancy Watkins was a lean and sophisticated thirty-five-year-old blonde who taught French at the high school. Adele knew that Nancy was an excellent choice and felt encouraged that Reilly was recovering his ability to plan and act.

"We'll be home late tonight if the weather doesn't delay us. I'll call Nancy when we arrive."

Deep in the background, Adele heard the sound of boots climbing Reilly's cellar stairs, then a brief pause and a sharp knock.

"I've got to go. The detective is back. Please remember how much I love you."

Adele whispered her love in reply and said goodbye. As Adele turned to her family to explain her sudden need to drive north, Reilly's internal ice jam returned and started to expand.

2.

Jolted

Canaan, Vermont's most isolated village, was often far removed from the law and worked by rules of its own. Avery Clark, the town constable, often said "Canaan is a one-horse town, and he's me." Avery solved most local problems, providing they came one at a time. With Canaan's low crime rate, he worked another full-time job. This meant that he might not be near a phone when needed. Canaan's police force also consisted of Paul Marshall, the resident outpost state trooper, but during most days, Paul was in Derby or cruising between the Northeast Kingdom's isolated towns an hour or more from home even in good weather. Winter roads, wayward storms, or trouble elsewhere stretched response time further. In most emergencies, residents were likely to get their first help from neighbors. When authorities finally arrived, those same neighbors were on hand to rubberneck and tell officials how to do their jobs.

For a place with two guns in every closet, murders were historically rare. Brazen extensions of "personal freedom" were common along this isolated frontier, but these didn't normally extend to capital crime. So this day was the gossipy exception, and murder was the topic of choice. Gerty Gray, the village newshawk, deciphered the police call codes on her scanner late in the morning, did some snooping, and then started to spread rumors by telephone. Secondary dispersal was vocal and bilingual, radiating from the Northland Hotel, Gulf station, Maurice's Diner, and those few other places folks happened to meet on a snowy Saturday. The story became garbled as to when and where, but whether in Canadian French or English, the core story remained: Reilly Bostwick had discovered a woman's frozen body.

By the time Conner Murphy pulled his asthmatic Land Rover into Solomon's Store just across the bridge in West Stewartstown, New Hampshire, news of the murder had jolted around the village. Conner's engine sniffled to a stop and gave one last defiant kick before expiring. He ratcheted the emergency brake and stepped into the new snow. He was a wiry, tall, former athlete with an eager, handsome face, thick brown, unruly hair, and a Boston Irish accent. He had come from the high school shop where he taught during the week and where he was building a table for the kitchen he was remodeling at home. With the snow picking up, he hoped to get the shopping done in time for Nancy Watkins' party. Conner worked his way through his wife, Karen's, list of staples, picking up eggs, bread, milk, and some pork chops while thinking about beer, potato chips, and a Hershey's bar. The beer would be waiting at home, and he could make the candy and bag of chips disappear on the drive with Karen none the wiser. God, he was hungry. He'd lugged three cords of firewood into his cellar that morning with the hope that he wouldn't have to move another load until February school vacation. They had moved into the place that fall, and, as with many local homes where wood was plentiful, the insulation was optional.

Through the window beyond the cash registers, Conner could see that a near white-out was already starting to make his Rover look like a lumpy marshmallow. As he approached the checkout line, he realized something was in the air. Francine LeGrand turned to tell Conner the news as excited conversation spread through the line at the register. Reilly Bostwick had found the frozen body of a woman who appeared to have been murdered. Word was that she had been shot in the face. Conner masked his pained surprise as he listened for the details, which were not forthcoming. He was a man who took his friends' emergencies as his own. He and Karen must visit Reilly right away. *Maybe we should take Reilly to Nancy's house. All his friends will be there. We'll surround him with the help he needs.*

Nancy's party was planned as a marathon of the Clint Eastwood Westerns filmed in Italy. Conner knew that the group attending was, aside from family, the wealth in Reilly's life: his first experience with so many mutually caring and widely entertaining friends. They called themselves "the gang." Their support had helped Reilly and Amy heal from the divorce and abduction. Conner knew them as exiles from debts, minor scandals, ex-boyfriends, ex-girlfriends, ex-wives, ex-husbands, and civilization in general. Several of them were single parents like Reilly. They were a stellar group of intellects, practical jokers, and home-brewers, and although misfits elsewhere, they cohered famously in Canaan. Most were good, and some were great, teachers. All were assertive, self-confident, and, as the old-timers would have it, "full of piss and vinegar," but between them, they had the skills to do almost anything. Conner claimed eminence as group storyteller. He always had a tale five steps taller than the previous one, and, as Reilly was fond of saying, almost half of them were true.

Later that evening, Conner was uncharacteristically serious when he picked up Karen and headed to Reilly's home a mile west of the village. They were determined to uncover what had really happened and to help distract Reilly from what must have been an awful experience.

The unlit winter entrance to Reilly's house was the cellar door. Visitors who successfully navigated his snow-walled driveway and found the door had to fumble for the light switch and ascend the steep stairs that led to the kitchen. Karen flipped the light switch, and they stomped the snow off their boots as they walked to the base of the stairs. The sound of their boots echoed in the dank and dusty cellar. At the top step, they knocked on the door, then opened it a crack and quietly called "hello."

Trotsky, Reilly's golden retriever, was rousted from a kitchen corner and let out a couple of embarrassed barks. An unenthusiastic "Come in" was the only spoken reply from within. As they widened the door and stepped into the room, they saw Reilly sitting at the kitchen table, sipping Scotch from his one snifter, the fancy bottle snug to his elbow. The room was in uncharacteristic disarray, with jackets and sweaters thrown over chairs, gloves and scattered papers on the floor, and unwashed dishes on the kitchen counter. Reilly was still wearing his snow boots, and his hair was disheveled. His blue-checkered wool shirt was partly tucked in to his old blue jeans. He had written several pages in a yellow legal notepad. He finished writing a sentence and looked up.

"So, how are you doing?" asked Karen gently as she got on her knees to receive Trotsky's kiss and give him the expected hug. She looked back to the kitchen table.

Reilly perked up a bit and turned toward her. She was a lovely woman, almost Conner's height, with deep blue eyes and curly, light-brown hair that accented her smile.

"We heard about the body you found," said Conner. "That must have been god-awful ghastly. Any idea who she was?"

Reilly's eyes widened, and he leaned back abruptly. "I'm damned surprised you haven't heard! I was sure the word would be out by now. Avery Clark's not a dullard, and she's worked with Constable Clark several times."

"Who is she?" questioned Karen as she pulled a ladder-back chair up to the end of the oak kitchen table and sat.

"I'm sorry," said Reilly. "Klarissa. It was her body I found....or at least I'm pretty sure. Her face was destroyed. It was sickening!" Leaning forward to the table while slowly resting his head on his crossed arms, he whispered, "Oh, how I wish it was somebody else."

"Oh shit!" Conner exclaimed as he slumped into the chair opposite Reilly.

Karen and Conner both sat thinking for a few seconds of loud silence as the magnitude of Reilly's woes became evident. Worse yet, they thought of Amy and the horror that awaited her.

Karen broke the joyless pause. "Where's Amy? Does she know?"

"Not yet. She's visiting my mother in Richmond, just east of Burlington. I just talked to my mom. We agreed that I should be the one to tell Amy if Klarissa is dead, but I don't want her to know anything about this until she is identified.

"I don't know what this will do to her," Reilly continued. "Amy just started to recover from the previous mess. She has been so passive for months, but lately I've begun to see smiles and some sparks of personality. She finally has a couple of good friends at school, and there's a local farm boy she likes to play with. Fortunately, she adores Adele and is becoming fast friends with Lottie. But to tell her that her mother is dead? I can't imagine putting her in that world of misery. I feel helpless."

Reilly slumped forward again. Karen moved her chair closer to Reilly and put her arm on his shoulder. "Well, we're here to tell you you're not helpless." Karen had known Klarissa briefly during her last months in Canaan but had never known the two as a couple. Klarissa's death shocked her, but her real concerns were for Amy and Reilly.

Reilly looked up as Conner continued Karen's thought, "Buddy, you won't be hopeless, either, not if we put our heads together. Your friends will take care of you and Amy. But tell me . . . how long do you think it will take the authorities to identify the body? I'm sure we can find some way to keep Amy from knowing until then."

"I have no idea about the identification, but Adele already has an idea for protecting Amy. We'll need help. She didn't say so, but I think she wants us to do some investigation on our own."

"Where's Adele now?" asked Karen, realizing how unusual it was not to see them together on a weekend. Since Reilly and Adele had fallen in love, she'd been his companion to all North Country events. "The best discovery of my life" Reilly called her. Adele was a thirty-eight-year-old widow with a daughter, Charlotte, whom everyone called Lottie. Lottie was the same age as Amy. Reilly had barely recovered from his fractious divorce when he and Adele had met. Reilly's buddies, who knew his emotional fragility, had feared how quickly and completely he was falling for Adele. They had patiently put up with his rambling about her lovely brown hair, open, sensitive face, and deep, dreamy blue eyes. They knew he was completely smitten when, after a couple of brews, he would babble about her beauty and grace. But before long, Adele had earned the gang's trust and affection. Now everyone was delighted to see how Adele had adopted Reilly and Amy with humor and poetic love.

"Adele and Lottie had to leave town quickly Wednesday," Reilly replied slowly. "You know her uncle, Josh Johnstone. His cancer took a turn for the worse, and he wanted to go to a hospice near his family in Rhode Island. I talked with her an hour ago."

"So Lottie didn't have the pajama party she kept telling us about . . . and Amy went to your mother's house," said Karen.

"Right."

"But you say that Adele knows about Klarissa?" asked Conner.

"Yes. She has her uncle settled and is driving back tonight."

Conner had a new thought. "Hey, I thought Klarissa was still living in England."

"I did, too, but I guess we were both wrong."

"What happens if it really is Klarissa?" asked Karen.

"I'm sure I'll become the prime suspect." Reilly leaned back in his chair and put his pen down. His face was paler than usual and new lines were visible around his eyes. He shivered briefly despite the crackling wood stove behind him.

"It's no coincidence that I found the body. I'm the only person who walks the back hill regularly. Hell, I was *supposed* to find her. Someone left her up there on display just for me. Don't spread the story, but this was really weird. She was frozen in place, sitting on a log. I can't imagine why, or who, or anything that makes sense, but someone intends to have me in jail."

Conner was curious for more details, but hearing the agony in Reilly's voice, he decided to lighten the tone. He nodded to the bottle. "Well, that might begin to explain the Scotch, but what are you writing?"

Reilly blinked and deferred the question as some distant part of his hazed mind recalled good manners. "Speaking of Scotch, would you like some?" He started to tuck in his shirt and stand.

"Sit still. I'll pass on the Scotch, your story doesn't do much for my thirst," said Conner.

"What about you, Karen? Would you like some wine?"

"No thanks. Listen. The gang is gathered at Nancy's. All your friends are there. This could be the best time to organize the help you'll need. We've come to take you there."

Karen stood and gave Reilly a hug, saying gently, "Grab a jacket. Pronto...don't think about it."

Reilly nodded, "OK. I'd like the company, and I need to decide what the hell to do next. That's what this is about," he said as he reached across the table to pick up the yellow legal pad. "I'm so worried about Amy. I'm trying to figure out what we can do if I'm arrested."

"Bring your notes. We can do some planning," said Conner. "I'll step in ahead to let folks know what's happened. That'll save a lot of yammering."

"Thanks," agreed Reilly, finishing his last sip of scotch. He stood and reached for his green parka as the wall phone rang. Reilly reluctantly picked it up and was shocked to hear a woman's slow, almost slurred, voice, which he recognized at once.

"It was Klarissa you found, wasn't it, Reilly?"

"Hello . . . Rita," Reilly replied slowly and cautiously. "I don't know what you have heard in the village, but the police have no idea who I found. I couldn't identify the body." Reilly paused a moment to think.

Reilly was disturbed by the question and the voice, which evoked unwelcome memories. How could Rita Webster know any-thing specific about the body he'd found? She couldn't...unless she had some source of knowledge that he and the police didn't. Could it be a lucky guess? Soon after Reilly's marriage had broken up and Klarissa had left town, Rita had started to call like this, never identi-fying herself and starting with a question, usually "Are you lonely?" Though Rita had been Klarissa's friend and confidant for years, Rita had had eyes for Reilly as soon as the ink had dried on the divorce decree. In the months that followed, Rita would join the teachers' parties, drink herself shameless, and dance a raw mating ritual aimed at Reilly. He had come close to giving in one boozy night when she had kissed him deeply, groping him with her free hand. Reilly's instinctive response had been countered by guidance from friends and the increasingly persistent thought that he was being seduced by a spider. *Beware those spinnerets*, he had told himself, as he could almost imagine the sticky threads surrounding him. On that night and all others, he had remained determined not to wake in her web.

Reilly knew that Rita indulged many excesses, sometimes at the expense of her children. Molly, age seven, and Sam, age nine, had been damaged by her antics. Back then, Reilly's rejection had been as gentle as he could make it, but not gentle enough. Now Rita could hardly mask her dislike for Reilly. They still talked occasionally so the girls could play, but Reilly had no illusions of friendship. When Adele had come into Reilly's life, he'd introduced her to Rita so their three daughters could play together. Reilly had chosen not to explain his experience with Rita.

Reilly continued talking while collecting his thoughts. "Rita, let me be honest with you. I need your help. There may be some chance that it's Klarissa, but please…please don't say that to anyone. Think of Amy. A false rumor would devastate her. If it's Klarissa, I need to be the one to tell her. Have you told anyone?"

"No."

"What gave you the idea that it was Klarissa?"

"I just . . . had an intuition that it was Klarissa when I heard the news. After that, I was completely distracted. I found that I couldn't think or get anything done until I knew. That's why I called you. Sorry I bothered you." Rita's voice retained its depressed tone as she abruptly said goodbye and hung up.

"What was that all about?" asked Karen.

Reilly explained the call, then said, "I don't trust Rita. Some of the damaging testimony that Klarissa used in the London court came from Canaan. I've always suspected Rita. I only hope she keeps her word this time and doesn't spread rumors about Klarissa's death."

"Hey, we need to forget that for now. Let's head down to the village," said Conner as he stood and put on his coat.

Reilly stoked the woodstove, and Trotsky bolted down the stairs to the cellar as Karen opened the door.

The Rover started reluctantly. Before they had gone the mile to the village, all knew that the chance of the heater working was zilch. The snow had tapered, and the sky was clearing to make way for another frigid night. The Rover slowly crunched snow all the way to the village as Trotsky frosted the windows with his warm breath.

Meanwhile, at the southern edge of the same small storm, Adele was driving north.

3.

Resolve

Adele's right tires drifted onto the road's shoulder and hit a bump. The muffled thud jarred her and raised her nodding head, now wide awake. She pulled the steering wheel sharply left as the Subaru wagon lurched away from the snowbank and jumped back onto the interstate highway's rightmost lane. A surge of adrenaline hit her as she straightened the car's wavering course and started to regain speed.

"Damn it!" Adele exclaimed. Then, seeing her sleeping daughter stir, she repeated the phrase under her breath. Lottie raised her head slightly, but as the car resumed its steady hum, she slipped back into her current dream, free from the worries that had a vice grip on her mom's mind.

Adele was shaken and disappointed with herself for having come so close to endangering their lives. She hoped adrenaline would keep her alert until she could stop to rest for a few minutes, rub some snow on her face, and drink another strong black coffee. She was beginning to realize how exhausted she was. Although they had completed over half their journey, the miles left ahead would be the difficult ones. It was dark now, and the North Country forecast was snow.

Twenty minutes later, Adele, coffee in hand, drove into the near-opaque curtain of snow squalls north of Concord. As she slowed to thirty-five, she reflexively checked that Lottie's seat belt was fastened. She knew the New Hampshire roads from there to her home would be heavily snow covered. If the storm became severe, she could hope to find a snow plow to follow. She was relieved twenty miles later when the new snow, which now amounted to four or five inches, started to taper off.

Adele's trip to Rhode Island had been an opportunity to settle her beloved Uncle Josh into the hospice he had chosen for his last days. His turn for the worse had come suddenly, and Adele scrambled to get time off from work. The events of the trip and Reilly's anxious call started a concert of worry in her heart. Starting at her parents' retirement home in Rhode Island and continuing for the taxing drive, the discordant music of grief threatened to overwhelm her natural optimism.

Adele recognized this as a forced hiatus in her life, as if God had commanded her to stop and take stock of her feelings. This personal test was unnerving. Wednesday last, she'd been living the simple, grateful life of a single working mom with a loving daughter and a wonderful boyfriend. So much had changed by Saturday evening. Now, both the impending death of her uncle and the possibility of losing Reilly inflamed memories of the tragic accident that left her a widow. She remembered her husband Doug and realized that she still longed for him deeply. When he died, her blessed and lucky life had been abruptly changed in ways that made it difficult to trust and love again. And now, when Reilly needed her more than ever, her fear of losing him was somehow threatening her resolve to save him. Her rational mind cursed it as a stupid trap.

Adele Johnston had been a year out of nursing school when she had met Dr. Doug Clayton in northern New Hampshire. She had chosen Columbia University for the lure of city life, but by graduation, she had grown averse to the city's hectic pace and impersonality. Northern New Hampshire had let her regain the comfortable and authentic rural life she had known as a child. Uncle Josh had influenced her selection of the job in Colebrook. He was a retired newspaper publisher, and his love of the North Country and fly-fishing had led him to split his retirement years between his large home in Colebrook and his camp close to the Canadian border in Averill, Vermont. Adele was his favorite of three nieces, and she had visited him whenever her nursing program would allow. Like many of Adele's high school teachers, Josh had encouraged her to earn a medical degree. Adele had preferred to be a top-notch nurse with the goal of becoming a nurse practitioner and someday running her own clinic. Uncle Josh hadn't argued the issue, even when Adele graduated at the top of her class.

Doug Clayton had been a young resident doctor in Colebrook when they met at the hospital. Adele had broken a few hearts but never thought of marriage until Doug. She believed in him completely, and after two years together, she wanted his child. How they enjoyed trying to make it happen.

Although Adele's life had become more complex after Lottie was born, still she thrived. Lottie's had been an easy birth, and she was a joyful child. As Lottie had grown, so had Adele's nursing career. Adele's relationship with Doug had evolved in harmony as life became all the little daily struggles of work and home, but still, he had been the romantic, bringing Adele flowers and listening to her feelings with an open heart. He had also been a great dad who had prized nothing more than playing with Lottie. She could still picture them rolling in the summer grass or adding finishing touches to a classic snowman.

It had been three years since Adele had gotten the almost-paralyzing phone call. Doug had been overdue returning from a trip to Gorham, New Hampshire, and Adele had been waiting up. She'd answered the phone on the second ring. The state police told her that there had been an accident and that Doug had died instantly. Adele had felt the abrupt visceral sensation of falling and an overwhelming sense of desperation. Grief had surrounded her and slowed her motions. Then, a few instants later, the horrid realization had struck: She'd have to explain to Lottie and then to the world that Doug was gone; yet she had not begun to imagine or accept it herself.

Those painfully out-of-focus times had led Adele into more profound depths of being human. She had learned how faith, ritual, friends, family, and the kindness of strangers offered strength and resolve. As clarity had slowly returned, so had self-sufficiency. She had learned to master the family tasks that Doug had always managed—car and house repairs, tending the finances. Over time, she'd learned to make decisions alone and have faith in her own competence. She'd struggled to be the best single mom she could. At times she was exhausted and frazzled, but generally she could remain patient and fun-loving with Lottie. She had still found the strength to be an exemplary nurse. Single-parenting and career had often left Adele's personal needs as low priorities. She had been tired to the marrow and precariously overextended. She'd worried at the time that she'd never trust as deeply again. Death had wounded her innocence, and now death's umbra had returned.

Thoughts of love and loss had accompanied this last trip south with Uncle Josh. They had agreed at the outset to speak about "important things." To them, this was family code of sorts that referred to Adele's father. Adele had been raised in the Society of Friends and found strength in the community and wisdom of their gatherings. One of her dad's Baptist friends had asked him why he enjoyed Quaker meetings so much, because, from his friend's point of view, they were painfully unexciting. Her father had said that at meeting, people finally talked about important things. Adele had known her last trip with Uncle Josh was in this spirit, and that, as with a Friends service, even the silences would be laden with meaning.

During their visit, Uncle Josh had told Adele that she would be in his will to receive his camp on Lake Averill as well as some of his other assets. With tears in her eyes, she promised to forever toast him at sunset from the porch facing the lake that they loved. He somehow made her feel at ease accepting his wishes, because he had a great skill in making others comfortable. As she drove north through Lancaster, New Hampshire, she remembered their conversation as the seeds planted by his wisdom started to germinate.

"Don't you find loss so much greater, the more deeply you love someone? I love Reilly so much, but I don't know whether I dare to take him as deep in my heart as I did Doug. I fear the great pain of losing again."

Her frail uncle had smiled. "Darling, I know how deeply you love me and I know that you have no regrets about that now or later. The grief will be natural and as it should be." He had paused thoughtfully and continued, "As you know, I've outlived two wonderful wives. After Martha's death, I had determined never to remarry. The thought of that loss was too painful to think of repeating. And, of course, I fell in love again. I married despite the reservations and fears I secretly carried. After Lydia died I finally realized that love is more important and enduring than loss. Love outlives the grief. I still love Martha and Lydia, and in my heart they're always with me. I seldom remember the grief, but I easily recall the love.

"Also, honey, I want you to know that there have been few men in my life I have enjoyed knowing as much as Reilly. He's your man. You two are truly beautiful together. I'll go on my way happily knowing that you have found each other."

As Adele peered through the snow, she repeated Josh's words as the thought blossomed slowly as a rainbow-hued epiphany. *What if I hadn't married Doug and therefore never felt the awful pain of losing him? Would that have been better?* She thought of Lottie and the wonderful times they had had as a family: that fabulous bouquet of memories in her heart. She recognized the laughable absurdity of the question. Of course, she should risk loving again. Her life would always be richer because of extraordinary people like Doug and Josh . . . and now Reilly.

And just as swiftly as the fear and confusion had burst forth, her grief vanished. Her heart slowly settled as her mind opened to the tasks ahead. She took a few deep breaths and drove on. Over the next hour, she felt her anger and determination return and surge through her. As she thought of Reilly's plight, she moved one step deeper in her commitment to him. She wasn't going to just free Reilly; she felt determined to make someone pay for this crime. This wasn't an act of nature or the caprice of some wayward God that a shattered human must accept. This was a man-made abomination, and it could be stopped. This wasn't a loss she needed to adjust to. This was a loss that didn't have to happen.

She would accept failure if she must, but as she sat forward in her seat and peered ahead to the snowy road approaching Colebrook, she was resolved . . . resolved absolutely to save her love.

Then slowly, as in prayer, she whispered, "Thank you, Uncle Josh."

4.

Sofa Surfin'

Waves of music pulsed from Nancy Watkins' cottage next to the almost-frozen Connecticut River on Power House Road. The smell of pizza was starting to radiate from the kitchen. Accents of basil, tomato, and parmesan mingled with the aromas of the hops and yeast from home-brewed beer. The party was well underway. Big Frank Gershwin and Gene Jackman were standing on the couch, knees bent and arms balancing, waving, and gyrating to the music of the Beach Boys. They called it "sofa surfing." Gene, who was about half big enough to be Frank's shadow, was teetering at the edge of balance as Big Frank wildly rocked the couch. Gene taught history, and Canaan's first graders knew and loved Big Frank as Mr. Gershwin. He called them his "munchkins." The rest of the gang, about fifteen in all, were sipping red jug wine and home brew while disposing of the world's affairs, all in good cheer as they relaxed in every nook, cranny, and niche of Nancy's small rental.

The party was taking a break midway through the marathon of spaghetti Westerns. No one cooked spaghetti, but lots of pizza was ordered. Unfortunately, Leo Richards slipped on the walkway ice in view of the picture window and tossed three boxes of pizza high in the air. Some wedges stayed in the box, but many descended into the snow. Leo, meanwhile, lay flat on his back, screeching about the slice that landed on his face. His feat was observed by the surfing crew with a mix of hilarity and alarm. Ross McAlistar and Big Frank Gershwin ran outside and, ignoring Leo, grabbed pizza left and right, rightside up and upside down, and stuffed the slices back in the boxes along with a quart of snow. They lugged the pizza to the kitchen, where the pizza scramble was put in the oven to heat and dry. Leo limped to the front door and stumbled inside, grumbling. Looking up, he saw the living room crew lined up against the opposite wall, each holding up his scores on scraps of paper. They said 5.5, 5.6, 4.5, and 9.9. Katie Griffin (the 9.9) gave him a big kiss and hug.

Less than fifteen minutes later, Nancy was using her red-check-ered wool shirt as a potholder to remove the warm, slightly moist pizza from her oven when the living-room lights blinked on and off. Everyone turned to look at Conner, who was standing just inside the front doorway with his hand on the wall switch and Trotsky by his leg. He seized the brief silence. "Listen up. I want you to hear the news before Reilly comes in." Big Frank stifled the Beach Boys as Conner continued. "You probably heard about the body he found. Karen and I just talked him into coming here tonight. They're still in the car. I told Reilly I'd step ahead to tell you what you need to know. It comes down to some scary news. Reilly thinks the body he found was Klarissa." He paused to let that sink in. Frank killed the stereo, and the room went from muddled attentiveness to shock-induced sobriety. Almost everyone knew the saga of Reilly and Klarissa. Conner went on, "Worse than that, Reilly figures he's the prime sus-pect. We don't know what this will mean for Amy, but she and Reilly are going to need our help."

A few moments later, as the group noisily discussed his quandary, Reilly stepped into the living room. Welcomed with hugs, handshakes, and vows of support, he soon found himself sitting by the woodstove with a plate of pizza and a mug of home brew, sur-rounded by a cluster of his closest friends.

Joanie Maynard stopped Karen at the kitchen door. Joanie taught fourth grade and had recently been inducted into the gang. She had met Reilly but didn't know his history with Klarissa.

"Is Conner saying that Reilly found his ex-wife's body and that she had been murdered?" After Karen's grim nod, she continued, "But why would he be the main suspect? I've heard Klarissa's name, but no one in the village ever pointed her out to me. I'm confused."

"Joanie, it's a long story, and this chapter doesn't make much sense. Klarissa filed for divorce two years ago last fall and got an apartment in the village. It was going to be an amicable Vermont homegrown, lawyer-free agreement with joint custody of Amy. In fact, all that winter, Amy went back and forth between the two households. In the spring, Klarissa suddenly shifted completely. She hired a lawyer, wanted sole custody, and resolved to take Amy to England to live."

"But, how could she do that?" said Joanie.

"Klarissa was born in England to an English war bride mother and an American G.I. father. She has . . . I mean had, dual citizenship. Klarissa's parents have a second home in England. They were living there at the time of the divorce, and they wanted Klarissa and Amy with them. Anyway, Klarissa quit her job, and she and Reilly went to court in early August that year. Reilly fought tooth-and-nail to keep Amy here. A couple of weeks later, the court announced its judgment giving Reilly custody. Klarissa left Amy and Canaan the next day and was in England a week later, apparently devastated by her own foolishness."

"Wow, poor Amy! I had no idea. That was a rough way for Reilly to start single parenting wasn't it?" said Joanie. "But, if Reilly won, where's the murder motive?"

"Last summer, Reilly sent Amy to England to be with her mother. The week before school started here and a day before Amy's flight back, Reilly got a call from Klarissa saying that she wasn't returning Amy and that she had enrolled her in an English school."

Karen paused and then continued, "The next part was extraordinary. Reilly somehow managed to bring Klarissa to court in London. Late that September, he flew to England for a week. It took a lot out of him, but he won the case and returned with Amy. We were frightfully relieved for both Amy and Reilly. Klarissa was flaky, and we all felt Amy's best bet was with her dad. So you can understand why Reilly wouldn't be pleased to see Klarissa in Canaan and why some folk might think he'd want her dead."

"Wow," said Joanie. "There's more drama in this tiny village than I suspected."

In the meantime, the next Western was underway in the subdued living room. Reilly, Karen, Conner, Ross, Cisco, and Suzanne, who had been seated at the back of the group, quietly repaired to conference in Nancy's bedroom carrying a few kitchen chairs. The phone rang as they closed the door.

Nancy went pale within seconds of picking up the phone. She cupped a hand over her ear and quickly dragged the phone's long cord into the kitchen. She shut the door and slid downward to the floor with her back against a kitchen cabinet. Minutes later, her eyes were dilated and she looked in shock as she joined the group in her small bedroom. The light spilled out into the living room as she entered.

"Damn it!" she exclaimed. "I've got more scary news!"

Reilly sat at the end of Nancy's bed nearest the door. Suzanne and Cisco fully occupied one side of the bed. Conner and Karen were on chairs, and Ross stood leaning against the wall near the room's far corner. The group turned toward Nancy as she shut the door.

"I just got a call from Pat Black at the hospital in Colebrook. Last night, she stopped by Adele's house to surprise Amy and Lottie with a treat for their pajama party. She didn't know about their last-minute change in plans. Pat saw a light in the girl's room, but nobody answered the bell. She decided to step in to leave the treat and a note. When she opened the door, a tall, burly man in dark clothes and a ski mask shoved the door into her, jamming her wrist and knocking her clean off the porch and down the front steps. She said he ran behind the house and a few minutes later she heard a snowmobile. When Pat looked around inside, nothing seemed to be missing or out of place. There was no sign that the guy was about to walk off with the TV or that kind of thing. Pat then found that the phone didn't work, and when she tried to start her car, it had been sabotaged like the phone. She walked a half mile to a neighbor's house to hitch a ride to the hospital. Fortunately, only her wrist is broken. They have the pain under control, but she's pretty shook up. Today she tried to find Adele, with no luck. She also tried to call Reilly but was using the wrong number. She called here figuring that I'd know where Reilly was. Apparently, she didn't know about Klarissa."

Reilly stood up abruptly, shocked by the image of horror and surprise in the wall mirror. He recognized a man at the marginal edge of coping. "Oh, my holy God!" he exclaimed. "This all has to be connected! Amy would have been there if Adele had stayed home. I think this was another attempt to abduct Amy!" I need to call my mother to make sure she and Amy are all right."

"You may be right," cautioned Conner, "but there have been a few break-ins in Colebrook looking for drug-buying money. Maybe he was just about to take the TV and stereo but got interrupted."

Cisco's deep voice added, "When it comes to safety, sometimes it's best to jump to conclusions. Reilly's right. We need to act as though these events are connected. It could be thievery, but screwing up the phone and car suggests a professional's touch."

Nancy put a hand on Reilly's shoulder, saying, "I agree. Let's figure out how to guard Amy when she returns. We should also protect Adele and Lottie."

When Reilly's adrenaline surge began to subside, he explained Adele's ideas for protecting their girls. He told Nancy to expect a call from Adele, then before excusing himself to call his mother, asked his friends to consider the best place to hide Amy and Lottie.

After returning from Nancy's kitchen, Reilly said, "My mom and Amy are fine. I believe Sal Blanchard, who gave her the ride, is the other person who knows exactly where Amy is, and Sal is still out of town, so things should be OK for now."

In the meantime, Karen and Conner had volunteered their home in Pittsburg, New Hampshire, a few miles to the north. Reilly agreed, then took out his yellow pad and, after a pause, continued.

"If this is another kidnapping, I don't see who benefits. I was bled white by the last affair, so the idea of ransom from me is ridiculous. With Klarissa dead, who would want to kidnap Amy? It makes no more sense than the bloody body on the hill." A dejected tone resonated in Reilly's normally self-assured voice.

"My worst fear is that I'll be arrested. That's why I've written down some ideas . . . things you might do if I am."

"Unfortunately," added Suzanne, "we don't have enough puzzle pieces to see the picture. We need to uncover some new pieces on our own. Let's not just sit around waiting for this SOB's next move."

"One more thing," added Reilly. "If I'm sent to jail, please let Adele take the lead? You won't believe how fast she comes up with ideas. Give anything you discover to her. She'll fight like a wounded she-bear to protect the two of us, but I also don't want her to place herself or Lottie in danger. So please protect her. This murderer is a cruel, soulless bastard."

Within half an hour, they started to implement their plan. Conner and Karen went home to prepare for guests. Nancy set out to visit Pat Black at her home in Colebrook. Ross would contact Trooper Paul Marshall in the morning. Before he left to guard Adele's house for the night, Ross also volunteered to have a talk with his old friend and occasional bed-mate Rita Webster. The group would meet again at two o'clock the following afternoon at Cisco's and Suzanne's house. Within minutes, the group had dispersed through the trailing edge of the storm now reduced to the occasional snowflake.

5.

Beak

Reilly's return home in Conner's Rover was watched by the same cruel eyes that followed the departure of other gang members from Nancy Watkins's house. Back in the village around midnight, the man barely visible in a second-story turret window was easing himself out of his latest fit of rage. *"Montgomery Mitchell,"* he mumbled slowly. "Monty" had a dignified, if uppity, ring to it. He rubbed his strong hands through his thick brown hair while he repeated his new name slowly several times. Sitting in the dark, looking down at the Canaan Gulf station, he stretched his muscular arms, popped his knuckles, and reviewed his new identity. His small gray eyes were close set, and his strong beak nose suggested an iron resolve. He reassured himself that if he could get the abduction back on track, Monty could still be more than a borrowed name. *"Identity and money, identity and money."* He repeated the new chant softly as he adjusted the fit of his new blue shirt where it was binding with his shoulder holster.

The backlit turret showed growing signs of Monty's setback and recent regression. The neat bed and carefully dusted sills were at odds with the overflowing ashtray and beer bottles dripping on the floor. The small living room behind the turret had not yet been soiled by the mood that Monty struggled to escape. It provided better evidence of his secular conversion. Here, his tools and toiletries were visible and available for use. A folder, notepad, and travel brochure were precisely stacked on the table. His new wardrobe, much unworn, was neatly folded in an old oak dresser. His possessions were few, but truly there was a place for everything. For now, remnants of his prior and occasionally revisited persona were lodged in the closet. These included his shit kickers—a mud-clogged pair of frayed hunting boots—and a massive, red-checked wool jacket. Two ragged flannel shirts were crucified on hangers, and three more were pushed into the corner of the upper shelf, covering several yellowing pairs of underwear. A surprisingly clean set of white coveralls separated the hung shirts from two pairs of jeans that must have served several years of unwashed duty.

Monty scanned north to the tall snowbanks centering the road from Beecher Falls. He could easily see both ways on Route 114, which bordered his outpost and the north end of Fletcher Park. The snow by now had ended in a clear sky, and the park was white with reflected starlight. His chair was next to the turret window in the old three-story blue Victorian rooming house on the corner of the commons. From there, he could scan and track his prey below. This position easily revealed travel to and from Bostwick's house west of the village. If he pivoted to his left, the other windows were well situated to observe across the town commons and the road south. His surveillance task, despite its view of all Canaan's comings and goings, was painfully boring apart from his excursion out earlier in the evening. The most exciting event revealed from his turret was a car with a flat tire limping irregularly into the Gulf station. Time was punctuated by the progressively less frequent passes of the plow truck with the rushing, scraping sounds of metal on pavement. The plow men by now were asleep. His watch was nearly over for the evening; nonetheless, Monty was on full alert because he knew the scheduled call would come in five minutes, and his news for the old man wasn't the best.

Identity and money. That was the deal, and for him, the perfect motivation. More than that, they were the last two remaining values in his system designed for one simple outcome: survival at any expense. If the old man's scheme worked, the equation would change. Then a new identity, plus abundant cash, would equal years of freedom to savor and squander.

"Montgomery Mitchell," he repeated, trying to engrave the words into memory. The old man had taught him that identity isn't just the magic of documents and disguise. It's behavior. Monty already had the documents, and they were perfect. He had used them on his trip to Springfield, Massachusetts, to rent the apartment and leave off ransom letters and photos. He trusted that now the money would follow. It was uncanny what the old man knew about him and what he must do unerringly to become Montgomery. He knew that for the rest of his life, he'd still leave a trail of fingerprints that didn't match his identity. Any false step could undo him. Nonetheless, the old man had taught him how and where to beat the system. Still, he knew that all bets were off if he couldn't snatch the girl.

With each phone call, Monty practiced this name and the affectations peculiar to it. The old man was a perfectionist who had shown Monty more ways to kill a person without a weapon than Monty knew with one. He had come to the commune as a stranger and recited the details of Monty's California crimes. Monty had been determined to kill the old coot and flee for new shelter. Then, when he took out his gun, the old man had calmly mentioned papers that would be mailed to the police upon his death. The old man was always faster and smarter and, unlike Monty, able to defy legal retribution. This was a man to follow . . . at least for now.

"Yes, this is Monty speaking," he muttered as he untangled the phone cord. "Yes, sir, just as you requested. I've been watching all evening. His car never went by. I did see a Land Rover come from Bostwick's direction and returned that way later. I think I've seen it in the school lot. I've been working on that list of teachers and registration numbers you wanted. I think the Rover belongs to Conner Murphy. I couldn't see in the back. Bostwick could have been there. I went across the bridge to West Stewartstown, got the truck, and drove by the houses in town where I have seen groups of their cars in the past. There was a gathering on Power House Road, and the Rover was there. Then I drove by Bostwick's house. There were no lights on and no fresh tracks in the snow in front of the garage. There were tracks at the mouth of the drive, so I think I know where Bostwick has been. I didn't see any sign of the girl. I know we're looking for a babysitter where he keeps his daughter, so I decided to watch the party as it broke up. I parked nearby and followed several cars around the village to see if any of them picked up their kids from the same sitter. Two of the cars stopped at the first trailer in Boutin's trailer park and picked up kids. I think one of the other teachers lives there. I'll find out. Then another car stopped on the village commons almost in view of my front window. Then a fourth car made a pickup at the same house. The Rover headed toward Bostwick's place an hour ago just as I expected. I've been listening to the scanner all day. Through late afternoon there was lots of coming and going from Bostwick's, but I didn't hear any mention of his daughter. He wouldn't have her at home now, so I'm looking at his friends, but I still haven't found that Clayton lady who has looked after her in the past. It's a small town, and there aren't many possibilities. I doubt that Bostwick will be free tomorrow, but if he is, I'll be on his trail, and I think he will lead me to the girl."

"Listen." The voice on the line was self-assured. "Like I told you . . . we have two, maybe three, days to pick up the girl. And I emphasize at your peril that she must not be harmed. You need to know that after three days, we'll abort the plan and hide all our tracks, or both of us will be at more risk than when we started, both from the police . . . and from each other." He dangled that last phrase in the air, letting Monty know that he was still one step beyond the obvious. "Here's what I want," he said in a low, commanding tone as he laid out detailed plans with contingencies for the surveillance, the next contact with him, and exact instructions for what Monty should do once he found the girl.

6.

Fifteen Stitches

Early that Sunday morning, Ross McAlistar stood in Adele's slippery driveway with a water-soaked left pant leg. The cloth was getting stiff as it froze. Although he was amused to watch Adele speed-exercise her golden retriever, a warm living room was beckoning. Ross was waiting to make sure that all Adele's questions had been answered before she left for Reilly's. Fortunately, Miss D'Ory, the pup, was beginning to slow down. Successive tennis ball retrievals in nostril-deep snow were getting a bit much. It wasn't anything like running. It was more like solid-state dog paddling, and D'Ory the Dog was flagging.

Ross showed his typical exuberance for all such nonsense. As he stood watching, he squinted his sparkling brown eyes and formed a mischievous smile that was framed by his bushy brown hair and roughly trimmed beard. While no more than Reilly's height, Ross had a chunky build and remarkable strength. In the opposite season, he'd exercise this trait by donning his kilt to compete in regional tournaments of Scottish games. Nancy Watkins had once witnessed a wide-eyed pack of fourth graders as they rounded the corner of the elementary school near the shop entrance. There, they had seen Ross practicing the event called tossing the caber. Later, Nancy had heard the group walk off exclaiming how Mr. McAlistar could balance and throw telephone poles. His friends had collected a slew of "Ross stories." Leo Richards' latest was from the week before. He swore to the gang that that he had seen Ross challenge the full clientele of the Cedar Lounge in Colebrook (alias The Swamp) to a "bonnie-good bar fight." Apparently, a logger at the next table had heard Ross braying about his fine home brew and had chosen to comment loudly that "home brew tastes like dog doo." The guy's whole table of giants had roared, and Ross had got pissed. Ross had stood and began to pick up the table. Leo had tackled him just in time to drag him to the sidewalk. According to Leo, they were lucky to have escaped alive.

Ross had been lured to Canaan by Conner Murphy. Reilly would say that it was Conner's hyperbole that had turned the trick, although Ross wasn't sure what that meant. Ross and Conner had conspired to do abundant mischief as college buddies. To classmates, they were best remembered for their extravagant style when streaking the halftime show of the centennial homecoming game. Each had worn only black sneakers and carried a small American flag aloft on a pole. Their paint jobs had been especially notable. Conner had been in red face, Ross in white, and both had painted their genitals blue. Fortunately for Ross, Conner, and the Canaan school system, their reputations had never caught up with them. And now, marriage had toned Conner down to an acceptable level of hyperactivity. Ross, who had arrived still recovering from a nasty divorce, seemed to have tethered most of his loose-cannon ideas, but the occasional prank was to be expected. Reilly, although quiet and intellectual, had always seemed to attract friends "writ large in spirit." Ross filled that bill. Both Reilly and Ross were enthusiastic for their home brew. Before Reilly had met Adele, he and Ross had spent many hours sampling their bubbly product while decrying what Reilly used to call "the dearth of Canaan pulchritude." Ross preferred to call the problem 'lack of nookie.'

Ross could see that D'Ory was now exiting the high snowbank on spaghetti legs. The dog sat awkwardly next to Adele as she prepared to throw again.

"D'Ory is looking at you like you're some madwoman," laughed Ross as she wound up and made her longest throw yet.

This time D'Ory ignored the ball, never taking her eyes off Adele. Her ears were cocked, and her face expressed a slight sense of puzzlement. She had worked up a lather making umpteen successive retrievals, and she had just decided that she had had enough of this stupid game . . . reputation be damned.

"Well, maybe. . . . I don't know about madness, but I'm wound-up. When I'm in a hurry like this I need my special shortcut to dog exercise. Unfortunately, I think Miss Pup has caught on to me."

"I think she doesn't care if that ball is lost 'til the spring after next."

"Maybe you're right. I had Reilly try this game with Trotsky. You know, the old boy looked absolutely disgusted and wouldn't even make a first try. Reilly calls him a 'treiver and says he's usually only interested in bringing himself back. That is, unless there's a partridge, woodcock, or duck involved. Reilly says in that department, he's a genuine re-triever."

"So tell me," continued Adele as they walked toward her car, "is there anything else I need to know about the plans you made last night?"

"The only thing I didn't mention was the strange call Reilly got from Rita Webster." Ross explained what had happened and how he planned to visit Rita later that day.

His explanation had a clear innuendo of some connection between Reilly and Rita that Adele, to her discomfort, didn't know about. She had witnessed a strange coldness in Reilly's and Rita's interactions like those she had seen in former lovers. She suddenly felt conflicted that Reilly had never mentioned any feelings for Rita. That sharp pain of doubt was most unwelcome. She would have to put it aside. Reilly had enough problems. She would save her questions until after Ross had talked with Rita.

Ross had arrived late the previous evening after Lottie was asleep. He had told Adele about the break-in and the gang's plans and then camped out near her front door on guard duty. He also had promised Adele to spend the morning with Lottie so she could visit Reilly. Because of this arrangement Lottie woke to an unexpected opportunity for mischief. While Adele and Ross were finishing their conversation Lottie sat watching TV cartoons with a faint smile and an unusually deep sense of satisfaction. She had been delighted after waking to find Ross fully dressed and snoring in their living room. He was overflowing their small couch, and this made him the perfect target in Lottie's mind. Ross was the gang's most notorious practical joker, and both Lottie and Amy had owed him a good one. Two weeks before, Ross had talked them into believing that Bigfoot's first cousin lived in the deep woods behind Conner's house in Pittsburgh, New Hampshire. Reilly had straightened them out after a fearful evening punctuated by high-pitched screams. That morning, Lottie had felt that she should give Ross a special, well-deserved wake-up call, so she scrambled back to her room. After a quick search through her desk, she had found a partridge feather and a stout rubber band. She hitched the feather to her mother's broomstick. Ross was happily snoring and snorting when Lottie had begun tickling his nose with the feather. She figured that water torture would be far more fun, but this would have to do for now. She knew Amy would be proud of her, as she had ever-so-lightly brushed the feather across Ross's nose and then paused to give him time to snooze again. She gradually increased the intensity of the tickle, and Ross made logy motions with his arms as if slowly swatting flies. His balance on the couch had been precarious, and he rocked as he moved. With that pattern established, Lottie's precocious mind returned to water torture. She stifled a giggle, quietly put down the broomstick, and tiptoed to the bathroom, where she soaked Adele's bathrobe with ice-cold water in the tub. She snuck back into the living room and, ever-so-carefully advancing on her knees, pushed the soaked bathrobe so it was laid out lengthwise below the couch. She returned to feather duty and induced Ross to rocking again. After a few minutes, Lottie's efforts had paid off richly. Following one particularly effective feather –to-nose contact, Ross made a more vigorous swat, the momentum of which had carried him off the couch and splat onto the icy terrycloth.

Ross had known immediately that he had been had, and by whom. He jumped up, half soaked, hooting and hollering, then playfully chased Lottie to her bedroom, where she locked the door. She screamed happily all the way.

Adele had been unaware of the hullabaloo until she had heard the thump of Ross hitting the floor and the ensuing screams. While peeved about her bathrobe and the puddles, Adele realized that the event satisfied some deep inner need for poetic justice. For his part, Ross seemed to enjoy all the teasing and assured Lottie that he'd get even. The interruption was a relief for Adele.

Prior to the living room uprising, when Adele had thought the household was still asleep, she had been quietly making phone calls. She talked with Pat Black about her injury and the break-in. Then she called Mary Hubbell, her supervisor at the hospital. Adele made an emergency request for her two remaining vacation days. Mary was fond of Adele and pleased with her work. When she heard of Reilly's plight, she granted Adele's request and wished her luck. Now Adele talked with Ross to settle other details.

As they stood talking next to her car, Adele gradually found the merriment of the morning displaced by deeper concerns. It was time to visit Reilly. She turned to Ross and signaled D'Ory to return to the house.

"So, Ross, maybe you ought to get inside while I warm the car. Your leg is soaked. Thanks for looking after Lottie. See you this afternoon at Suzanne's.

"I'll help that wild Indian of yours clean up. Good luck with Reilly."

"Thanks, Ross."

Ross went back to the house while Adele started her Subaru. Within a mile, she was deep in thought about the challenge ahead. She was still distressed with the uncertainty and fear that had visited her the day before. Now the violation of her own home heightened those feelings and focused new concerns for Lottie. The sum of these thoughts conspired to make her painfully aware of the risks she was about to take.

She knew that she'd need information from Reilly, but she also wanted him to feel hopeful. She had laid awake much of the night thinking about how to protect Reilly and Amy. She wondered how

deeply the police investigation would probe. After all, the trail liter-
ally and figuratively led to Reilly. How hard would they look for
other suspects? Adele was now certain that Reilly needed an inde-
pendent investigator.

She had some doubts about her competence in this role. She
knew Reilly needed a superb detective. Her only prior experience
with murder was the dozens of mysteries she had read and the crimes
she followed in the papers. *Not the best training*, she thought, *but
still not hopeless*. Despite her qualms, she knew that no one else
would volunteer for the job. So that made her the most qualified
applicant. Reilly would protest, but she was starting to regain the
energy and determination she'd need. This was a bluffer's game, and
she was damn sure she wouldn't show her doubts to Reilly.

Sunday morning had come at Trooper Paul Marshall far too fast.
His infant daughter was yowling in the crib next to their bed. His
wife, Francine, was frying eggs in the kitchen at the other end of their
snug log home in Canaan village. "Please check on Jenny," she
called out. Paul tripped on a shoe as he entered the bedroom and
bounded off the near wall. When he regained his balance, he cursed
Francine's white Angora cat, which had been asleep atop his uniform
on the ironing board. The ruckus put the cat on full alert. Paul
cursed, picked up the offending shoe, and winged it across the room
as the white furball disappeared into the closet. This triggered Paul's
last memory of the evening before, when beer bottles had been flying. Two drunks had been lobbing empties in the Northland Hotel
bar, then slugging out their differences toe-to-toe in the parking lot.
On the sidelines, a shop-worn brunette, the apparent object of their
desires, had watched the joust with glee. A developing headache
reminded Paul that this only happened just a few hours before.

"Damn cat," he yelled again as he went to pick up Jenny.

"What did you say, dear?" Francine called from the kitchen.

"Nothing, honey," Paul lied as the cute baby cooed and
squirmed in response to her dad's attention. The cat was the bane of
his home life, and the feeling was mutual. Francine had picked the
name Evenrude because she purred like the family's outboard motor.
Paul had shortened it to Rude.

The morning continued in the same theme when the phone rang insistently just after he sat down to breakfast. It was the second call that morning. He had just been on the line with a local teacher named Ross McAlistar about a break-in across the river in West Stewartstown. The guy had the crazy idea that it had been a kidnapping attempt. Paul had politely reminded him that this was New Hampshire business. Now it was Detective Sergeant Roland Coté, and no, he couldn't call back. Roland was about to leave Derby to drive to the morgue in Burlington, and Paul's eggs would wait.

"What did you find about Bostwick?" Coté began.

"It was like Aubry, the constable, told us yesterday and Bostwick himself hinted. The woman could be his ex-wife. People in town reminded me that she moved to England after they divorced. He got custody of their daughter. That may have something to do with his motive."

"How so?"

"Last summer they had a battle over the girl. Bostwick had full custody and sent her to England for a summer visit. She wasn't returned. He flew to England and somehow brought her back. Must have cost him a mint. From the looks of his digs yesterday, it was a mint he didn't have. The abduction was a violation of the Vermont court orders that gave him custody, so technically, the ex-wife could have been arrested if she reentered Vermont.

"Wait, this is strange," he continued. "It didn't cross my mind at the time, but I just got a call from another teacher who said there was a break-in across the river Friday night at the house where Bostwick's daughter was supposed to be staying. She wasn't there due to a last-minute change in plans. This guy thought it might have been a kidnapping attempt. It sounded screwy to me at the time."

Coté cleared his throat. "All that adds to the reasons I want you to question Bostwick again. You remember that the woman had some clothing with British labels. Our working assumption should be that it's Klarissa Bostwick."

"From what I hear," Paul interrupted, "it should be Klarissa Wilcox. The people I talked to say she left the state using her maiden name. It's possible that either name could be on her passport."

"Let me tell you what's going on here," continued Coté. "Klarissa Whichever's father, Fulton Wilcox, is coming to the morgue this morning to attempt an identification. I'm driving to Burlington to talk with Susan Prescott afterward." Paul knew that Susan was the state's chief medical examiner.

"Chances are," Coté continued, "without a face and with her teeth scrambled by the blasts, we won't have an answer today. Yesterday when we compared notes, most of us believed that the woman was killed elsewhere and hauled up the hill to where she was found. If so, we lack the site of the murder as well as the weapon. We found two spent twenty-gauge cartridges in the snow near the body. Assuming they killed her, we'll be able to identify the shotgun if we find it. I want you to question Reilly. You saw his guns yesterday. Take another look at the twenty-gauge. I see that you recorded its make and model. I need serial number too. The lab says the cartridges were reloads. See if Bostwick loads his own ammo. If he does, ask him for a few cartridges that have been fired through that gun."

Coté told him to call the New Hampshire State Police about the break-in. Then he dictated a list of specific questions for Bostwick. Trooper Marshall printed them carefully, one after the other, as his fried eggs approached room temperature.

The call came soon after Reilly had finished shoveling his driveway. Trooper Marshall was making sure he was home late morning before stopping by with a new set of questions. Reilly hung the phone on the wall while gazing out his living room picture window that faced east toward the village. His mood brightened as, finally, there was some good news. It came in the form of a green Subaru station wagon turning in to his freshly shoveled, snow-walled driveway.

Adele, tired yet perky, followed the smell of coffee up Reilly's cellar stairs and opened the door. Trotsky and Reilly both rushed forward for attention; Reilly won.

After an extra-long snugly hug, she looked down and said, "Sorry, Trotsky."

Reilly took her coat and gazed at her shapely figure in new blue ski pants. Her short, chestnut-brown hair caught the morning sunlight from the kitchen window. He couldn't resist saying, "Did I ever tell you how truly callipygous you are?"

She turned and lightly grabbed his collars with both hands and looked at him nose to nose.

"Listen, Buster, that had better be a compliment."

"Oh, it is, my love," said Reilly with a limp grin.

She bit his nose lightly and said, "Well, I'm glad you haven't completely lost your sense of humor." Adele sat at the old oak kitchen table, spread her elbows on top, and rested her chin on her hands. Reilly threw a few logs in the living room woodstove and then sat opposite her.

Adele looked across the table and gave her best imitation of Oliver Hardy, "Well, here's another fine nice mess you've gotten us into, Stanley."

Reilly's smile faded. Although he was extremely happy to have her company, his mood began to plummet again as his mind returned to the hill. Reilly gave Adele a more complete telling of his morbid discovery and the plans the gang had made the night before.

He explained the call he had just received from the state police and that he expected Paul Marshall to arrive soon. "I'm afraid that I'll be in jail and not able to fight back or take care of Amy." Reilly rested his head on his arms as tears came to his eyes. "She's so sensitive and has been through so much already. . . . I thought her life was starting to improve. She doesn't need this."

"So, wait a minute. Just relax. You're not guilty, agreed?" Adele stated.

Reilly reply was muffled. "Agreed," he said without lifting his head.

"So that becomes our first and most important fact. I need to ask you some tough questions . . . bear with me. When we talked yesterday, you said it was Klarissa. How do you know?"

Reilly sat up abruptly as gruesome memories flooded his mind. "Her face was sickening, bloody, and changed beyond recognition, but it was her . . . size . . . shape. . . . She was wearing the blue winter parka I gave her . . . . The rest of her clothes were typical of what she wore. Here . . . take a look. I just found it." He pulled a snapshot from within the pages of his notepad. It was a winter picture of Klarissa standing on their snowy, windblown porch, not ten feet from the camera. "See, that was the jacket she was wearing. It's just too big a coincidence."

Adele studied the photograph carefully, then handed it back to Reilly, who tucked it into the yellow pad. Adele had never met Klarissa, but she remembered other pictures of her pretty, long blond hair, wide-set blue eyes, and upturned nose.

"Well, you're probably right, but the medical examiner will be looking more closely than that." She reviewed for Reilly what she understood would be needed for an identification.

"Too bad they can't take genetic identification beyond blood type," said Reilly. "You know, in the sci-fi I read, they do it with chromosomes and DNA. It should be possible soon, but it seems to be some kind of biochemical problem."

"Maybe someday," said Adele as she got up from the table, walked into the kitchen, and turned to face Reilly. "From what you tell me, I think she wasn't murdered on that hill. So there's a bloody crime scene elsewhere. We'll also have to see if the police find the murder weapon. If they find either . . . that could take the heat off you. So this isn't the time to get discouraged. You have been set up with some clever evidence, but frauds leave their own clues. That's what we'll search for. We just need to focus." Adele walked next to the table.

"Tell me about where the body was found. You showed me that log when we hiked your back hill last fall. I remember the cant-dog. Funny, we sat that same place talking about log drives and lumber barons. What a creepy thought that is now. We know you walk back there all the time . . . and that your approach can be seen from the road. Someone could probably predict that you would find the body. Could the killer have gotten the body there in any other way than your toboggan trail?"

"If the police found another trail, they didn't mention it. I doubt they did. All the tracks out there seem to lead back this way."

"From what you've said, do you have any doubt that it's Klarissa?"

"I assume she's dead or . . . there would have to be some dark, elaborate fraud. That's hard to imagine. Still, I think we need to check a few things on our own. While I was waiting between police questions, I tried calling Klarissa's number in England. It would have been late in the evening their time. There was no answer. Maybe I'm just trying to hold off telling Amy and want to find something less horrible to say. I just pray that we'll find the evidence that keeps me out of jail."

Adele sat again and replied, "there's a lot happening here. We need to view this crime, knowing you're innocent and being set up. Now tell me the ugly part. How bad was Klarissa's face, and what does this tell about how she was killed?"

In Burlington, the face that Reilly was graphically describing was about to be seen in the cold flesh by Klarissa's father, Fulton J. Wilcox. Susan Prescott, the state's Chief Medical Examiner, wasn't happy when she met the tall, dour man at her office door within the medical complex. The identification of a deceased family member was the least pleasant of her duties. In a small state, it's often difficult to delegate such work, particularly on weekends. When the duty was hers, Susan couldn't find a way to escape it. Everyone in her office flattered her as the best: the most empathetic, the one most able to comfort in the worst of circumstances. Susan knew that a morgue didn't usually hire people for their diplomatic skills and suspected that such compliments were their way to get Susan to do more of the dirty work. She didn't like dealing with bereaved people, but sometimes, like today, she had no choice. Coming to the morgue directly from church struck her as particularly odd.

Susan knew that the identification of a corpse that has been burned, decayed, or mutilated might not be definitive. Such events, which would be traumatic for an uninvolved person, are a nightmare for relatives. The family members desperately want the body not to be the husband, wife, son, or daughter they are looking for. They fear uncertainty almost as much as the terrible certainty of identification. This viewing promised to be one of the worst: a middle-aged woman shot repeatedly in the face at close range with birdshot. Clearly, someone was trying to obscure or delay her identification. Susan knew she'd be in no rush on this one, despite the pressure she anticipated from Detective Coté.

To Susan, the man who walked slowly beside her fit the stereotype of a mortician rather than a grieving father. Wilcox was lean and hard. He looked to be about sixty, with gray hair thinning to baldness. He was well dressed and had commanding body language. He was anything but friendly: a suitably unpleasant man for the task ahead.

When she'd called Fulton to set up the viewing, she'd expected inconclusive results. However, when he arrived, he surprised her by presenting a set of his daughter's fingerprints as well as some old health records and a childhood lock of her hair. She wasn't used to getting prints for noncriminal victims or from relatives. She made a mental note to try to obtain an official set from the office where Klarissa Wilcox had worked before she had left Vermont for England.

Fulton explained that he had had his daughter fingerprinted at thirteen when they had lived in the UK for a year. The police in Lyndhurst fingerprinted children as a service to parents. There had been several high-profile kidnappings in Hampshire, while in London, police had discovered a boy raised by another family ten years after he had been taken. A number of departments around the country had made this service available to discourage abductions and help in recoveries. *And of course*, thought Susan, *they knew that the prints in many such crimes would be used in morgues like this one.*

The fingerprints had been marked and dated by the English police. Susan made another mental note to call there tomorrow. She asked Fulton if Klarissa had any scars or body markings, moles, tattoos, or the like that he could identify. He described a scar on her left arm and its location. She had received a deep cut in an automobile accident three years before she had married, and he thought she had had around fifteen stitches to close the wound. This was a good sign from Susan's point of view because it opened the possibility that if this wasn't Klarissa, Fulton would be able to leave with that knowledge. Susan had seen far too few happy endings after such viewings. But it gave her the illusion of optimism. She knew deeper down that it would just be some other poor father shedding the tears, and she would likely as not be on duty then as well.

Fulton shivered when he entered the morgue. The chemical smells and cool air were so familiar to Susan that she didn't notice them. When she switched on the full lighting, Fulton winced. She knew that the only way to proceed was quickly and professionally. She approached the far wall with its grid pattern of body-length drawers and pulled out number sixteen. The body emerged feet first and was obviously naked under a sheet. Fulton stood on the right side of the drawer. Susan asked him if he was ready and suggested that he might want to brace himself on the locker wall. He just nodded his head, and Susan raised the sheet to reveal the head and shoulders, and then folded the cloth away to expose her left arm.

Although Susan was accustomed to such sights, she chose to focus on Fulton. He looked pale and drawn but didn't show any observable change. He seemed stoic. She had seen such nonreactions before and didn't necessarily judge them as indifference. She knew the pain would be there, and in a man like Fulton, it would probably be released slowly over time.

The face, which had been washed clean of blood, was punched in and severely distorted. Though there had been sufficient force to cave in her face, it hadn't been enough to break through the back of the victim's skull. Susan knew Fulton couldn't make a valid identification at this point. His rising elation or crushing sorrow rested on what they would find on the victim's left arm.

Susan walked around to Fulton's side of the tray and examined the woman's left forearm, where the lateral surface revealed a well-healed scar. It was right where Fulton had described it and sufficiently long as to have required the number of stitches mentioned. She slowly looked up at Fulton.

Fulton looked pale and faint as he leaned back on the wall with his right arm and then raised his left hand to cover his face. He sobbed quietly while Susan stepped nearer to comfort him.

She escorted Wilcox to the edge of the parking lot, feeling drained. Back in her office, she made notes for the morning. She had directed her technician to take fingerprints of number sixteen and compare them to the set provided by Fulton. Her assistant was also to do a microscopic comparison of hair samples. In a note to herself, she planned to call Lyndhurst to ask about their program for fingerprinting children. "Call before eleven AM," she wrote, remembering the five-hour time difference. Now she thought they might be able to confirm identity by early Monday afternoon. She wished she could just go home, but she knew that Detective Coté would arrive soon, eager for a review of what she suspected as well as what she knew. Atop all that, Susan's rumbling stomach was berating her for skipping breakfast.

7.

Chips

"Hi, Dad."

Amy, her freshly washed hair tied back with two blue ribbons, sat in an old New England rocking chair in her grandmother's living room. Her smile was pixie-like and luminous as she tried to keep the phone cord from tangling. Her grandmother's bathrobe, which overwhelmed her tiny frame, would occasionally catch under the rocker, making a bumpy ride. Elaine Bostwick's cozy house had treasures an eight-year-old girl could appreciate, especially when they came with the attentions of a loving grandmother. Amy liked her grandmother's Currier and Ives prints and her collection of Hummel figurines, proudly displayed in a glass corner cabinet. Most of all, Amy loved the large Victorian doll house in the corner, now in its fourth generation of use. The room was warm with shared affection, and Amy was more relaxed than she had been for several weeks. The joy in Amy's voice raised Reilly's spirits more than he had thought possible.

"Oh, Dad! I'm having such fun with Grandma. We just had a tea party, and yesterday we sewed dresses for her antique dolls. Last night we went to the best movie. It's called *Dark Crystal* and it was really scary. I loved it. I want to see it again, but I'd like you to be there."

"I heard about that one. It has lots of fairies and strange creatures. Right down your line, I'd say. Did you like it as much as *E.T.*?"

"I don't know. I loved *E.T.* and, I know I said that was my all-time favorite. Dad, do you think I can have two all-time favorite movies?"

"I don't see why you can't have three."

"Grandma asked me to call you this morning before we started home. She said you wanted to talk to me."

"That's right, my dear. I've had a change of plans. How would you like to stay with your grandma a few more days, but not there in Richmond? Adele's going to give Lottie a mini vacation from school and has been trying to persuade me to let you join her."

"Could I really do that, Dad?" Amy looked up, wide-eyed, to her grandmother.

"Well, I didn't like the idea at first, but you know Adele. Lately, she seems able to talk me into most anything."

"I know, but, Dad . . . doesn't Adele have lots of great ideas?"

"Oh, I agree. I just didn't like you missing school."

"Dad, I promise . . . I'll make up any work. I think it's a great idea. Please."

"I told Adele this might be OK if your grandma was willing to look after the two of you. Adele talked with Conner and Karen. They have some extra room and have invited your grandma to stay with you until Thursday morning, when you'll go back to school. If we decide to do this, Grandma would drive you there later today.

"I'm going to be wrapped up in a big project. I'll tell you all about it afterward. I might even be out of town. That would mean that I probably wouldn't see you for a few days. That's the part of the idea I don't like. Adele would be around to visit. I'll stop by, too, if I can.

"Dad, I'll miss you too. Won't I see you on the way to Karen and Conner's?"

"Honey, I just don't know yet. I'll visit you tonight if it's possible. Are you OK with that?"

"Yes, but how about Trotsky? Can he come to Conner's? Please, Dad."

"I don't know, dear. That'll be up to Adele and Conner. You can ask. Adele was planning to look after both pups for a few days."

"Oh yes . . . please ask Adele to leave D'Ory with us too!"

"Well, I can't promise you the dogs, but I will let you have your little vacation with Lottie. Now I need to speak to your grandma. I love you, dear."

"I love you too, Dad. Bye-bye."

Reilly explained the plan to his mother, who quickly agreed. Elaine had to carefully mask her worries when she hung up the phone and returned to Amy's world.

Reilly turned back to Adele and sighed. "That was hard. Amy can read me so well. She was happy over the phone. I hope somehow we won't have to destroy more of her childhood. For all we know, her mother may be dead and her father about to be jailed. I've never felt so Christly uncertain in my life!" Reilly looked fondly into Adele's eyes as tears welled up in his own. "And I also can't bear the thought of losing you. You and Lottie are family for me now, and I was beginning to feel that our lives had a fresh start. Now I just don't know."

"Reilly, we haven't been beaten yet. Not by a long shot. We'll protect the girls for a few days and get to the bottom of this. I won't have it any other way. We have to solve this," and then with emphasis on each word, "*so we will.*"

Adele paused before continuing, "If the break-in at my house was really an attempt to kidnap Amy, can you think of any way that might be related to Klarissa's murder?"

"No. The two don't add up. Klarissa is the only person I know who might kidnap Amy. As little as I respect her, I can't imagine her hiring some thug to do the job."

"But you've told me that Fulton Wilcox is wealthy and sometimes involved in shady deals. Couldn't someone try to force a ransom from him using his granddaughter?"

"I never thought of that," said Reilly. "It's possible."

Adele added, "It's a brutal thought, but suppose the kidnapper murdered Klarissa to make her father more susceptible to paying the ransom."

Reilly slumped in the chair again and lowered the pitch of his voice as he said, "I want to doubt that."

"Nonetheless," replied Adele, "if this murder is related to Amy, I suspect Klarissa's dad would be the guy to investigate."

"I agree. . . . And maybe there's a second reason. Fulton once merely disliked me. He hated me after we went to court. And remember, his side lost both times. Fulton J. Wilcox doesn't lose gracefully. This guy hates my guts and would love to see me in jail. I don't know how he could be involved in this, but we need to know more about him. He once made some slips about his mysterious past. That's why I've written these notes. I'd like you to give them to Suzanne. See if she can make sense of them. I think they're clues to his role in World War II and why he seldom talked about those years. They may tell us what he's capable of today."

Suzanne Foster was an English teacher who had begun raising her kids in Greenwich Village before torching bridges and moving to northern New Hampshire with her husband, Cisco, and family. The gang knew she was widely read on WWII spy stories and history. Suzanne was a wizard at finding obscure information.

Adele sat opposite Reilly. "Another possibility," she said slowly, "is that someone else knew Klarissa was coming here and found a way to kill her while having you take the blame. Who has an interest in seeing that happen? I want any ideas you have about local people who disliked Klarissa or might feel threatened by her return."

"I have thought of two candidates. Maybe we should to learn more about them. We need information that directs the police toward the true killer. Also, if I'm arrested, I'm more likely to be released on bail if there are other suspects out there. I'll try anything that keeps me free to help Amy."

Reilly explained that the connection to each man came from Klarissa's job in Colebrook's mental health agency and her work helping battered women. Her agency work had been mostly administrative, but on weekends, she had covered their emergency phone line from home. Although it's a New Hampshire clinic, many clients came from Canaan. This is why Klarissa was sometimes privy to the seamy side of local life.

"The first guy is Donald Houle," Reilly continued. "A few years ago, his wife called the hotline for help. It didn't take Klarissa long to see that this wasn't a mental health problem. The woman was being beaten. The agency alerted the police, which led to a restraining order. When Donald learned that it was Klarissa who had first mentioned the police to his wife, he vowed revenge. He probably subconsciously scheduled it for his next binge. One summer night, about two in the morning, this bastard got me to think about mental health services in a whole new way."

Reilly described the night three years before. He and Klarissa had been sound asleep in the front bedroom. He vividly recalled the startling crash and explosion of glass shards across their bed. The brick had smashed their front window, traveled over their bed, dented the far wall, and dropped to the floor. There had been an unearthly screaming roar outside the window. An impossibly deep voice had cursed Klarissa in a crazy, almost unrecognizable mix of French and English. Klarissa had immediately jumped up and said, "Donald Houle." That had meant nothing to Reilly. He had whispered to her not to turn on the lights as they scrambled out of bed and into the living room. Both had cuts on our arms and faces and were trailing bloody footprints. Reilly had told Klarissa to call Paul Marshall and had then run to the spare bedroom for a shotgun. Meanwhile, Amy had begun screaming in her bedroom. Reilly shifted in his chair, pained by the memories.

"Like a lot of folks, our front door is blocked and never used. So I just had to lock the back door and latch the kitchen door to the basement. While Klarissa was dialing, I managed to find and load two cartridges. I made sure Houle was still in the front yard, then slipped out on the back porch as Klarissa locked it behind me. She went to Amy, who was still screaming. Fortunately, the moon was almost full, and my eyes were fully adjusted. I walked slowly and quietly in the moon shadow along the far side of the house toward the road as Houle's rant continued. I paused at the front corner of the house with my gun ready. Then I jumped around the corner. He wasn't more than fifteen feet away. I aimed at his chest and yelled his name. He turned, and I could see the wild look in his eyes. He staggered toward me, and I thumbed off the safety. He heard the distinct click and recognized the twin tubes leveled at him. One more step, and I'd have shot. He stopped and swayed to and fro, looking surly and confused. I heard a siren and knew we were fortunate. Paul Marshall was in Canaan that night. He arrived a minute later and took Houle away in cuffs.

"Amy was traumatized that night. After I tended to her wounds, Klarissa slept with her. Nancy Wilkins looked after Amy the next day while we restored everything to normal—visually, at least. It was probably the first event of many that conspired to rob Amy of her childhood. We were all shaken. At the time I tried to get Klarissa to change jobs.

"That happened quite a while ago, but I'm sure Donald Houle would be one person who would prefer Klarissa dead. I haven't seen him for some time, and he could be in jail, for all I know.

"I'm sure that the second bastard is still in the area. His name is Jake Paulson. His wife also came to the mental health agency after talking to Klarissa on the emergency phone line. She also was being beaten. This happened more recently . . . during the time we were separated. Jake has a violent streak and threatened to kill Klarissa in a drunken rage. I learned about Paulson from Rita Webster. She was friends with Klarissa and me before we split and was there when Jake confronted Klarissa. The peculiar thing is that Klarissa didn't report the threat to her agency or the police. She even told Rita not to talk about it, which, as far as I know, she hasn't, except to me. I still think Jake is muscle-bound and dangerous. In fact, the whole Paulson clan has an awful reputation around town."

When Reilly had finished his account, he slowly walked to the large picture window in the living room. Adele stretched and glided gracefully behind him. As her body came to rest against his, he felt her arms wrap around his waist from the back. The two paused a long moment, captured and calmed by their love and the winter's sparkling white beauty outside.

"So, Reilly, like it or not, you now have a smart and pretty detective on your side. That's me. Don't even bother protesting. I promise I'll be careful and you and the gang will always know what I'm up to, but I'll do whatever I have to. I think Jake will be the first person I visit.

As Reilly started to protest, Adele put her finger to his lips. "Leo Richards would be just about big enough to be my bodyguard. He certainly has the right attitude."

"I know you well enough not to argue because you have a distressing tendency of winning, but be careful. Work with Suzanne and our friends. They'll want to get involved. And if I can't make the meeting this afternoon, please tell everyone what we have talked about."

"Uh-oh," interrupted Adele, looking toward the village. "It's time for your personal detective to leave. Don't worry about Amy. I'll make sure she and Lottie are settled at Conner and Karen's. We'll talk again this afternoon."

Reilly turned back to the window just in time to watch the state police car awkwardly turn in to his driveway. He gave Adele his yellow notepad and said, "I have the feeling that it would be best for you to keep this." He wrapped his arms around her, resting his hands on the small of her back and inhaling the scent of her curly brown hair, the hint of lavender in her light perfume. He stood there, motionless, feeling her body against him, for a long and desperate moment of tenderness, security, and desire. Then he released her very slowly. "Thank you so much, my love. Please protect every part of your lovely self, because I want all of you for my own." He kissed her again at the top of the stairs.

Karen reached down to pet Trotsky, then left.

When Trooper Marshall drove out from Canaan beneath a mild azure sky, it was a comfortable fifteen degrees with light crisp wind. The five or six inches from the passing storm had been cleared from the roads. The snow piles at the mouth of Reilly's drive were approaching ten feet tall, and the opening was so narrow that the cruiser gouged out a quarter panel of snow as he turned.

Adele backed her car to the side of the drive so the cruiser could pass. She nodded to him as she backed the tricky blind exit onto the road.

Trotsky gave the handsome officer at the cellar door his equal-opportunity welcome. Soon, he and Reilly were seated in the kitchen, bathed in winter sunlight. The trooper declined a cup of coffee, and although Reilly had known Paul socially, the pleasantries soon passed.

Marshall was soft-spoken. "Yesterday, you told Sergeant Coté about the resemblance between the woman you found and your ex-wife, Klarissa. We're making inquiries based on that possibility. She had no identifying papers, but some of her clothing had British labels. Last night we notified Klarissa's parents. The medical examiner has arranged for her father to view the body today. We also made inquiries in England. I just learned by radio that we have been able to confirm Klarissa Wilcox's flight to Canada. Her landlady says she left England Wednesday. There are flight records of her arrival at Mirabel, northwest of Montreal. So far, we have no indication of her crossing the border."

The trooper methodically went through his list of questions and took several pages of notes, printing them so precisely that they looked typed. Then he looked up and paused before changing topics. "I'd like another look at your shotguns."

Reilly led Marshall around a corner to the spare bedroom he used as his study. He was proud of his small collection. Although he'd occasionally hunt deer with friends, he didn't own a rifle. Reilly had an old Winchester 12-gauge pump gun for hunting ducks and two more elegant guns for his upland bird hunting. The Newton, with its external hammers, although suitable for bunnies, was a challenge on partridge, whose tricks included the ability to dart through thick woodland and disappearing in twenty yards or less. The Arietta 20-gauge boxlock, a true bird gun, was third on the rack. Marshall carefully focused on the Arietta and observed it while recording notes. Then he looked up.

"I'd like to see your ammunition."

"Would you like to see where I reload?" After Marshall nodded, Reilly said, "The reloading press is in the far corner of the cellar. I haven't used that area since before bird season."

The officer did one more inspection of the smaller shotgun without touching it, then walked to the top of the cellar stairs. Reilly flipped on the light, and they descended, leaving Trotsky behind. Aside from an entranceway and tiny garage, most of Reilly's cellar was unused space in the cold seasons. The space included his workbench, a storage area under the stairs, and a windowless corner walled off into a small room sealed with an old wooden door. The air was musty with the faint smell of root-cellar vegetables. When Reilly approached the door, he yanked smartly on the knob, then reached in and jerked the pull-cord, lighting one bare bulb.

Below the cobwebs, he was surprised to see that the table that held his reloading machinery had been jarred. The empty yellow hulls and wads he normally had neatly organized had been scrambled, with many on the floor.

Reilly's and Trooper Marshall's eyes adjusted to the light as they gazed to the floor. A large brown, almost dry, stain was evident. Marshall raised his flashlight, which revealed a splatter pattern of dried brown droplets that roughly defined the shape of a person's upper torso and head with arms raised. Around the head, there was an incomplete ring of pea-size chips in the weathered concrete-block wall. In the flashlight's beam, each chip appeared as a light-gray spot. Collectively, the chips formed a sick halo to a body's dying outline. The officer seemed to grow steadily taller as the aftershock hit Reilly.

Trooper Marshall read Reilly his Miranda rights and collected his guns. He radioed Waterbury for a team from the Vermont Bureau of Criminal Investigation and then called the Canaan Constable to seal off and watch over the crime scene until reinforcements arrived. Before driving Reilly to jail in Newport, Marshall was kind enough to let him make a local phone call. He'd save his jail call for his lawyer, Bob Newton, but for now, he was desperate to speak with Adele.

Across the river in a rented garage, the metal was as cold as moist air wafted from open pools of the nearby Connecticut River. Monty's fingers were numb as he replaced the last bolt on the new set of license plates. He was nervous about the surveillance the old man wanted, because in the sparsely populated North Country, a single unknown vehicle can appear out of place. But he was resigned to the risk in the old man's plan. He needed to find the girl today, give the old man enough time to position himself, then snatch her and head south with a good head start. Friday would have provided a clean break, but now things were messy. Risks against the plan were multiplying and time was growing short, but he knew the price of failure. Just as his thoughts were becoming gloomy, good news arrived by scanner. Bostwick was on his way to jail, and his friends wouldn't yet know. This set in motion one of the old man's contingency plans, and Monty knew he needed to get to Colebrook quickly to use a pay phone.

Twenty minutes later, he tightly filled the small roadside phone booth. "Hello, I understand you're a friend of Reilly Bostwick. This is Fulton Wilcox speaking. I'm Reilly Bostwick's ex-wife, Klarissa's, father and Amy's grandfather. It's extremely important for me to speak with Reilly. Is he there?"

Then there were the muddled awkward replies: condolences on his daughter's death, hopeful responses that the body wasn't Klarissa's, and so forth. And of course Reilly wasn't there, so his real question came next.

"Is my granddaughter, Amy, staying with you? I need to contact her right away. Can you help me? Who should I call next?" After five calls, Monty cursed this ploy, as it had yielded nothing but had heightened his risk profile.

Paul Marshall's cruiser was in sight of Norton Pond, approaching the dip where the school superintendent's son had flipped Conner Murphy's driver's ed car the previous spring. This stretch was one of the state's most fertile grounds for frost heaves. The damage from last season's crop was still evident. Reilly felt nauseated in the cruiser's malodorous back seat, thinking about the gore in his basement. He was horrified by the story it told. This had been a brutal execution. He forced himself to imagine what it had been like for Klarissa. She hadn't deserved to die. She may have angered a few people and made some sad mistakes, but this was no justification for brutality and death. She was the mother of his daughter. He mourned for the love they had once had and for his memories of her finer nature. As Reilly struggled to imagine what breed of degenerate human animal could do this, his best friends held counsel.

8.

Kaleidoscope

The Foster clan lived in a small farmhouse at the end of a steep, snow-packed dirt road in the outback of Pittsburg, New Hampshire. It was six inches deeper in snow than the surrounding hills and virtually free of modernity . . . sans phone, sans power lines, sans everything ordinary. Cisco and Suzanne were in their fifties and were the senior members of the gang. Their house was an intellectual oasis and a frequent gathering place for the group. It was a land of giants. Suzanne was an elegant six-foot-tall blond with green eyes and delicate hands. Cisco topped six-foot-six, with the physique of a recently retired bodybuilder. He was a large-framed bear of a guy with a flowing brown beard, deep brown eyes, enormous hands, and a warm heart. More than once, Reilly had described them to Adele as the brightest couple he'd ever met, and to the gang, they were legendary. Exiles from New York City in the late 1960s, they had bought a hardscrabble farm which hadn't been tilled in years. They had resolved to reinvent parenting for their two daughters and son, having suffered through unhappy childhoods themselves. Theirs was a demanding land of hauling boulders, milking goats, feeding geese, and living with frozen waterlines, yet it was a place with a sunny intellectual climate of the highest illumination.

In this parable realm, where ants prepared for winter by storing food while grasshoppers merrily fiddled, Cisco was a confirmed hopper: The Foster woodstove tended to smoke and hiss from the green wood it burned most of the winter. Behind Cisco's easily misinterpreted brawn was playful genius. He was skilled in numerous trades from scuba diving for abalone to tree surgery. His current reinvention of self was as a rural postman.

Cisco's restless creativity was hard for most people to believe at first. Klarissa, for instance, had doubted his ability to the day she left Canaan. But Reilly's skepticism about Cisco had dissolved long ago. The gang knew Cisco as a marvelous, slightly cockeyed encyclopedia of ideas and a solid friend.

Suzanne was a different tome, equally bright, but of another dimension. She would irritate the hell out of Cisco when some messy problem arose and she had its best solution before him. It wasn't the solution that bothered but that Suzanne just jumped directly to it; she didn't have intermediate steps, no list of reasons. Nothing. To Cisco, this didn't seem fair or even possible, but there it was. Suzanne had done it again. Hers was a genius of emotion and intuition. It rested securely on a granitic foundation of academic research, literature, art, and history. The gang admired her brightness of spirit. She was a finer manuscript, whose pages abounded with wild-colored patterns and tales of irreproducible magic.

The house was a dusty piece of original art framed in a shell of dubious country carpentry. That Sunday afternoon, the Fosters' Round Oak stove was belting out heat while voraciously eating green logs. When she'd arrived, Adele had told Suzanne and Cisco the shocking news of Reilly's arrest. Now she sat at the kitchen table trying to decipher Reilly's notes about Fulton Wilcox as Suzanne listened carefully, standing at the kitchen counter.

"Beaulieu," said Adele, "that's the place where Reilly heard the clue. We think Klarissa's father may be involved in all that has happened recently, but we have no idea why or how. We'd like to know more about his background. Reilly thinks Beaulieu, may be the key."

"You say it's somewhere in southern England?"

"Here, let me read what Reilly wrote."

Klarissa's grandparents were living in Lyndhurst in an area called the New Forest. It's in southern England. We were there with her parents vacationing about four years ago and went to an estate called Beaulieu. That's what the French would call it. The Brits call it "Bu-lee." It's the manor house of Lord Montague and the site of an antique automobile museum. When we toured the manor house and museum, Klarissa's father mentioned that he worked there during the war. I knew he didn't mean in the museum. Klarissa's mother mentioned a town that might mean something. Fulton went there often and on one trip bent orders and took her along. Apparently, it turned out to be an adventure. They drove into the village in the middle of an air raid. She told that story several times. I think the town was Briggens. One other odd phrase used to come up. Something about fannies, but the word was used in strange ways, like Fulton would say to Dianne, "That's something a fanny would know." It was like a fanny was a person.

"Suzanne, does this make any sense to you?"

Suzanne paused for a moment while thinking. "There's something familiar in that. Many estate houses were used for training during the war. I have a friend in New York who was a British officer. I'll go down to town and give him a phone call after we meet. I also know of some reference books that might help. No promises, but I'll try to have some answers by tomorrow night."

Gang members started arriving and trooping into the living room, where a lifetime collection of art objects hung from the exposed beams. Cisco repeated the news of Reilly's arrest as they entered.

When Ross arrived, Adele pulled him aside. "Remember telling me about the call Reilly got from Rita? We think she somehow knew that Klarissa was coming to town. Reilly just told me about two creeps who hated Klarissa. I'm going to ask everyone what they know about Jake Paulson and Donald Houle. When you talk with Rita, see if she has any connection to them. That could explain how one of them knew she was coming."

Adele soon joined the group and sank deep into one of Cisco's oversized chairs. She began by describing Trooper Marshall's grisly discoveries and Reilly's new problems. It was clear that finding the weapon and murder site had accomplished the exact opposite of what she had hoped. Adele reviewed the forensic evidence the police could use to match the body on the hill to Reilly's basement, saying it would be an easy match. Whoever had set Reilly up had done a masterful job.

Meanwhile, Joanie was chatting with Suzanne in the kitchen, trying to catch up on Reilly's end-of-marriage debacle. "I still don't get it. What possessed Klarissa to leave Canaan after she lost custody of Amy?" asked Joanie as she sliced a wedge of extra-sharp cheddar from the large wheel on the table.

"It's hard to understand...I'm not sure even she knew, but I think maybe it was an emotional breakdown. Her parents were living in England that year and it probably seemed a safe nest. She risked everything on the court case. When she didn't get custody, she had already quit her job and prepared to move. The momentum carried her mindlessly forward. I guess she'd have been mortified to stay in a village she had declared herself too big for. The sad part is that when she failed Amy, she failed herself. How she must have suffered, essentially as her own victim. I used to dislike her for her actions, but I eventually came to feel sorry for her."

"But what about the abduction in England? Is that forgivable?"

"Well, I don't think of either case as mine to forgive. Reilly thought that Klarissa's father played a large role in everything. He believed that in her weakened state, Klarissa caved in to her father's schemes. They had no idea the work that Reilly had done to straighten out Amy's life. So Klarissa was convinced she was rescuing Amy from a dreadful life here. Again, everything depended on her winning the case, and she had never considered the possibility of losing, so Amy was again the victim. It's tragic. And now if Klarissa's dead, it's more tragic still. And this sad drama could have a third act if Amy were to lose Reilly as well. So we need to work heart and soul against that."

"Amen," chanted Joanie as she picked up the cheese-and-cracker tray and carried it into the living room.

The group was discussing the unusual phone calls five of them had received just before driving there. None of them had ever met Klarissa's father and couldn't recognize the voice. They agreed that the calls could be legitimate but could also be from someone investigating where Reilly was hiding Amy.

"Did it sound like a local call?" asked Big Frank. "Klarissa's parents live in Burlington."

"That's right," Adele said. "Did you hear any background noise that might tell you where the call came from?"

"It didn't sound like someone's living room," said Shelley Roberts. "There was a hollow or open sound to it, and there were faint scraping noises in the background."

Nancy added, "That's right. I heard the hollowness, too; it sounded like snow-moving equipment way in the background."

The others concurred, and all agreed that the calls were suspicious.

"Couldn't we phone the real guy to find out?" asked Joanie. "We could confirm whether he made the calls."

"Here's a different idea," Adele interjected. "Reilly believes that Fulton Wilcox, Klarissa's father, is a potential enemy even now. He supported and funded Klarissa's legal escapades and, from all indications, clashed with Reilly from the start. I've asked Suzanne to look into his background. I think we can learn more about him if he doesn't know we're suspicious. I suggest that Nancy, or anyone else who received a call and thinks they remember the voice, give him a bullshit call, wrong number, try to sell him *Reader's Digest* . . . whatever, but get him talking enough to compare voices."

"I'm up for that," joked Nancy. "My dad always said I'd end up selling magazines."

Cisco spoke up. "I suggest that you forget the magazines and give the guy a break. He may not have made the calls and he may have just discovered his daughter was murdered. Maybe a simple call to express sympathy from one of you who knew Klarissa pretty well would be better."

"Thanks, Cisco," said Nancy. "You're right, of course. I'll still make the call. I knew Klarissa."

"Yes, thanks Cisco," Adele added. "Nancy, please tell me what you learn. Now let's look at what we can do to assist Reilly. I can look after Trotsky most of the time, but I'm sure that sometime I'll need backup for both him and my dog. OK, thanks Nancy. Reilly's house is a crime scene, but we need to somehow keep his fire going, or else his pipes will freeze. His furnace is broken and he was hoping to get through the winter without it."

"I know Trooper Marshall," said Cisco. "I'll see if I can talk him into letting me drain Reilly's pipes. The crime-scene people will freeze their buns off if they don't keep a fire going. I may not need to drain the pipes quite yet, but I'll see what I can work out."

Adele continued, "In a few days, we may need another safe-house for Amy, Lottie, and Reilly's mother. For now, they'll be with Conner and Karen."

"We're good for most of the week," said Karen, "but we'll need some backup Tuesday afternoon and evening."

"Bring them to my place after school on Tuesday," chimed in Shelley. "It's in the village, but we'll keep them inside while my zoo keeps them entertained."

Everyone smiled, remembering Shelley's three crazy Siamese cats and her grinning Saint Bernard, Scooter, that all referred to as Slobber.

"And if it's early afternoon and I'm not home from school, they can visit with Sam and baby Sarah downstairs."

"Fine. Call me if you run into a problem," Adele continued. "As you know, a man broke into my house Friday night. That was where Amy would have been except for my last-minute trip to Rhode Island. Reilly and I think that this might have been a kidnapping attempt and is somehow related to this murder. These phone calls could mean the same thing. We have no concrete evidence, just a healthy paranoia. Anyway, I want everyone to be extra alert. If there's someone out there searching for Amy, we're the folks he will probably watch. Take down any information and give it to me. No, wait. Give it to Ross, too. We'll probably want to tell the police what we learn. Ross has been talking with Trooper Marshall."

"Right," agreed Ross.

"That reminds me," said Leo, "when we left the party last night, there was a truck down by the bridge. It followed us past the North-land and turned south behind us. When we stopped at the trailer park, it drove past. It must only have gone to the edge of the village, because it drove by not more than a minute later, heading north."

"Yeah," said Conner, "come to think of it, there was a truck with a guy in it parked in front of the Northland when we drove Reilly home. That's kind of a strange thing to do at close to midnight in Canaan when it's below zero."

"What do you remember about the truck?" asked Adele.

"Only that it was dark-colored, maybe black, and I think there might have been a snowmobile on back."

"Well, that should rule out about a third of the trucks in the North Country, but nonetheless, let's keep an eye out for Mr. Pickup Truck. And, for what it's worth, the guy who busted into my house escaped by snowmobile. Now, there are just a few more details I need covered. Who would like to call Ronny to bring him up to speed?

"OK, Frank. Tell the boss Reilly's situation and tell him to expect Amy to be absent from school all week. Don't mention where she's at."

Ronny Freeman was the jovial principal who ran Canaan's combined elementary and high schools. His skill of eliciting creative teaching from his motley crew rested on his tolerance, patience, and personable cajoling. He had been invaluable to Reilly when Reilly had had to miss school to fly to London.

"One last thing," said Adele. "Reilly has identified two locals who might have their own reasons for wanting Klarissa dead. I intend to investigate them and to try to stir things up. I hope to interest the police in one or the other. Reilly told me to ask you what you know about the two: Jake Paulson and Donald Houle. What can you tell me?"

This triggered a free fall of information. To school people, the Paulson clan was legendary. Adele heard animated descriptions of three generations of notoriety. There was such enthusiasm to the stories that Adele had to cut them off when the tales started to wander far afield from Jake. Houle provoked a similar reaction. He was apparently personable when sober but potentially lethal when soused. The gang mentioned recently seeing them both around the village.

The meeting broke up in a surprisingly businesslike fashion, with the group quickly tidying up and leaving. On their way out into the snow, Adele talked Leo Richards into bodyguard duty for her visit to Jake's home Monday evening. Leo was a math teacher at the high school. He was more than six feet tall and had black hair swept back from his face, keen eyes, and a strong chin. Leo had a middleweight boxer's confidence and seemed to enjoy confrontation. This had served the teachers well in salary negotiations and would serve Adele equally well in her talk with Jake. Leo even liked the idea.

9.

The Whole Pond

The Sunday light faded quickly from Reilly's east-facing cell window amid the faint smell of chlorine and urine. The high rectangular window illuminated the coverless toilet and two beds that filled the soulless room. He sat on his uncomfortable rack, head in hands, as the hall lights, then the cell lights, came on. In the discouraging ambience of faint clanks and muffled conversation, Reilly blinked twice as he suddenly remembered lesson plans not written. *Not this Sunday evening,* he told himself. The only writing at hand was in his own journal, which the authorities had allowed him to keep after inspecting. He decided to reread a section as he stretched out on the hard bed. For several hours, his effort to cope and further plan had become a battering ram of mental exhaustion. He was beginning to realize that you can't plan the forces that control you.

Reilly turned to the journal, searching for some fabric of normalcy. He had started the journal soon after moving to Canaan in

1974 as a means to record and extol his family's new home and its North Country way of life. He would mail his early journal descriptions to old friends before they came to visit. Inviting and lively, these narratives were the thread, weave, and cloth behind the family pictures he loved to take. Optimism had been the sustained tone until two years ago when Klarissa had demanded a divorce and moved out three weeks later. The tone had then changed to reflect his personal struggle: the separation, divorce, custody fight, and, later, challenges of single-parenting. When hell had surfaced a year later, the journal had become a stark narrative describing the international abduction, the second trial—this one in England—and then the ongoing single-parenting in an insecure world. Recent entries flowed with a renaissance of spirit thanks to Adele. Reilly and Amy were beginning to trust the world again, and recent journal entries no longer sounded like they had been written in a bunker.

He remembered writing to friends who were planning their first visit to Canaan after home snows had melted in Massachusetts. He had told them to prepare to go back twenty years and one season in time. "You may think it's spring, but be prepared to arrive in late winter. You may think it's the garish 1970s, but I'll welcome you to the best of the 1950s."

Before his divorce, Reilly had often thought about life on the Canaan scale and how isolation, climate, and smallness lent unique character to what he considered a frontier community. He watched immigrants, with their outlanders' conception of civilization, come to what they considered a backwater only to discover that the natives thought Canaan the main channel, if not the whole pond. The village absorbed the people but left their ideas to evolve through a natural-selection mill turned by necessity. Reilly thought that to understand this process, one had to understand the location. Reilly called it the Land of Milk and Honey. It was a land with dairy farms and apiaries. More importantly, it was a promised land for those like Reilly who had lived elsewhere in modernity's constant, meaningless change. Now his description of Canaan set the background to a new and unfamiliar drama. Reilly felt himself calm and his breathing return to normal as he read from the first chapter written in the summer of 1976.

*Halfway between the equator and the North Pole lies this dou-
blet of villages that stitches together Vermont, Quebec, and New
Hampshire. Canaan town includes the village of Beecher Falls to the
north and forms the west edge of the Connecticut River, which, apart
from the impoundment between villages, can be waded as a trout
stream. In Canaan proper, the Connecticut is joined by Leach
Stream, which drains Wallace Pond to the west along the Canadian
border. Further to the west is the edge of the great watershed whose
rivers run north to the St. Lawrence River and east to the Atlantic. A
drop of water to the near side is southbound for Long Island Sound.
Water leaves the area due to gravity and altitude. People come and
go for other reasons. Both cycle more slowly in winter.*

Reilly rolled over and looked at the window as he remembered
Klarissa's chaotic emotional state when she'd left Canaan that late
August day a year and a half before. It had been a retreat in full emotional disarray when she had received notice from the Essex County
Court that she had lost custody of Amy. Her rage had led her to England less than a week later, leaving Amy's world in fragments. "Read
on," he told himself. "Look for the good. Those were ugly times, but
life improved. Read on."

*Canaan lives in Vermont's Northeast Kingdom, which is highly
populated with trees, hills, rivers, and ponds. People, mostly in small
clusters, are few and far between. The largest city, St. Johnsbury,
would be considered a town elsewhere. Poor, rural, and Yankee were
the descriptors that came to mind for the smaller northern villages.
Canaan, however, leans north more than most towns in the Kingdom.
Over half its residents came in recent generations from Quebec. It is
common for conversations in the village to leap back and forth
between rural English and 17th-century French. Vermont towns have
their own distinct personalities. Some are ingrown, laconic, and suspicious of strangers. Canaan is open and accepting with civility and
has a self-effacing sense of humor.*

*Twenty miles north, they grow luscious strawberries, but here,
apart from the outer influence of the St. Lawrence River, Canaan
grows green tomatoes. Our first winter it reached 43 below, and
there was a two-week spell when the temperature didn't rise to 0°.
Waiting for spring, our family witnessed spitting snow on high-school
graduation day in mid-June and had potato plants in our garden*

frosted ten days later. Winter was greedy for the days that summer gave up all too capriciously. While recommended as the first place in the state to see peak fall colors, this is arguably the last place in Vermont to look for spring.

Twelve hundred is a number you can easily hold in mind. Twelve hundred or so Canaan citizens means that you say hi to everyone you meet. If you don't know them already, there is a reasonable probability you will soon. There is little duplication of role—room for only one village idiot, so to speak. For instance, I'm the school's Science Department. Over a few years I have gotten to know every student in the high school. The transience of families is so low that veteran elementary-school teachers know almost all students in elementary and high school. In this I have found a personal truth. When everyone knows you, you know yourself better. So, in the Canaan microcosm, everyone gets a chance to be authentic. Here there is no second string. Everyone gets to play.

Reilly had discovered that, in one sense, Canaan was a terminus as far north and east as the state offered. In another sense, it was an international passageway. Canaan had two customs posts, one west of the village and the other in Beecher Falls; yet somehow, Canaan stood unique from Quebec and much of Vermont.

Our village is more than fifty miles from the nearest shopping center or sit-down theater. It is the corner of nowhere and the end of the supply chain for gasoline, food, and teachers. At least this, plus mud and black flies, is what immigrants tell friends from whence they came. However, these negatives, when flooded with North Country sunlight, project Canaan's strengths. Canaan could be better understood if you look for the obvious. It is a place of immense natural beauty, with thousands of acres to explore for hiking, boating, fishing, hunting, snowmobiling, or just picnicking. The snow is whiter here, the fall colors more spectacular, the air cleaner. Even the pulp truck that drives by leaves you the scent of balsam fir rather than diesel fumes. This picture finds few comparisons elsewhere if you, like the partridge and the hare, have found your niche.

In those early Canaan days, Reilly had thought about what he called the geography of the soul. He had felt more alive and at home with himself in Canaan than he ever had before. Maybe it was being married, parenting, owning a home, or having new friends, but it had felt like more. It was as though experiencing village life as true community had transformed him. He and the village folk he had met knew where they belonged. His science training said that there were many other variables, but the truth seemed to require no proof. This was a most pleasant place to live. People belonged to the land and to each other. In his journal, he had wondered how people are changed by where they live: What marks are left by geography, by climate, by storm? And if the place won't change, will its people? What are their deeper indicators of having done so?

And then, there was the singular peculiarity. The person Reilly lived closest to had defied all his generalities. From her first clerical job at the furniture factory and her short stint at the Colebrook country club to her longer-lasting job at mental health, Klarissa clashed with her supervisors. Reilly believed that her desire to rise to a leadership position was undermined by her condescension toward coworkers. He thought her position as a teacher's wife protected her as a tolerated eccentric within village life, but after they separated her social line of credit in all venues started to run short.

Klarissa had wanted to move to Canaan more than Reilly, yet she developed a growing aversion to its simple way of life. Reilly had been too close to her to know why, but he sensed that the storms, harbingers of complete climate change, had all been internal.

Reilly closed the journal, finding its familiarity diverting and comforting, but not enough to displace the creeping despair that led him to wonder about the firsthand experience of the partridge or hare when a hawk is aloft. A niche is not the same as a secure life.

10.

Wobble

The gentle beginnings of Klarissa and Reilly's life together were the opposite of its tumultuous end. Still, the unraveling of their lives was presaged several years before coming to the Kingdom.

They met in the August heat of 1967. He was mid-Masters degree in biology at the University of Vermont in Burlington and she, three years into a B.A. in sociology. He was a long-haired, scruffy, hardworking, and not-so-social young man having a sparkling affair with higher learning. He loved the academics but progressively lost interest in campus social life. She, an austere beauty, brilliant in eccentric ways, was about to start an oscillating adventure of harmony and dissonance that would mark her life. They were both a year away from the more serious outer world when they merged futures.

Romance ruled from fall through the next spring as she finished her B.A., but they both knew that romantic roads tend to part at graduation. Klarissa decided to go to England in September to work part time and informally study sociology. Her mother, Diane, was a British war bride, and Klarissa had dual citizenship. The family had lived for several years in England as Klarissa was growing up. Now she'd live with her grandparents in Lyndhurst, not far from her parents' second home. Reilly finished his degree in June. The carnage in Viet Nam was increasing, and he knew that his draft deferment, as a single graduate student, would soon expire. Given his anti-war stance, he considered becoming a teacher.

During that spring, his contacts with Klarissa's parents seemed harmonious, but there were faint pedal tones that didn't fit the melody. Her mother, Diane, was gregarious and a perfect hostess. Reilly liked Diane but was surprised how completely she deferred to her husband. The longer he knew the couple, the greater he sensed that fear played some role in her submission.

Klarissa's father, Fulton J. Wilcox, was a master of social distance. He never clearly described what he did for a living. Reilly believed he had worked in military intelligence in England during WWII, although Fulton didn't talk directly about it. Whatever the reality was, Reilly wondered if the experience had robbed him of an ability to feel empathy or pity. Maybe these traits, already present, had been the reason he had been recruited. He had power, self-confidence, and wealth but little time for family. He directed a company and traveled abroad frequently. As he explained it, he was an intermediary between developing countries and United States munitions makers and between the same companies and the American military. Reilly met several of Fulton's colleagues, and they struck him more as thugs than businessmen. Fulton liked to drop names and flaunt his connections. His influence extended into Congress and the Pentagon. He was known for his finesse, making deals and keeping them out of the media. With Viet Nam in flames, the good times were rolling for Fulton J. Wilcox.

Reilly's standing with Fulton became clear after a late-summer dinner with the Wilcox family and friends at their residence in Burlington. That morning, Reilly had been a participant in a Viet Nam protest at the local General Electric plant that made Vulcan machine guns. Fulton accosted Reilly in the middle of the meal, questioning his appearance, intelligence, patriotism, and courage in one brutal assault. Klarissa was mortified, and the other guests greatly embarrassed. Reilly was shocked and remained silent. After dinner, Fulton continued his affront, saying that he hoped Klarissa would marry an Ivy-Leaguer who could make some real money.

About that time, Reilly made his final decision not to become an instrument of war. This left his choices as jail, Canada, or teaching. He chose teaching in the hope of doing something socially useful while not severing ties with family and country. He had taken a few education courses in his senior year and that summer interviewed in the tiny towns of Chester and Danville. Small Vermont high schools had trouble finding science teachers. A Masters degree was quite a find, and Vermont could issue emergency teaching certificates. Danville offered a contract, but he connected better with the teachers he had met in Chester. He signed a contract right after the interview.

Strangely, though, Fulton became markedly friendlier just before Klarissa was to leave for England. Reilly was thinking about marriage and was willing to defy Fulton but felt that he first needed a stable place to live and a regular salary. Although the urge was immediate, realistically, the timing wasn't right. He knew if he did propose and she accepted, the two of them would face powerful opposition from home.

It was a difficult parting. Klarissa visited Chester one evening on her journey to Boston. They had just made long and passionate love. It was two in the morning, and while he drove her to the bus station in Brattleboro in the pouring rain, the radio played "Leaving on a Jet Plane." They said nothing and only realized years afterward that they both became emotional to that song.

Then she was gone. Reilly's job consumed him. Teaching high school was much harder than being a graduate student. The pedantic approach he'd used teaching labs at UVM failed him. The self-confident simplicity of Vermont kids came as a total surprise. He was accustomed to upper-middle–class, often neurotic, pre-med students. These kids were refreshingly normal. Neither height, weight, nor intelligence altered this appraisal. He found that his vocabulary left them confused. His satire exerted no force whatsoever; it just created sympathy for the victim. Lesson plans for a week somehow took a month to complete, yet he was totally dumbfounded how to fill the time except by talking. His little professor lectures only seemed to mesmerize the troops. Fortunately, these relaxed rural kids liked his active labwork and were reasonably tolerant of his inexperience. Gradually, he found that he needed to learn from them for them to learn from him.

Distance made the heart grow fonder. Reilly's teaching improved, but a slight loneliness hung over him. He and Klarissa exchanged letters. She wanted to come back, and he joyously agreed. It was mid-October when he called and proposed. She immediately said yes. She prepared to return in November, and they would marry in the spring. When Klarissa told her parents, they were against the wedding but knew not to say so outright. In their phone conversations they seemed to give her insipid encouragement they didn't feel. She sensed a steel wall of opposition behind the accommodating words and knew she'd be skillfully manipulated to reject Reilly. Klarissa realized that she'd be forced to cancel the wedding. Her parents were talking about events they wouldn't allow to happen. Klarissa decided to bypass these obstructions. She told them she had changed her mind and was returning in mid-February. She then quickly phoned Reilly, asking him to make plans to elope.

Reilly picked up Klarissa a week later at Logan Airport in Boston. With the help of their friends, sworn to secrecy, they married hippy-style in Burlington. His family was surprised; hers was outraged, but the deed was done. Klarissa's mother learned to accept the marriage and grew fond of Reilly. The frost on Fulton J.'s attitude never melted, even after Amy was born.

Looking back, Reilly thought the drama of that winter a fitting end to the tempestuous year of 1968: that cusp in time after the Tet Offensive, President Johnson's abdication, and the Martin Luther King and Robert Kennedy assassinations. Reilly had seen it as a time when civility was dying. The children of the placid, idealized 1950s nuclear families had become the enraged hellions of the nuclear 1960s. He had thought that the United States were becoming a nation of protests and riots with all shades of rejection and denial. The war supporters had had the power of government, but the war protesters had gained power on the streets. The Civil Rights Movement had demonstrated how deeply entrenched and essential prejudice was to maintaining the status quo, but Blacks had found a louder voice. Women had discovered a clear and angry new voice. The violently maligned gays and lesbians had found the beginnings of visibility and identity. A very few had started talking about humankind's egregious treatment of the environment. But at that time, most people didn't get any of it. The racially prejudiced didn't get it. The traditional males didn't get it. The sincere patriots didn't get it. The industrialists didn't get it. What was absolutely heretical then (before the storm had passed) now had promise of becoming mainstream. Reilly had read and believed true that those alive during a revolution couldn't see the revolution happening. That was a year of multiple revolutions. In that time of challenge and violent upheaval, neither side of 1968 could envision the outcome. The wind gauge was in the eye of the storm.

Now, sitting in his cell, Reilly considered how his marriage had taken twelve years to spin out of control. Maybe it had been the loss of speed as love waned that had caused its wobble and eventual fall. Maybe it had been the gusts of the external storm that had robbed its momentum and stability. Maybe it had been the failure of two people to pull toward the center, but whatever it was, there had been nothing so unusual in its demise as to predict the explosions that followed. Looking back, it now seemed to Reilly that even the curative powers of rural Canaan never had a chance.

11.

Riverbend

Brad Mungeon took a long last swig of beer and then crushed the can effortlessly end-to-end with just a thumb and two fingers. A hook shot out the truck window sent the can backward over the cab. As he drove northward, the mashed aluminum flew through the sub-zero air, buffeted by the truck's turbulence. Brad rolled up his window as the can cleared the guardrail and bounced off the steep riverbank. From there, it slid onto the ice covering a Connecticut River trout pool just above Canaan village.

He took a slow cruise through Beecher Falls as a precaution before doubling back to the bar, then parked his truck against the snowbank in front of a run-down hardware store and warily observed the drab building across the street. His watch ticked off five minutes before he stepped into the cold, walked to the snowbank, and unzipped. Even in the dark, it entertained him to slowly pee a steam-ing capital M in the clean snow. After he stretched back to his full height, he pivoted toward the bar a bit too quickly. The six beers he'd recently slugged were sloshing against his day's bad luck. The mix was generating enough dizzy heat to keep his anger simmering.

Even from a few feet away, the bar was almost as dark as the cloudy sky. He noted the sign's burned-out neon bulbs. At the front door, he could see the faint glow at the edges of the window shades and hear the thump-thump of an out-of-date country tune. He rubbed his gloved hands after knocking on the wooden door. When the response was slow, he knocked harder and kicked the door solidly for good measure. *This must be the place,* he thought as he listened to the flowing water below and behind the building.

"This building's ass does hang over the river."—That's how his stupid neighbor at the commune had described the place. For Brad, the important feature of the Riverbend Inn certainly wasn't water, but, then again, it wasn't booze, either. The owner of this dive didn't consult the State of Vermont on its Sunday hours of operation. His future wealth and freedom depended on the information about Bostwick's daughter he hoped to find here.

The short, wiry Frenchman who opened the door squeezed aside to let Brad's giant frame slide by. Mungeon knew he was surly enough to pass as normal clientele, so he ignored the pip-squeak's questions while he looked over the guy's balding head to scan the open room. The bar and kitchen behind were to the left. An open floor with scattered tables completed the setting. The walls were amber-streaked knotty pine, and the tables, covered with red-checkered oilcloth. A few beer signs and a tattered poster from a long-ago rock concert completed the minimalist décor except for a homemade wooden sign that said "The Elbow Room." Brad saw that the windows were fitted with oversized draw shades. He liked the ambient smell of smoke, beer, and rye whiskey. As his eyes adjusted further, he noted small groups of men at three tables and a couple hidden in the corner of the dimly lit room. He spotted his commune neighbor Raven and walked toward that group. He detested small talk. Tonight he'd force himself, although there was no need to shed habitual rudeness. As he grabbed a chair, he looked over his shoulder and snapped an order, "Get me a beer."

The Riverbend's extra hours fit several Beecher Falls traditions. Canada and New Hampshire define this far corner of Vermont.

Although no bigger than a small city neighborhood, Beecher Falls, the subvillage of Canaan, was a bastion of enterprise—most of it free, but not all of it legal.

The area's legitimate money flow was associated with a massive furniture factory. The other economy was geographic. The town was intersected by Bridge Street, which led to New Hampshire, just a stone's skip across the river. There, the availability of low-priced booze and cigarettes was a boon for smugglers. Less than half a mile north of the bridge, the road led to a crossing point to Quebec replete with questions and restrictions. The highly permeable border from Beecher Falls west to Norton and beyond offered no such problems. With booze and cigarettes heavily taxed in Canada, even short-distance travel could be lucrative.

That Sunday evening, the tradition of malleable law continued at the Riverbend, where the beer was frosty and the whiskey was New Hampshire cheap. For another night, the faithful could gather to escape unpleasant households, nurse their booze habits, and squander their kids' futures. Brad, by disposition and profession, was familiar with this side of free enterprise. As he sat, a skinny pox-faced man in coveralls looked up and smiled with beer foam on his lips.

"How're they hanging?"

"Fine. . . . Just where they should be," Brand countered.

Raven's standard greeting had been expected. The thin man, some variant of precancerous hippy wastrel, swept the dirty black hair out of his eyes. As with other commune squatters, Brad didn't know if Raven was a first name, last name, nickname or some crazy-ass totem. Not that it mattered. There wouldn't be much to learn from this bird, but for a guy whose brain was fried on rotgut, Raven was at least occasionally funny.

Suddenly, Brad's danger antenna got a signal through the beer fuzz . . . something about that big man talking to the broad in the corner. As the guy's face caught the light, Brad felt the acute visceral anger that marked many of his interpersonal relations. Meanwhile, no corresponding identity rose to consciousness. He turned to Raven.

"Who's the SOB in the corner? I know I've seen him before."

Raven copped a look. "That's Paulson. . . Jake Paulson. I shoot pool with him at *the swamp*. Funny, we've just been talking about him. You see," Raven leaned forward and continued in a hushed voice, "that ain't Jake's wife. That's Nancy, Giles Vachon's wife. Things could get real interesting when Giles comes back to town."

Brad began to relax again and thought to himself with a smirk, *That bastard probably wouldn't remember me even if he can see past her tits.* He knew that Paulson was thinking with his balls. This evening, he would be nearsighted, if not deaf, dumb, and blind.

Brad spent the next hour pumping locals for information. He bought a round of drinks for his table and let them bum cigarettes. Soon, they were yapping about the murder. When a guy from the nearest table chimed in, he bought them a round. It didn't take long to expand the blather to everyone except the couple in the corner. Before long, he had sucked dry their meager information. He easily confirmed that the cops had swallowed the bait and arrested Bostwick but no one knew a damn thing about his daughter. Disgusted, he got up to take another piss.

A few minutes later, Brad stopped, slammed the men's room door, and stared. A pudgy thirty-something slob was bent over on his chair, with the barkeep two steps behind with a pail. Probably a load of puke . . . just what he needed! Nothing would piss him off more. He sniffed defensively as he approached, only to find the malty smell of spilled beer. Dubois, looking grim, stood holding a bucket of potato peels topped with beer-soaked paper towels. Brad braced his legs in a fighter's stance, waiting for the man to stand. The guy's red head bobbed back and forth as he sopped up the last of the beer. Just as Brad prepared to exorcise his fury, Ike Blanchard looked up, smiled, and said, "Hi." Brad's surge of anger dissolved as he realized his good luck. He knew this guy. Better yet, he knew this guy was married to a teacher.

A few weeks earlier, Brad had met Blanchard in a Colebrook bar. He had discovered that a few beers made Ike a spigot of useful information. Now was the time to prime the flow. Brad gave Dubois the cost of Ike's refill and dragged another chair to the table. After Ike had had a chance to settle, Brad asked him, "What have you been hearing about Bostwick and the woman he found?"

Ike told what he knew. It was common knowledge that Bostwick was in jail and that the murdered woman was his ex. *So much for old news*, Brad thought. It was the time to get serious; his life plans hinged on one essential piece of information.

"So, I hear that Bostwick has a daughter," Brad pressed. "This must be a mess for her. If he's in jail, I wonder where his kid is."

"Well, I don't know much, but I think I know that. My wife, Sally, went to visit her mother in Burlington on Friday right after school and took the girl . . ."

Brad's antenna suddenly caught the loud disturbance at the door. He turned to see the barkeep shouting in French at a stocky, middle-aged lumberjack in a tattered, green-plaid wool coat. The drunk with a ragged black beard started arguing back in so loud and unusually low a voice that every else shut up. This coincided with a scratchy hiss from the jukebox, which trailed a song about trucks and heartbreak. For some reason, the sudden near-silence and start of "Don't It Make My Brown Eyes Blue" caught the guy's attention and quieted him down. Meanwhile, the smaller man reached behind the bar.

Brad turned to Blanchard and asked, "What was that all about?"

"That's Donald Houle. The bartender, René Dubois, is pissed at Houle for blabbing around town about this joint's illegal hours. At first, he wasn't going to let him in. Donald was about to start a fight, so René backed down."

Ike explained that Dubois had recently bought the Riverbend. Houle had liked this because it would be the only bar within twenty miles that hadn't banned him for life. Donald had a reputation for broken-bottle bar fights and had been banned years before from the old Riverbend. René had decided to collect Donald's money until he crossed the line. From the look in René's eyes, that could be tonight.

Brad now noticed the wooden club on the bar by Dubois's right arm. This guy was small but obviously knew the price of keeping his liquor license. Meanwhile, Donald was drifting toward their table with a shot and a beer.

Brad wasn't pleased with the interruption but had reasons to remain peaceful when Donald arrived. Ike, who vaguely knew everyone, made introductions. Donald said, *"Comment ça va?"*

Brad grunted the outer limits of his French, a polite *"Ça va bien."*

"We have been talking about the murdered woman that teacher found yesterday," said Brad, trying to intercept any change of subject. He knew he was close to pay dirt with Ike and didn't want this loud-mouthed dickhead to prevent him from digging more.

"Well, mister man," Donald blurted in a deep, heavily accented voice. "I hear about that. I hear she was frozen...bent like a pretzel, she was. *Maudite*!" he added excitedly. "They ses she don't have no face! Might make someone sad. Not me, I piss on her grave."

This caught Brad's attention. He decided to see if the blowhard knew anything useful. He turned to face Houle and asked him, "What did you have against her?"

Donald chased a swig of beer with a shot of whiskey, farted loudly, and took a slow, deep breath. He told his long, rambling story about Klarissa's influence on his wife, who had moved out on him two years before. Brad had to smother his laugh when sad-eyed Donald told how he had arrived home at his trailer only to find that his wife and former friends had emptied the trailer completely, even including the light bulbs. Donald moaned about how nothing had happened when he had flicked the switch and how he had had to sleep in a corner like a dog. Houle then said that Klarissa had some-how got him thrown in jail. Brad found all this mildly amusing but useless. He was still impatient for the one piece of information he hadn't pried out of Ike. He was determined to try again.

But Ike had already started to tell more stories about Klarissa. The common theme seemed to be that she was excitable and erratic, and even Ike, who hung around with that liberal teacher crowd, con-cluded that she must hate men.

Brad pressed his long-awaited moment. "So, what were you about to say about your wife and Bostwick's daughter?"

"Oh yeah . . . Sally planned to visit her mother in Burlington on Friday right after school. Reilly asked her to take Amy to her grand-mother's along the way. It was in Richmond. Sally came back late this afternoon without the girl, so she's probably still there."

Bingo, Brad said to himself excitedly. Then with an internal sigh of relief, he decided it was time to head to the apartment. It still might be possible to salvage their plans, but timing would be crucial.

René looked relieved as he propped the door open for Brad to slide out. A parting glance showed Jake and Nancy quietly playing footsie in the corner. Houle, across the way, was getting more animated. He was loudly spewing a string of stories and blasphemies, but at least so far, the bull in him hadn't been otherwise provoked.

The blast of frigid air focused Brad's thoughts to the tasks ahead. It was time to shift the operation to Richmond and plan a break-in for tomorrow night. He'd call the old man to research Mrs. Bostwick's Richmond address. This time, they wouldn't fail.

12.

You're It!

A scuffling noise down the hall shifted Reilly's mind back to the reality of jail. He stood slowly and watched as a guard briskly escorted a staggering late-Sunday-night drunk to the adjacent cell. Reilly stretched and walked to the small window to look up into the clear, frigid night. The stars shone brilliantly down from their black dome above. Light from the full moon highlighted the thick drifted snow on the flat roofs like meringue on great rectangular pies. Teetering on the edge of self-pity, Reilly was once again rescued by Adele. The thought of her brightened his mood and made him think about the joyous shoots and ladders of their recent romance. As he returned to the bed, he remembered how Adele filled his senses with the floral essence of hope: the feeling that his distressed life would heal again. He slowly stretched, closed his eyes, and went to the room in his mind that held cherished memories of their romance.

What a difference love can make. Reilly had undertaken what he called "attempted dating" six months after becoming a single parent. He had quickly found that romance in the North Country was both difficult and sadly comical. Whether indigenous or in exile, it was tough sledding for romantics. He was forty, with an eight-year-old child, and reasonably literate, all to his disadvantage. The pool was exceedingly shallow in the Kingdom and northern New

Hampshire, and the probability of mismatch was laughably high. After his strange and brief encounters with Rita Webster, he had used an introduction dating service in Vermont to arrange a few awkward coffee-cup conversations with an array of North Country females. The outfit had published a booklet with profiles of the singles county by county. Starting with Vermont's Essex County entries, already a tiny group, he had bracketed the ones of reasonable ages, and in five meetings, he'd exhausted the list. Reilly had started calling romance a mind/body experience because each potential partner might, with luck, have one or the other. He had had a few promising flirtations with other single teachers, but because of their age differences and his single-parent status, things had not been likely to exceed friendships. Then one day, a walk in Colebrook had changed everything, as his expectations, which had been ill with mild winter depression, had finally kicked off their covers.

Reilly met Adele on a late spring Saturday afternoon. An unusually bright sun warmed the few shoppers walking past the wood and brick buildings that made up the east border of Colebrook's main street. Colebrook, across the Connecticut River and six miles south of Canaan, served as local Vermonters' main shopping area. The air was fragrant with the smell of manure and newly plowed moist soil. Reilly was dressed for spring cleaning in old jeans and a blue sweatshirt. He was preceded by the always-eager Trotsky on a lead when he spotted an attractive country lady walking from the other direction, led by a beautiful female golden retriever. Reilly shifted Trotsky's lead so the dogs would meet nose to nose. With a twist of the wrist that would change his life, he met Adele Clayton and D'Ory the dog. They immediately made friends with each other's pups, which gracefully launched introductions and a friendly conversation. She was close to his age, and he noted the absence of a ring on her slender left hand. He was enchanted with the flow of their small talk. After getting her name and good graces, he suggested that the dogs should go out on a date. She didn't say no.

Before their second meeting, Reilly tried to describe Adele to Conner and Karen, who had been urging him to begin dating. Fine scientific observer he was, he scolded himself—he couldn't describe her hairstyle, what she had been wearing, or even if a trim figure had likely been under her bulky coat. He just remembered her deep blue eyes. Though he was normally on the shy side, he'd locked onto those eyes for the whole conversation. She had been easy to talk with. Her smile was disarming, her laugh unforgettable. Though many of the details of their meeting were fuzzy, he felt immensely attracted to her and knew that she was the soul of beauty. After a marriage in eclipse and a long stretch of involuntary celibacy culminating in a romantically barren winter, Reilly knew from experience that low expectations were the ones most commonly reached. Nonetheless, this was undeniably exciting.

As he'd later see, no simple description would have done her justice, as no still picture could have captured her fairly. Her large blue eyes, dimpled chin, fair skin, graceful neck, and short, curly, chestnut-brown hair were all striking. But it was the dynamic of her movement that highlighted her grace, elegance, and distinctly feminine lines. Equally important to Reilly, Adele embodied the beauty of a fine mind and a loving heart. He was charmed from the outset. This was an unexpected turn for Reilly.

He called the following Thursday, and when Adele answered, he asked to speak to D'Ory.

"Who should I say is calling?" Adele inquired casually.

"Tell her it's Reilly calling on Trotsky's behalf."

"Oh," exclaimed Adele. "Please wait while I call her to the phone."

Reilly heard, "Come girl" in the background.

"Here she is," laughed Adele as she lowered the phone to her dog's ear.

"Hello, D'Ory," Reilly began with his special dog-encouragement tone usually reserved for Trotsky, who was now looking up quizzically from under the kitchen table. "What a good pup. Would you like to go for a walk?" Then, with rising pitch and enthusiasm, "Would you? How about a walk with Trotsky? Like that, girl? Good girl!" he exclaimed. He heard D'Ory shuffling around Adele's feet. After the dog had let out a couple of brief yips, Adele decided to answer for her.

"Miss D'Ory Dog wants to know where Mr. Trotsky would like to take her for that walk."

"Well, old Trotsky tells me he'd like to have both of us come along, too. I hope that is not inconvenient. He had in mind a walk near Quimby's to check the ponds and look for wildflowers." Quimby Country on Forest Lake was the oldest and best-known fishing camp in northern Vermont, but at that time of year, it was closer to mud season than tourist season. A path behind the main lodge led to the bigger of the two Averill lakes.

"Well, I'm most surprised at his love of wildflowers," she exclaimed. "And when did Mr. Trotsky want to take this walk?"

"He has been barking about Saturday morning. He says we could meet there at ten o'clock, assuming D'Ory can talk you into it."

They continued to laughingly act as their dogs' proxies and arranged to meet Saturday morning at the gate to Quimby's overlooking Forest Lake.

Trotsky and D'Ory sniffed and frolicked while Adele and Reilly settled into their hiking pace down and back Canaan Hill Road. Their walk to Big Averill and back was fine, but their curiosity about each other required a longer walk. They talked about their backgrounds and how they had arrived in the North Country. Reilly kept the story of his divorce as simple and accurate as possible. Adele, too, went lightly. He learned that Adele had been brought up in central Maine, where her father had run a dairy farm before retiring to Rhode Island. She had been educated at Columbia and was now a nurse in Colebrook. Like him, she had an eight-year-old daughter. Her husband, Doug, had been killed three years before in an automobile accident, and she fully understood the ups and downs of single-parenting.

When they returned to the cars next to Forest Lake, Reilly leaned on a large birch while looking out at the rippled surface. Adele tucked part of her jacket under her and sat on a damp stump. Both sensed that neither was in a hurry to leave.

Reilly looked to the edge of the lake shore before turning back to her and asking, "Did you know that up here, May flowers are really June flowers?" Before Adele could reply, he stepped past her, knelt, and began picking from a cluster of tiny white spring beauties. He returned to her with the small bouquet. As he handed it to her, he asked," Do you fly-fish?"

After admiring the delicate flowers and thanking Reilly, she replied "I've tried it a few times. My husband, Doug, liked to fly-fish, and the year before he died, he bought me a fly rod and reel and gave me some casting lessons. I only got to fish a few times before his accident."

"Would you like to try again? I have a canoe and would love to take you to one of my favorite ponds."

This was the start of a series of pleasant adventures. Reilly remembered how the growing heat of that spring and summer paralleled their affection. Their happiness had overflowed and warmed Amy's and Lottie's lives with its reflected glow. The full confirmation of love occured on a God-sent, bell-ringer of a Colebrook summer afternoon when Adele melted Reilly's heart with a single playful gesture. By then they had dated for two exquisite months, a renaissance of two ragged souls both moving past the mere habit of survival.

That day, as they walked side-by-side in a recently hayed pasture near a meander of the Connecticut River, Adele jumped away from Reilly, swatting him on the shoulder as she did so. "You're it!" she cried as she grabbed a two-leap head start. Reilly was astounded to find himself a forty-year-old adult drawn into a game of tag.

He had answered the challenge by turning quickly, lowering his head, leaning forward, and running straight toward Adele, who was twenty feet away and next to the sandy riverbank. He was certain he'd catch her with one burst of speed. Adele spun quickly and jumped to her left just as Reilly tried unsuccessfully to tag her. He overshot Adele and tried to slow while still tracking her over his right shoulder. His momentum carried him forward, causing him to dunk his left foot in the river. Only quick reactions prevented further embarrassment.

Adele had been most pleased. As Reilly dripped out of the water, he began to recall that there were some strategies to the game. This time, Adele zigzagged away from Reilly as he ran after her, sloshing each time his left shoe hit the ground. Adele darted back around toward the riverbank and turned to face Reilly, who stopped ten feet away, trying to anticipate her next move. This time, Reilly moved in slowly, first feinting to the left and then to the right. Adele dodged skillfully, but Reilly, in a double feint to the right, managed to give her a solid pat on the butt while bending low to avoid a counter-tag. "You're it!"

"Hey, buster, watch where you're putting your hands!" she shouted playfully as she regained her balance.

"I was. I was," Reilly had laughed.

Adele had moved to the attack by running straight at Reilly, who had now proved so adept at dodging that he taunted her while at close range. Adele faked slower movements as if she were tiring. This plus Reilly's overconfidence had been his literal downfall. As Adele charged again, Reilly's ankle had given out, and Adele swatted his shoulder as he fell.

Reilly had risen and circled Adele, whose back was now toward the sloping riverbank. He moved forward as he faked left, then right, then left again while ducking. She moved backward, and he raised his arms high as he had sprung up and forward, lowering them gently on Adele's arms. As he held her in a bear hug, she lost her balance and fell, managing to bring Reilly down with her.

Reilly had given her a long passionate kiss and said, "You're it."

Adele giggled and twisted to get loose.

Reilly, feeling mischievous, used her momentum to roll them over the slope toward the river. That worked so well that he enhanced their momentum with his shoulder to turn a second time, and then another. Adele's voice rose to a truncated scream as they rolled into the water. Adele recovered first and was in waist-deep water, splashing Reilly, who arose sputtering from the deeper water. He slogged through the subsurface mud, and they had wrestled and tumbled in again.

"Hey, buster," was then interrupted by a wet hug and a deep kiss.

An hour later, their bodies lay perspiring again, their clothes making absurd decorations on a string of bushes that formed a hedgerow perpendicular to the river. They were happily naked, entwined, and relaxed as the warmth of the ripe July sunlight had stilled their bodies. The air had been rich with the aroma of wild primrose and freshly mown hay. The murmur of the stream below mesmerized them as they lay exhausted and blissful on the grass.

Suddenly, they heard a babble of young voices upstream. They slipped on untied shoes, frantically grabbed soggy clothes, and beat a naked retreat across the small field to Reilly's car on a tractor path near a small grove of maples. They ducked behind the car and laughed until they hurt as they looked back to where three canoe-loads of Boy Scouts navigated the river.

Reilly had driven Adele home slowly that day. He had turned off in front of her cottage and pulled her over toward him on the seat. Adele had glided his way into a long embrace and kiss after which Reilly had looked deep in Adele's eyes and said, "You're it. You're really it."

Reilly remembered Adele's radiant smile as she waved goodby . . .*but, now something was wrong. . . .terribly wrong.*

A sudden clanking noise destroyed Reilly's fond memory. Adele's smile slowly faded…then vaporized as the reality of his con-finement returned.

The cell light blinked out as Reilly heard hollow footsteps at the end of the hallway. A moan rose from the next cell as the drunk rolled in his bunk. Caught in mid-reverie, Reilly had been abruptly forced back to the perils of his cage. The second jolt hit him as his thoughts returned to Amy. While Reilly lay in the hollow silence of shadows, panic again welled up in him. His mind returned to the same horrible thought as the remaining hall lights went black. He lay considering how much time was left before Amy would learn some errant version of events presented as the truth: the screaming lie . . . *your father murdered your mother.*

13.

Victorian Gothic

Reilly stretched his stiff back after awaking early Monday morning. He was somewhat surprised that he had slept at all, given his last memories of the night before. After a cold-cereal breakfast with acidic coffee, he was about to write an entry in his journal when he discovered the notes he had written on the last page. They were from London the previous fall. The brief scribbles filled his head with memories.

September 20, 1982
Royal Courts of Justice.
the "High Court" presides over the most serious civil trials.
opened by Queen Victoria in 1882.
the last Victorian gothic building
35 million bricks, said to contain 1,000 rooms and 3.5 miles of corridors.
88 court rooms. QB34

He could visualize the massive Victorian Gothic building on the Strand in London with its gray towers, arches, and massive doors. When he had been there, only the great monolith of the Royal Courts of Justice had been of any importance to Reilly. He had hardly been aware of the famous Strand, the Savoy, Drury Lane, and the royal this-and-that: some of the best theaters and museums in the world, all within a short walk. That first day in court, he had entered the massive building from the back through a labyrinth of alleyways from Gray's Inn, where he had met his solicitor and barrister the day before. It was when the court had broken for lunch on Tuesday that he had stepped into the London sunlight and turned to see its splendor. He had immediately recognized this building. It was probably the best-known courthouse in the English-speaking world. He had asked himself, how did a small town Vermont teacher ever land here? He remembered walking along the Thames, sitting on the grass, surrounded by people, yet utterly alone.

It all seemed to go back to London. Now that singular volcanic eruption of events and emotion had returned. Its aftershocks were so severe that his emotional shelters were crumbling. London had been a magical world, from bridges falling down in his young imagination to the birth of the Hamlet soliloquy; London was a home to the English language and a crossroad to American history. Reilly knew that the miasma spreading to engulf him emanated from there. The metaphoric fault line from London to Canaan was still active, but the connection defied logic as it defied geology.

The defining event of Reilly's life and the outcome of the custody trial in London had been decided in four seconds and about twenty small running steps, which had echoed in the marble-walled corridor outside the room called Queen's Bench 34 in the Royal Court of Justice. It was the third day of the trial. The judge had a social worker bring Amy to court to interview her that morning. Reilly had just left court after a discouraging session. The social worker and Amy were in the hall. Amy wore brown corduroy pants and a blue pullover sweater. Her blond hair hung straight to her shoulders. She looked tragically sad and confused. Then she spied her dad across the long hall. Her countenance changed completely. The cadence of her footsteps sounded joy to Reilly as his little girl ran to him and jumped into his arms. He wept as he held her, never wanting to let go. She was overjoyed to see him. Later, he was allowed to have lunch with her. They sat talking, not knowing when or if they would eat together again. Despite his fears, just being with Amy had helped him regain the energy and drive that had brought him to London.

Reilly felt surprising relief in that hopeful memory and turned again to his journal. He knew he had to reread the events surrounding the London trial. Maybe there were clues that would help him now. He'd barter his soul not to have to tell Amy of her mother's death. If Adele failed to make a breakthrough today, Amy would have to be told everything. Reluctantly, he picked up and cradled the journal while remembering the legal twists and turns that had surprised him in London.

He had wondered if the barrister and judges still wore wigs. They did, but not in family court. He had been shocked to discover that hearsay evidence was admissible in England, which had put him to a great disadvantage. He had found Klarissa entering as evidence conversations she claimed to have had with Amy about life in Canaan. How can you refute conversations that you don't know took place? He was going to have to confront a tangle of half-truths designed to smear him while the character witnesses he might have called upon were five time zones to the west.

The second day of proceedings had ended Wednesday with Reilly on the stand. He had been surprised to find that he was prohibited from speaking with his barrister. His solicitor had explained that he was still under oath. How different this was. In the States, lawyers coach testimony so commonly as to go unnoticed. Reilly had started to see that the English system was more objective. He had imagined the competing barristers as substitute prize fighters in the square ring of former marriage. In England, the actual contestants could never fight directly, nor would their testimony be manipulated. He knew by then that the convolutions of the law are not the same as the convolutions of the uninitiated mind. Here, common people had an issue that the law must decide. Their surrogate legal giants would fight cleanly by strict rules, and in the British family court, a brilliant judge would be both referee and jury.

Reilly decided to revisit events in his own words. He leaned back on his bed and opened his journal to read the one entry he had chosen to write in story form. As he read, he remembered all the surrounding events recorded only in the invisible ink of tears.

The most important event of my life started in late summer. A week before school resumed I received a call from Klarissa saying that she refused to return Amy and that she had enrolled her in an English school. This was both devastating and completely unexpected. Klarissa had complete advantage. I was broke from the divorce and property settlement a year earlier. It had been a financial squeeze to send Amy to England for the summer. I knew nothing about the resources and procedures that I might need.

I studied this bleak picture. I called Klarissa to reason with her to change her mind. There was no answer. I sent telegrams to her and to her mother. I couldn't locate Amy. As I was preparing to start the teaching year, I was also preparing to fight for Amy's return. The more I learned, the more hopeless the situation appeared. I found out that England wasn't a signatory of the Hague Convention on the Civil Aspects of International Child Abduction which would help return children across international borders after this kind of kidnapping. My United States senators and others offered encouragement but knew of no way to force Amy's return. This meant that my only recourse was to take Klarissa to court in England. I had received sole custody of Amy in an American state court. I didn't know anything about the practice of law in England. Add to this that my passport was out of date, the English courts were on vacation in September, and English courts rarely grant custody of female children to their fathers. Furthermore, I didn't even know where Klarissa and Amy were. Aside from that I only owned an old car and shared ownership of my house with the local bank. I had almost nothing in savings.

But more serious was my fear for Amy. Klarissa told me Amy wanted to stay in England. She had written this desire to someone in social services. I also learned that Klarissa bought her a school uniform in mid-summer, telling her that she would be attending school there. She enrolled her as Amy Wilcox, using her own maiden name.

Klarissa had waited to tell me until the day before Amy's return flight in that last week in August. So, Klarissa had been corrupting my custody for much of the summer and planning this abduction for months. I had no clear idea what additional pain and confusion would enter Amy's life, whatever I did next.

So, what in life is important and what is worth risk and ruin? To what extent had Amy already been harmed by this event? Would I only make things worse? These questions were heated by the knowledge that if Klarissa won by default, she wouldn't dare return Amy to the United States for visits for fear that I wouldn't return her. I might be able to see her in England, but she would be cut off from me, my family, and from the country of her birth.

This idea resolved my questions. Klarissa's actions were cruel and reckless, not just to me and my family, but, more critically, to Amy. I knew that Amy was the most important person in my life and worthy of any risk I might take. I couldn't change the harm already done, and I was well aware that my immediate actions could further traumatize Amy. I knew the years ahead would be rough for Amy. They would demand love and assurance from me. I was also certain that I was the more-stable parent, the one better able to earn a living and understand Amy's needs. The question remaining was how.

My folks and brother helped me financially. I worked with Bob Newton, lawyer from the divorce case a year before. He made contacts in England, and I hired a solicitor from Gray's Inn. She later picked a barrister to argue the case. So started a frenzy of spending and travel. Through phone conversations and wire transfers of money, I was able to initiate court action in London and have papers served on Klarissa. When a court date was set, I purchased plane tickets. Over the next few days, I completed a round trip to Littleton, New Hampshire, to pick up plane tickets, drove a round trip to Burlington (at the end of a school day) to mail documents to London, and traveled to the United States Consulate in Montreal to renew my passport. This was completed during the first week of the new school year.

One Saturday, late in September, I drove to Boston for an overnight flight to London. I was vague on both the geography of London and on English currency. I managed by trial and error to find a cheap hotel room near Russell Square. Monday, I met my solicitor and barrister, and Tuesday we went to court.

I had the Vermont custody decision, which would be valid in the UK unless their court lost confidence in me as custodial parent. I lost that round on Tuesday. Klarissa's barrister used my correspondence to Klarissa about Amy's well-being during her year with me as evidence against me. She said that they indicated that Amy was unhappy and unsuccessful in school. She also asserted that in some instances, Amy wasn't being properly cared for. They introduced statements they claimed came from Amy that cast me as inebriated and, on occasion, sexually indiscreet in her presence. These gross distortions caused the court to continue the case rather than reverting custody to me. Most of these slurs had to come from someone other than Amy. Who remains a mystery.

Reilly rolled slowly in his bunk, picked up his pen, and wrote in the margin of his journal: **Rita Webster???**

Then he continued to read.

I remember Wednesday as the worst day. I had no live witnesses to refute the hearsay evidence which was so freely admissible in the British court. Fortunately, the affidavits I brought from Amy's teachers told a different story. When on the stand, I defended myself forcefully, and my barrister was brilliant at showing the judge how to interpret my communications to Klarissa as that of a caring parent, keeping her informed, as I felt she should be.

Thursday, Amy was brought to the court building in the care of a court social worker. I couldn't wait to see her after the morning session. After we were reunited, the social worker took us to the restaurant so we could have lunch together. When we had to part before the afternoon session, the social worker told me not to be discouraged, because the British court would be fair. I was deeply discouraged, but I had no idea that the case had already turned.

The court social worker testified that afternoon. She had questioned Amy about her mother's behavior. It was clear that the court viewed buying Amy a school uniform, enrolling her in school, and using Klarissa's maiden name as especially damning. Likewise, Klarissa's disappearance with Amy after the fateful call to me was presented as irresponsible. She also described Amy's loving interac-

tion with me during our lunchtime meeting. Thursday ended with some hope to counter my profound dread of losing Amy.

The judge moved toward a conclusion Friday morning. He criticized Klarissa for setting her own interests ahead of her daughter's. It was clear at that point that I had won. The judge complimented me for saying that I still felt that Klarissa should be a part of Amy's life. He made it clear that any future interference from Klarissa would likely result in the total loss of visitation rights.

Then the judge dictated the court's conclusion verbally in what resulted in a twenty-page, perfectly cohesive document reviewing the case and its conclusion. With much gratitude, I shook hands with my solicitor and barrister at about 1:00 PM and called Gatwick Airport to book a second seat on the flight home. I then rushed to catch the next train to Winchester. Klarissa and her mother were on the same train. They emerged red-eyed at the station, and we shared a taxi for the final leg of the trip to a house Klarissa was sharing with her parents. Amy was OK with the court decision. In fact, she sang to herself as she packed her suitcase. At that point, she missed me more. The suspense was heightened when Klarissa had trouble finding Amy's passport. With the document finally located, Amy and I took a train back to London and booked a room for the night.

I called my mother in the States, which started a joyous phone chain with my friends. We arrived at Logan late the next afternoon, totally spent. We commenced the drive north and, when the exhaustion hit me, hunted for a motel. There were none; it was the peak of an especially colorful leaf season. I somehow drove the rest of the way home. This was how the second year of single-parenting began.

Reilly slowly put down the journal and thought about the trap he was in and how he might confound it. He knew he had beaten long odds before.

14.

Knot Much

Most of that night, ghosts from horrendous bloody scenes stalked Adele's mind—kidnapping and murdering dreams. Then as dawn approached, Adele's panic and paralysis gave way to deep insight found within the netherland of half-sleep. Now, rough ideas from the evening before condensed into a plan, and as Adele fully wakened, she was energized with a rush of new ideas.

She hopped from bed and walked barefoot across the cold floor to her closet, already thinking about her jail visit. She had pitched her first idea to Reilly's lawyer the night before. Her scheme would ensure special access to Reilly. She carefully selected clothes for this role. She would enjoy surprising him. As she dressed, she knew that her other ideas would play out as the day unfolded. Meeting with Reilly was the first priority. Adele expected to return to Canaan but didn't know which trail she'd follow from there. She threw a change of clothes in her backpack, then, looking beyond the thick frost on her bedroom window, added her heaviest sweater. She checked her appearance in the mirror and, when satisfied, dropped her pack by the front door and turned toward the kitchen.

The eerie silence as she ate breakfast reminded her that this wasn't a normal Monday. There were no dog sounds and no bustle of family preparing for work and school. Although she missed Lottie, she wanted her away from home. She'd need uninterrupted time for the strenuous tasks ahead. Also, the break-in still concerned her. The thug looking for Amy knew this house. Adele would be careful not to be followed on her drive to visit the girls before her trip to Newport. After a final check in the hallway mirror, she bundled up and stepped into the frigid sunshine.

Before visiting the girls, Adele stopped by the high school. Classes hadn't started, so she could debrief Ross after his visit with Rita Webster. Ross was excited with his find. They talked next to Adele's idling car.

"Rita was cagey with me. She wouldn't tell me why she thought the body on the hill might be Klarissa's. Like she told Reilly, it was just a hunch. But get this! I was looking around Rita's apartment and saw her address book open near the phone. I drifted over, and there was a notepad next to it where she had written a phone number. Rita came over and scooped up the address book and notepad right from under me. She acted pissed off, but I was able to remember most of the number. Guess what? It's an English number. I looked up the country code. Here, I've written it down for you."

Adele tucked the paper in her briefcase as she jumped into her car. The number Ross had written was "011-44-1962-??????" She'd see what it meant to Reilly. She also had a few questions of her own for him about Ms. Rita Webster. She shut the door and shifted into first gear when Ross rapped excitedly on the window.

"Wait, you haven't heard my other discovery!" Adele rolled down the window. "You know that Rita lives at the end of Kemp Hill Road. She bought that cottage from Bill Cowan a couple of years back. Bill's tree farm surrounds her property. When I left Rita, I stopped to shoot the shit with Bill, figuring that everyone who visits Rita had to practically drive through his yard. Get this! Last fall, Rita brought Donald Houle over to ask for a job. Bill knew Donald and wisely declined. I asked him what he thought about that strange couple. Bill just said Rita loves to get laid and Donald always needs a friend with a driver's license. Other than that, it didn't make much sense to him, either."

"Thanks, Ross. That's important. . . . Wow! This means that not only could Rita learn Klarissa was coming here, but Houle could also get that information. It could be the clue we need. Keep asking questions."

An hour later, when Reilly was drifting within his recollections of London, Adele was driving westward toward Newport. She was again teetering on the edge of pessimism and was annoyed that she couldn't free herself of the anxiety set to unbalance her. Despite the crisp beauty of the day, her worried mind only registered the road ahead. Then, a few miles past Norton, an owl swooped slowly across the snowy road ahead, its barred plumage clearly defined in the morning sunlight. In its wake drifted a single fluffy feather, distinct against the blue sky. The feather wafted downward and washed over her car as it passed. Adele experienced this rare daytime sighting as a token of nature's elegance. This, in turn, tipped a delicate emotional scale within. Slowly, her vision began to expand and register the magnificence of the day. And with that, her sense of hope began to return.

This emotional epiphany continued with thoughts of Reilly and their shared love of the natural world. That single feather also released a whimsical memory of their first fishing trip and her earliest spastic attempts to cast a dry fly. They certainly hadn't been graceful like that feather. She smiled as she remembered those awkward, out-of-control casts. Reilly had chosen to write a poem about that day. Adele's innate optimism began to regain its equilibrium through the same memories that had sustained Reilly the evening before. As she relaxed, those recollections flowed like a summer brook, and the miles to Newport whisked by.

Their relationship came as a surprise to Adele, but almost from the beginning, she had known this was the love she had never expected to feel again. Her playful side liked reeling Reilly in like a big fish. Her beauty soon had him hooked, and he was hers to play. *Such control*, she had thought with satisfaction . . . *the big lug. How he really wanted to get my attention in those early dates.* She remembered their hikes and fishing trip and the poems he'd written, the first of which had arrived with a bouquet of daisies the day after fly-fishing Little Diamond Pond.

Reilly had picked her up in West Stewartstown and they launched his canoe on that aptly named gem near Dicksville Notch, New Hampshire, in the early evening. He told her that he picked ponds based on wind conditions. Tonight was dead calm, and they could see the concentric circles radiating here and there on the pond surface showing the rising rainbow trout. Reilly inspected Adele's fly line after she assembled her rod and reel. They paddled the canoe toward an area with intermittent rises north of the launch.

Reilly fished the hair-wing green caddis dry and with two skillful casts landed the fly gently in the center of the ring of a recent rise. A rainbow hit the fly on the way up in a jump that cleared the surface by a foot. The thick, fourteen-inch trout put up a respectable fight before it succumbed to Reilly's net.

"You made that look mighty easy," exclaimed Adele, who was starting to whip her line wildly back and forth overhead. Reilly was worried about his right ear as the caddis and #12 hook whizzed by his head. Adele's timing had not yet developed, and she let the cast sag behind her as leader and line slapped the water. Then the forward cast shot high and collapsed with her fly not ten feet from the canoe.

Reilly focused on Adele's casting and quietly gave her hints on keeping line and fly aloft. Adele could make this work some of the time. Reilly paddled the canoe so that she could cast over the bow.

Soon, her line looped back on itself and snagged, tying the leader in a loose knot. The line dunked in the water in front of her. Adele reeled in the knot, picked strands apart, and prepared to cast again. Over the next half hour, she repeated this procedure six or seven times with the last knot being what Reilly called a "bird's nest."

Adele remembered spending fifteen minutes on that knot. She was never impatient or frustrated by a procedure that would have driven Reilly rattle-headed crazy. Reilly volunteered, "Would you like me to replace that leader? It would get you back to fishing."

"No thanks, I'm making good progress," she said, totally engrossed in her task.

Reilly landed three trout before the intricate knot was unraveled and the line ready for use.

The sun was setting in a lavender-and-pink glow. The pond's surface echoed the colors shimmering around scattered rings from the rising trout.

Adele managed a perfect cast to a splashy rise as the light was fading. The strike surprised her, but the hook was sufficiently set to withstand two bold jumps and a jerky retrieve. Adele was giggling, and beside herself with excitement, when she managed to position the splashing fish above Reilly's net so he could lift it aboard.

In the dusk, back at the car, Adele served lobster bisque, home-made bread, and a cold bottle of Sancerre. On the trip back, they continued exploring each other's worlds. Reilly learned that Adele was a weaver and that weavers are not fazed by tangles that would drive the uninitiated distraught. He learned more about Lottie and how Doug had died in a winter car crash when Lottie was five.

That evening, Reilly tried his hand at poetry, which he hadn't done since high school. Feeling fanciful and romantic, the idea had appealed to him. Her beauty was sufficient motivation. He hoped the verse in the form of a conceit would provoke one of her radiant smiles.

Knot Much
graceful loops and loopy casts
the fly that neither flies nor bites
cast to play a stage on air
would rather hatch a midair snare
than barb a fish that fights

He had sent the poem with a bouquet of daisies on Monday. Tuesday evening, he received an encouraging call from Adele. The venue of their next date was Adele's choice; they would have a picnic on Beaver Brook Falls near Colebrook.

They had met that following Saturday and hiked upstream with the dogs. Adele picked a large granite boulder as their picnic table next to a waterfall on the brook. Reilly had baked bread, and Adele brought a light spring salad. The sun had streamed through the trees and warmed their noisy perch above water. It was a hypnotic moment. The water had whispered its promises, and the rising moisture from tiny waterfalls caught misty rainbows midair. They talked about the books they loved, their daughters, and their experiences as single parents. Reilly, more determined than ever to win Adele's heart, wrote his second poem. He still hadn't found his romantic voice, but he loved to puzzle over the words.

Air, Water, Life: An Ode to Beaver Brook
awash, aware, away, to flow
brooks branch with braided stem
tenacious moss soft thunder knows
with interface of air below
speaks foam with life therein

Adele remembered thinking that Reilly was getting cosmic, but she had loved how it had sounded when he read the poem aloud over her second glass of St. Emilion. Then she had fallen on the floor laughing when he'd assured her that if she would view it from the perspective of a trout, she'd have no problem with the poem.

Adele remembered how they had first made love. They were staying in a camp owned by one of Reilly's friends on the east side of Wallace Pond. It had been a windy early-June evening. The waves were from the west. They were on the porch, almost above the waves rhythmically folding onto the shore with a rushing, near-hypnotic sound. They could faintly hear the Bach cello concerto playing on the stereo inside. They sat on the couch finishing their wine, and as the light waned, Reilly lit two bayberry candles that flickered to the music.

Reilly had put his arm around her shoulder and held her close to his chest.

"Did I ever tell you how much I enjoy being close to you?" He had slowly and tenderly touched his lips to hers.

Her sigh had been slow and deep, a profound sound of intimacy. He had been aroused as she melted into his arms, stared deeply into his eyes, and returned a kiss whose message was unmistakable. They had undressed and lain on the narrow bed on the porch moving slowly so as to sense and cherish each moment, made deep love, and then, as the sensual world accelerated, climaxed exquisitely and entwined in sublime peace, to a sense of fulfillment . . . and a delicious falling sensation.

Adele remembered the third poem as the sweetest: the one that had made her think there might be some hope yet for Reilly the romantic. She recited it from memory as she drove past her first stoplight in forty miles.

On the Reflection in Your Eyes
When taking trust by storm,
we ride sensual waves of chance.
Afloat and pulling together,
we rock love in a deep water dance.

So music enfolds the process,
as trust uplifts the theme.
Like-souls navigate eye-to-eye
to merge each other's dream.

The dream's heat swells in candle light
as waves lap the misty shore.
Pleasure taken meets pleasure given
amidst trust and joy and more.

As she drove past Gardiner Park within sight of Newport's small downtown, Adele happily realized that she had no recollection of the drive since Norton. Likewise, she didn't have the plan of approach she had intended to compose during the drive. Although the memories had been therapeutic, now she didn't feel quite ready for her debut at jail. It was time to stop for directions and sip a slow cup of black coffee. She saw the huge stuffed bear in the café window on Main Street and pulled into a parking space across the way. As she stepped inside the heavy door, she studied the mounted black bear as it glared out the frosted window at the few denizens of Newport's almost deserted sidewalks. If this mangy guy was the token of anything, Adele couldn't imagine what.

15.
Trickle

Twenty minutes later, Reilly's mood brightened when he heard Adele's melodic voice approaching along the prison hallway as she chatted with a guard. Adele was dressed professionally in a black wool skirt and jacket, white blouse, and small silver earrings. On her arm, she carried a briefcase and a long, black, quilted coat. She was wearing glasses that Reilly had never seen before. The guard unlocked the door to let her enter. Reilly read her eye movement and body language correctly and didn't approach with a hug and kiss. As the guard departed, Adele said in a clear voice, "Hello, I'm Adele Clayton, Bob Newton's new paralegal assistant, and . . ." She waited until the guard turned the far corner before she whispered, "Bob says he will disbar me if anyone catches us smooching."

"OK," Reilly said with a smile Reilly. "That is if they catch us."

"Hold your horses, Romeo." Adele sat on the bed and motioned for Reilly to sit opposite.

"So how did you con Bob into this . . . arrangement?"

"I called him at home last night. I told him I'm filling in as your detective and needed access to jail. That got me nowhere."

"I'm not surprised."

"Well, he didn't quite laugh. He just made a sarcastic comment about me coming to my senses. I ignored that and got him talking about the evidence against you. After a while, I had him agreeing that the police had little motivation to look for a different killer. Still, I couldn't get him to budge. So I changed tack and talked about Amy. I told Bob about the abduction attempt. I explained about the counseling and custody arrangements we need to make. Eventually, I convinced him that I needed this special access to protect Amy. He was a hard sell. By the way, Bob will be stopping by this afternoon."

"I'm impressed! I just wish your clever mind had figured out some way to make our jail relationship more . . . intimate. You do look so kissable."

"That may be, lover boy, but you're going to have to wait." Adele smiled as she folded her dark coat beside her on the bed. So how are you doing?"

"I'm OK, I guess, but I'm worried sick about Amy. After what that kid's been through . . . I keep trying to think, but worry shuts me in like a fog. Someone has me caged, and I can't figure out a damn thing. Maybe the killer wanted to eliminate Klarissa . . . maybe he wants to dispose of me. I suppose it's possible he wanted to get rid of both of us. Which . . .what . . .why? It doesn't make any sense. This seems like the perfect crime . . . like someone invisible is stacking the evidence against me."

"Well, I can't see anything perfect about murder, but I know what you mean. Still, there has to be a flaw."

"I hope so, but I feel like I've been made part of a goddamned magic trick where I have been substituted for the real killer.

Vermont State Police Derby Station

"Sergeant Coté speaking." By a stroke of luck, Roland Coté just had been reviewing the ballistics lab report on the Canaan murder while Susan Prescott had been completing her paperwork on Klarissa.

"Susan Prescott here. I had told you this morning that the fingerprints and hair Wilcox provided match the body but that I needed to do more research. I found out that the regressive agency Klarissa Wilcox worked for in Colebrook doesn't have employee fingerprints on file. I called England and was able to confirm that Klarissa was fingerprinted when her father said she was. With the matching prints and her father's knowledge of an identifying scar, I have concluded that the deceased is Klarissa Wilcox. Did you hear anything about lab results and ballistics? I know that's not my domain, but a case like this makes me curious."

"You probably know that the blood found in Bostwick's cellar matches the victim and the medical records you gave me yesterday. The ballistics report shows that the cartridges found near the body were fired by Bostwick's gun. What was your final determination of time of death?"

"That's a little tricky. We know that, given the temperature, rigor probably set in slowly after her body was moved outdoors. She was frozen solid when found and not insulated for a twenty-below-zero night. From that and the fact that there was no predator damage, I'm saying she died sometime between Thursday afternoon and late Friday morning."

"We know that Reilly was home all evening Thursday, but so was his daughter. They arrived at school at eight on Friday morning like usual. However, he was home alone Friday afternoon and evening. That's when we think he killed her and hauled her up the hill. Could she have died as late as that?

"Yes. We really don't know exactly how cold it was where she was left. Our estimates could be off. I understand that Canaan is often the coldest town in the state."

"Bostwick claims his dog was acting strange on Friday night. Like he didn't want to wake up and had no interest in food. He claims the dog was drugged earlier in the day by the murderer. By the time he told us this on Sunday, there was no way to detect drugs in the dog. I think he made it up, and like everything else Bostwick told us, there isn't one bit of supporting evidence that anyone else was involved."

"You don't sound surprised."

"Nope. Hey, thanks for your help," Roland said with a slight smile.

"No problem," was the response as Roland hung up the phone happy for such a quick, air-tight conclusion in a capital murder case. *This will look good with the press and certainly won't hurt the well-deserved prestige of the VSP.*

Adele turned from where she had been standing next to the small cell window in Reilly's cell. "That brings you up to date on Amy and the gang except for one thing. That's Rita Webster. You mentioned that she was Klarissa's friend, and Ross told me how she called you soon after you found Klarissa. How is it when I first talked with Ross about her, I had a feeling that he was hiding something?" Adele felt somewhat peeved at Reilly but kept her voice unemotional. "Is there something between you and Rita that I should know?"

Reilly blinked in surprise. "Well, I never mentioned it after I introduced you to her because I thought you might become friends and it would affect your feeling toward her. Stupid me, I should have known you would see it differently." Reilly smiled and continued. "I guess I should have told you about my precarious escape from Rita's clutches." Reilly then explained how Rita had pursued him right after the divorce and was now irked at him having her advances rejected.

"You should also know that Ross had a brief fling with Rita after she lost interest in me. That may account for his roundabout way of explaining things. And if I detect a hint of jealousy in your questions, don't worry about me. I'm as loyal as your bird dog."

"Well, does that make me your master?" Adele replied with a smile. "Oh, I almost forgot," she continued, "what do you make of this number?"

Adele pulled the slip of paper from her briefcase and handed it to Reilly while explaining where the partial phone number had come from.

"Well, that explains several things. Zero-one-one means it's an overseas call. The forty-four is England's country code, and nineteen-sixty-two gets you the Winchester area. Just add the right six digits, and you have the number of Klarissa's apartment," said Reilly. "I knew there was someone in the village still in contact with her. Damn her! I'll bet Rita gave Klarissa the false information that showed up in the English court! She partied with us and had plenty of chances to spy on Amy and me."

Adele then explained Donald Houle's link to Rita Wilson and added, "This might also explain how Donald could have know about Klarissa's arrival. I'll pass this new information to the state police on my way through Derby."

"Right, but I'm still puzzled," Reilly replied. "I don't understand why Klarissa would return here in the first place. She couldn't visit Amy without my permission. If she kidnapped Amy again, she couldn't keep her legally in the US or England even if she found a way to get her out of the country. I didn't dare let Klarissa see Amy over Christmas, but as I mentioned before, my lawyer was working on an indemnification agreement with Klarissa's parents that would make a summer visit possible. If they double-crossed me, I'd have their money and English law on my side getting Amy back, and both Klarissa and her parents would lose total contact with Amy."

"So obviously, someone knew Klarissa was coming here. She was murdered for reasons unknown. From this angle, Donald Houle is my top suspect. The problem is that he was fired from the factory early last week and no one seems to know where he is. That's why I'm starting with Jake Paulson. I know where he lives, and Leo Richards and I are going to stop by later today. Yesterday I heard an earful about Jake from the gang. I'm curious to meet him. I'll let you know what we find tomorrow."

As the guard approached, Adele stood and said stiffly, "Well I've got to go, Mr. Bostwick. Mr. Newton will be visiting you this afternoon."

As Adele drove past Norton Pond, Bob Newton left the venerable white wooden county courthouse in Guildhall deep in thought. He drove his Jeep cross lots toward the Newport jail through the black spruces and sphagnum-moss lowlands of Victory Bog, one of the least-populated sections of Vermont. Intermittent snow and ice-packed roads slowed him until he reached Interstate 91 north, where he could cruise safely at 45 mph. This was his first uninterrupted chance to mull over the murder in Canaan and what defense he might offer. Even before hearing the details from his client, he was worrying about a misstep.

The call from Reilly had been a rude surprise. Bob had seen strange happenings in his career, but he couldn't imagine Reilly as a brutal murderer. Then that request from the Clayton woman was unusual, but he had decided to grant it. Now he wasn't sure. He had never defended a client in a capital case. The sudden press interest had come as an unsettling surprise. The first calls had come at his home the night before. He had just checked his office and had more than a dozen calls to return. He had sensed that this was but a trickle and that the flood was yet to rise.

He realized that he had misread the scope of the problem at the outset. These calls from newspaper and television reporters meant that the heat of scrutiny was probably about to burn him. The lead article in that morning's *Burlington Free Press* mentioning Reilly and Klarissa had done nothing to lessen his apprehension. So far, the brutal and twisted nature of this murder wasn't common knowledge, but it was probably about to burst as a tabloid-style favorite.

As he adjusted the Jeep's heater, he thought of Reilly's ill luck, which so contrasted the completely routine divorce case he had just argued. The parents had sought and been granted joint custody of their ten-year-old daughter. Wasn't that what was supposed to have happened for Reilly, Klarissa, and Amy too? He remembered counseling Reilly that you don't win a custody case. One way or another, you'll be connected with the mother of your child. *Connected*, he thought. *How ironic. Reilly has certainly remained connected to Klarissa, but what an odd dance. First, he fights for sole custody to keep his daughter in this country, then he confronts an international abduction, and now they're linked again, this time by murder.* Based on what he had heard, Reilly's third trial could make the other two look benign. He had talked with both Reilly and Adele about the murder and then phoned the state's attorney to inquire about Reilly's status. He was still puzzling about the basis for Reilly's legal defense as he pulled into the jail parking lot.

After Bob Newton identified himself, a guard led him directly to Reilly's cell. His first questions were about Amy and her well-being. Then he turned to darker matters. "Well, the news isn't good, and you may want to get an experienced criminal defense lawyer," Bob said as he sat on the cot opposite Reilly.

"Bob, you're my good news. I know you and trust you. When Amy was abducted, we didn't know a solicitor from a barrister, but somehow you connected me to the best legal team in London. I need a fine lawyer, and that's you."

"The case in England was family law, but this is likely to be first-degree murder. Don't make that decision quickly."

"Bob, I don't have much chance in court, whoever represents me, unless we find what really happened to Klarissa. I'm sure the carnage in my cellar will match the body on the hill. Likewise, I'm sure the investigators will find she was killed with my gun. Of course, I've been home the last few days except for my time teaching. So there it is. I have a revenge motive and no alibi. It certainly appears that I had the opportunity to kill her and was sloppy about the evidence I left behind. Not much room here for a good defense."

Reilly sighed and continued, "I have no doubt that you'll defend me well, but you won't have anything to work with unless we can uncover what has really happened. By the way, thank you for letting Adele be your temporary assistant."

"Look," Bob said softly, "that is no casual matter. And I'm beginning to regret the decision. Adele was persuasive that this would be the best way to protect Amy. I still think that's true, but we have the press to contend with, and if they find out about this cozy arrangement, it won't look good for me or you. I'd feel terrible if I've somehow compromised your defense."

Reilly smiled. "She's pretty tough to argue with. Right?"

"Yeah, she'd probably make a good lawyer."

"Tell me what the press thinks. Maybe they know something useful."

"Well, TV and newspapers were slow to get started, but today they're hungry for the story. There will be live reports by phone from Canaan this evening and reporters interviewing people around the village. You can expect pictures of you, Klarissa, and your house in tomorrow's papers. This could become a field day: 'Public school teacher accused of killing his ex-wife by shooting her in the face with a shotgun.' Right now they'll be digging into the history of your divorce and court struggle in England, too. That'll keep the story alive. So far, they haven't focused on Amy, but that is sure to be next."

Bob shifted his sitting position on the uncomfortable bed and continued, "Look, even if Adele and your friends have evaded reporters so far, this won't last. As of tomorrow, I'm going to have to revoke her law degree and hope the press is none the wiser."

Reilly rolled that over in his mind and then asked, "What have you heard about the police investigation?"

"I understand from talking with the state's attorney this morning that they have tentatively identified the body as Klarissa's. He thinks the identification will be confirmed sometime today. I should know by tomorrow morning. I've also heard that the blood in your basement appears to match Klarissa's type. You and Adele told me your story over the phone, but I need to hear it from you in detail."

Reilly retold the story as completely as he could, including the break-in at Adele's house. He also brought Bob up to date on the plans to protect Amy. Bob left the jail just before noon with his mind filled with quandaries, while in several locations around Vermont, newsmen puzzled over the logistics of covering a juicy murder up in isolated backcountry Canaan.

16.

Un-fucking-believable!

Late Monday afternoon, St-Jovite, Quebec

A string of brightly colored cabins punctuated the serpentine road's ascending passage through the spruce grove. Whether by clever planning or extraordinary luck, all these snow-frosted structures could be seen from the largest glacial boulder next to the base road. In summer it was common to see someone scrambling atop the boulder with a camera. This frigid afternoon, there were no tracks to that boulder, although someone must have succeeded in winter. Many Québécois would recognize these cupcake-like Laurentian cabins . . . not from a map, but from a popular Christmas card.

The afterglow in cabin number two wasn't from a day of skiing. Klarissa Wilcox sat with red eyes and tear-stained cheeks, staring back and forth between the empty glass and the almost-empty wine bottle. The phone rang. She jumped as though someone had read her thoughts.

"Hello . . . Dad?" she asked breathlessly. "I can't stand another day of this!"

Fulton Wilcox's steely reply was no surprise to Klarissa. "I couldn't call earlier today like I promised. I know you want to see Amy, but we've had problems. Dealing with that bastard Reilly is complicated, so you'll just have to be patient. I think you'll see Amy tonight. Monty and I'll bring her there. Can't say what time. Plan to be up late," and then with a familiar edge in his voice, "Make sure you're ready for her."

Klarissa made a sarcastic expression and poured the last of the wine.

"This cabin is driving me crazy. I need to see Amy. Damn it!" She looked at the wine bottle in her hand, then clunked it on the table. "I swear, I've been depressed for months. Even the meds aren't doing much."

Fulton's tone was unchanged. "Look. You'll be OK once you see Amy. Hold yourself together. We may not succeed tonight. If not, I'll call. That'll make tomorrow our last chance. In case of a delay, I've advanced your flight another day. And remember, don't call me at home or work, no matter what happens! With any luck, Amy and I'll see you soon. Got to go."

The click in Klarissa's ear was yet another reminder of her father's odd social graces.

Canaan Village

If old buildings can be old friends . . . Adele daydreamed that the houses around Fletcher Park were elderly Canaan ladies. As she looked across the snow-covered green, she could imagine the houses talking as if they were preparing lunch for town meeting. They had endured the same storms and heard the same babies cry. They remembered the cursing loggers with their sledges and the clip-clop of horses pulling buggies and wagons. They knew the town's stories, even those that predated most living memory, like the time when Abigail Holbrook had first voted in town meeting. And, they would be sure to tell you, it wasn't because she was a woman. She had been a property owner. Through countless summers, these elegant ladies had celebrated the mysterious springtime rebirth of the hardy lawns, trees, and gardens. They had been safe nests cherishing generations of their human families. Survivors of slow yearly cycles of storm and cold and the numerous facelifts with the tickle of paint brushes, they had learned long before to tolerate each other's wear and decay as merely the price they must pay to protect those within. And Adele had no doubt that they remained affable and complementary. This was how Adele's weary mind viewed them that Monday afternoon as she listened to the old ladies talking. That day, they were exclaiming how proud they were of their yellow jewel: the Alice Ward Library across the way.

The timeworn, yet comfortable, two-story apartment house on the southeast corner of the town commons looked directly across to the arched front portico of the town library. Adele was enjoying that viewpoint from the bay window of Mark and Samantha Wilson's ground-floor apartment. Adele knew this old building for many more than its two stories. Its apartments were frequent gathering spots for Reilly and his friends. Just a few steps from Canaan's combination elementary–high school, and housing two teachers, it was everyone's first stop after a hard day. Shelley Roberts and her excitable pets lived on the second floor of the old Victorian, where she had an excellent view of Van Dyke Hill beyond the south edge of town.

Adele was briefly relaxing as the sun descended in the western sky. She could see snow-crowned Van Dyke casting its long, sneaking shadow north-eastward, covering the houses at the edge of the village and spreading its darkness toward New Hampshire. She and Reilly loved local history. They knew that Van Dyke had been a powerful and sometimes ruthless lumber baron who had once cast his own large shadow in the North Country. She fancied that the village houses still remembered his red Stanley Steamer. *How strange,* she thought, *how quickly, even measured in village time, the shadow of the hill completely eclipses the shadow of the man who once ruled the hill.*

Adele was visiting Samantha Wilson and her young daughter. Adele needed little excuse to visit baby Sarah. A hug from this lovely child and another chance to make her laugh provided the uplift Adele needed for the tasks ahead. She used Sam's phone to make a series of calls to friends asking about the Paulson clan. In the back of her mind, she was trying to deduce what Jake Paulson would be like. She and Leo Richards would visit him later that afternoon.

"So what do you think of the gang?" asked Sam as she washed her seven-month-old daughter, whose tiny body was squirming playfully in a green baby bathtub.

Adele responded, "I was amazed by them. I was brought up on a farm that was being taken over by suburbia and wasn't used to a sense of community. The gang's generosity and practical joking were new to me, too. I've learned to love it. I think it has made me more alive and feisty. I remember last October when Cisco and Suzanne were approaching winter with a bad roof and Cisco didn't have it in him to ask for help. Our band of friends spent the weekend putting on the new roof. Conner called it a beer-inspired barn raising. That Saturday was a classic morning! The gang arrived at sun up with a tractor hauling a hay wagon piled with roofing material. They formed a procession up the Fosters' driveway. Ross led the way in his kilt, with bagpipes wailing. Cisco met us in his underwear just outside the woodshed. He stood there, scratching his head. I'll never forget the puzzled look on his face. What a hoot!

"And speaking of beer," Adele laughed, "I was initiated early last summer with beer-powered high jinks. It was soon after Reilly and I started dating, and one of the first things we did together with Lottie. It was just after we had put Amy on the plane to England. We went to visit Conner and Karen. Conner had just knocked down most of the sheetrock in the bedroom he was remodeling. After the fragments stopped flying, Conner rested and apologized that he was out of brew. He then had a home-brewer's revelation. He remembered that Ross had just bottled a fresh batch. Conner told us his plan, but he said we'd have to be stealthy. At that time, Ross lived in a camp on Back Lake. He made and stored his brew in a dirt cellar which, fortunately, had a bulkhead. Conner led the three of us on our mission. It was dark by then. We drove and parked down the road from Ross's camp. We quietly approached the camp from the backyard, opened the bulkhead, and climbed down into the cellar. Reilly helped Lottie down the steps. There, we lifted two freshly minted six-packs of Ross's finest. We then sneaky-petered out to the car and drove back to Conner's dust palace. The true genius of Conner's plan was apparent when he called Ross and invited him over to drink some brew! We laughed and laughed when it finally dawned on Ross that he was drinking his own beer. It might have been a shady lesson on personal property for Lottie, but a first class one on practical joking."

Adele looked out the window to the south. The advance of the hill's shadow prompted her to check her watch. "I'm going to make one last try to get Linda Cowen."

This was the fifth call she had made to friends in town to gather more information about Jake Paulson before her visit.

"Yes, Linda, this is Adele." While they talked for a few minutes, Adele jotted down some sketchy notes. When they had finished, she thanked Linda and turned to talk with Sam.

"The more I learn about these Paulsons and Houles, the less I care for them. Reilly really likes the kids up here. He says they are like Becky Thatcher and Tom Sawyer or the Little Rascals with French accents. But these folks could still be cave dwellers. "

Adele slowly turned and gazed out the window over the snow-bank. She noticed an old car slowly approaching from the north. "Oh, here comes Leo Richards. He's going to be my bodyguard for my visit with Jake."

Sam lifted Sarah from her bath and wrapped her in a thick towel while saying, "Invite him in. I can't wait to hear what was going on in school today. I must have seen state police cars drive by five times."

"Un-fucking-believable!" exclaimed Leo. Then, looking apologetically at Sarah, he amended, "It was an unbelievable day. Every damn kid knew about Reilly even before they arrived. The noise level in the hall was deafening. And the teachers' room wasn't much better. The arrival of the state police caused an uproar. And then the kids would get completely riled up again every time another police car left or came back. . . . We had kids rushing to the windows, pestering cops in the front hall. I couldn't get kids to focus on math no matter what I did. I threatened. I begged. I stood on my desk, swinging one of Reilly's meter sticks over their heads. Nothing worked. Ronny told us to go about business as normal. I told him after our brief morning emergency meeting, 'Yeah, Ronny, you just go about your principal's business as normal, too. What a joke!'

"The kids and teachers were agitated, but at the same time, really upset, and there was nothing we could do about it. Everyone wanted to know more of what happened. The teachers didn't have any news to help them out. The kids adore Reilly and are scared for him in jail. And just think, it's only Monday! When I talked with Ronny at the end of the day, I saw Phil Terry, the guidance counselor, standing outside Ron's office, pale and dazed. The guy looked completely shell-shocked. This is going to be a hell of a week."

"So what did you find out from Ronny?" asked Adele.

"Well, Ron was characteristically tight-lipped, and apparently, the state police did a lot more asking than telling, but I did learn a few things. We all sensed yesterday that the trap Reilly's caught in is almost too slick to be believed. Apparently, the police have that idea, also. So, even though they have him in jail, they're asking questions about Klarissa and who else might not have liked her. Of course, they're also trying to determine what would possibly turn a well-liked, nice guy like Reilly into a killer."

"Did Ron give any indication that the police were asking about Amy?" queried Adele.

"I take it that they asked if she was in school. They must have figured that out by now. I'll bet her grandparents on Klarissa's side want to know where she is."

"You're right, and I expect that they'll pressure the police to locate her. If I were her grandparents, I'd be panicked by not knowing. I'm sorry that we won't be able to tell them for a while, but that is part of the price of keeping Amy safe. What did you hear from our friends? Did they do much better today?"

"I didn't talk to everybody, but damn Ross and Conner," Leo said with a faint smile. "Sometimes I wish I taught shop. Those SOBs did business pretty much as normal. Being on the far end of the elementary-school building, their classes couldn't see the cops come and go. Their kids are all in the middle of projects, and that was just what they needed to do . . . working with their hands . . . to stay marginally functional. So Ross and Conner didn't sense the meltdown the rest of us felt. It seems that none of us who know about Reilly and Amy were questioned by the police, but then there was the press."

"What?" exclaimed Adele.

"Yeah. There were two reporters . . . one from St. Johnsbury and the other from Burlington. I don't know if they were newspaper or TV, but I know that Ronny gave them almost nothing. He politely told them to get lost, so there they were, outside the school with kids streaming out. Now that really . . . shall we say, enhanced . . . the atmosphere. They waited until we started leaving. A few teachers talked with them, but none of our close friends. They might have learned some background on Reilly, not much else, but you know they'll be back."

"I suspect my phone will be ringing soon, too," said Adele.

Leo looked at this watch and said, "We better get going. Jake should be home by now. The factory shift just ended. Maybe we can catch the slimeball before supper."

Adele and Leo suited up for the deep freeze beyond the mahogany front door. Adele leaned down and gave Sarah a parting kiss on the forehead, looked at Sam, and said, "Thanks Sam, I needed this hiding place. We're off to meet Jake. I plan to stop by Suzanne's later this evening. If anything comes up . . . if Mark has learned anything new, please have him pass it on to Suzanne. He may have to drive up there if she's left school, but I'd really appreciate it. See ya."

The air stung their faces as they climbed down the porch steps and into Leo's old Dodge Dart. No heat had been generated when the car had come around the block from school, and the one-mile trip north would do no better, but at least it stopped the wind.

17.

Darwinian in Nature

Before her interlude with Sam and Sarah, Adele had had a chance to compose her mental picture of the Paulson and Houle clans on her drive from Newport that morning. Her phone calls had only added shading to the already dark picture the gang had painted. She realized that she'd seen two kinds of poverty in the North Country. Plain poverty was pretty normal. To her, this meant folks of low income who still showed the industriousness to make life worthwhile. They lived caring lives of consequence. Jake and Donald, on the other hand, had a poverty of both heart and mind. They would still be broke if they had just won the lottery. Both men were wrathful, way-ward, and inconsistent. She thought about them as wrecking balls swinging wildly. They destroyed life's meaning for themselves, their clans, and those others whose lives they carelessly clashed. She knew that both clans had a strain of poverty that was heritable.

Apparently, Jake's training ground had been an emotionally chilled home dictated by a father who had been a failure at all things save his ability to extract obedience within four walls. Jake's mother had run a home to complement her husband's style. The children had been entrapped, wanting for any stability or praise that their world might (but seldom did) offer. Wounds had been awarded at random. The degree of damage was as unpredictable as the next surge of adrenaline. Jake's father had earned good money in construction. By

Canaan standards, it had been a fine job, but the Interstate highway segments he had helped build were far from home. He was gone for weeks, sharing cheap rooms with like-minded losers who had chosen heavy drinking and gambling as their entertainment options. Not much of his paychecks had made it home. He could be smart and personable when sober, but this wasn't the father Jake would know except in deep memory.

Jake was one among five children. Their mother had run the home and the family war. She raised her children by skillful attrition bounded by the rules of neglect. She cultivated family alliances and double-crosses. Her kids were often in trouble with neighbors, but family values meant loyalty to clan. Mother would tell the neighbor to go to hell and then would punish the accused depending on his or her birth order. Over those child-rearing years, townsfolk associated Paulson Lane with crass, dangerous people whose lives reflected their violent denial of a self-imposed inferiority.

The birthmarks from domestic warfare were different for each child. Jake's name could have been Menace. In his late twenties, Jake had been tall as anyone in town and weighed more than 250 pounds. He liked to use his size to push people a bit just to see what would happen. He backed off when he sensed personal power, whether physical, financial, or intellectual. He had been a bully on the school grounds. As an adult, he was a watcher. He was inept at social interactions, very slow at learning, and reluctant to trust. His organization principle seemed to be physical force, whether used or implied. He advertised his nature through his carriage and attitude.

Jake had married Chantal, a girl smarter than he, which is not much of a compliment. He had seen fit to run his family by example, that is, the example he had experienced. He had one son, who was about five the year Reilly's family moved to town. Chantal's wandering bruises and his son's foul vocabulary gave witness to the displeasures of home. This was a time when schools and social agencies were beginning to recognize the abuse that had always been there. Recent rumor had it that Jake was no longer abusing Chantal and that his love interests were elsewhere. He was still occasionally in trouble with the law and currently had a petty theft charge pending.

The Houle lineage was no better. Donald had three sisters and two brothers. His father had been a logger when he worked and an obnoxious drunkard when he didn't. His mother was a housewife of sorts. Donald's mother bad-mouthed her husband to the kids by force of habit. Over the years of Donald's childhood, her resentment had grown to the point of endemic insanity. By this time, she became a paranoid, foul-tempered, closet alcoholic. The home war culminated late one fall. Father had been logging in Maine. Demand was slow and work halted two weeks earlier, and he still hadn't come home. Mother was out of money and threats. In a paroxysm of drunken rage, she destroyed the basement sump pump. Their house foundation was porous to a hillside aquifer. Without the pump, the cellar started to fill. After a couple of days, water shorted and ruined the oil burner. This coincided with an early-winter cold spell registering fifteen below. Next, the pipes froze and the family had greeted winter without heat or water. Father rejoined the war at this point. The Houle kids tried to carve out their own safe, albeit freezing, bedroom territories as the battle raged. They barely survived the winter by hauling water and burning green wood in a leaky wood stove. The one warm room where the kids might have studied was the prime battle site.

After that winter, divorce had been in order. Mother got a loan, razed the old abode, and had a smaller house built in the same location. Father moved to Island Pond. Over the next few years, the kids grew up and settled in the North Country. Mother had her acreage subdivided so Donald, like her other offspring and their ill-chosen spouses, could settle, as Cisco described them, "like cluster flies."

Donald had been prevented from dropping out of school twice, and then, over a few months, was thrown out three times. The last exit was midway through his second try at eighth grade. He had been expelled for punching his pregnant English teacher. Donald never had any particular fondness for language.

Donald had followed his dad's example as a logger. In his middle twenties, he married by shotgun, but this lasted less than a year, when friends of the bride ganged up on him and rescued her, pending divorce. In the ensuing years, Donald's drunken belligerence was known to set a new standard for the North Country.

It was almost dark when Adele and Leo left Sam's apartment. On the way to the Paulson apartment, Adele gave Leo an overview of her plan to question Jake. She guessed that if Jake were into capital crime, he wouldn't talk with them at all. If they convinced him to answer some questions, he might make a slip or tell them something useful about Klarissa's other enemies. She and Leo agreed on the ruse they would use.

Jake and his wife lived upstairs in a small, dirty, yellow house at the north end of the village near the rail spur leading to the Beecher Falls furniture factory. It was one of the town's cheapest rentals, with a cluttered yard filled with old car parts. Leo carried a paper bag up the wooden steps. When they knocked on the door, Jake answered. He looked puzzled as if figuring out a threat. Adele was surprised at first that his face was almost handsome, but soon saw a default sneer appear as his face relaxed. Adele introduced herself and Leo, and then said, "We're here to talk to you about Klarissa Bostwick, who also called herself Klarissa Wilcox. We'd appreciate it if you would answer a few questions."

"She's dead and I don't see your badges, so fuck off." He started to close the door.

Leo put his foot in the door and forced it abruptly half open with his free arm. Leo and Jake were nose-to-nose. Jake pulled back to throw a punch but held back, seemingly restrained by Leo's absolute lack of fear.

"Jake, simmer down," Leo continued calmly. "We've come to help you. You have a court case coming up soon, and we can keep your life from getting unnecessarily complicated."

"We can almost guarantee that you're going to get hassled by the police this week," Adele quickly continued. "The cops will be on you big-time. They're doing a murder investigation, and you're about to become a major suspect. On the other hand, if you help us, we might be able to prevent that from happening."

"I don't believe any of that bullshit. My legal situation ain't none of your fucking business, and the police got nothing new on me."

Jake pushed back on the door, but Leo held his ground and continued, "Look, Jake, this isn't new business, but you still could get reamed for it. We promise to be much easier for you to deal with than the cops." Leo smiled with a self-satisfied mixture of pleasure and threat.

"Jake," Adele spoke up persuasively, "we know you once threatened to kill Klarissa Wilcox and that the police would find this really interesting."

"Goddamn it!" Jake yelled close to Leo's face. "That was a couple years ago. I never did anything to her. In fact I did her a favor last time I saw her. She left town months ago. Why the fuck would anybody think I'd murder her now?"

"We agree, Jake," said Leo calmly, "and we'd like to be on your side, but we've talked to the woman who was there when you threatened Klarissa. Reilly Bostwick told us he could never figure out why Klarissa never officially reported that death threat to the police or her agency. We know that she also asked the witness not to talk about it. That made us real curious. We wondered why Klarissa apparently wasn't afraid of you."

"That's right, Jake," said Adele. "We figured out two things. One, that the police weren't likely to hear about that death threat . . . unless someone told them, and two, that you would be a good person to ask about Klarissa. Look, we're only looking for information. None of us can figure out why she came back to town."

"Goddamn! You've got this all wrong. I was on good terms with that bitch before she left town. I even helped her out. I'm clueless why she came back, and you're just talking one long line of shit."

Adele looked up into Jake's eyes and spoke in a softer voice. "Jake, Reilly Bostwick is my man. Leo and I are investigating Klarissa on our own to help him out. I have a list of people who could have been a threat to Klarissa, and I am going to turn it over to the police tomorrow. The death threat has to put you number one on my list. So, with just a little bit of cooperation, your name might just disappear from that list. So ease up."

"Got it, Jake?" Leo continued. "If you can convince her that you really were on good terms with Klarissa, there wouldn't be any reason for Adele to involve you, particularly if Klarissa chose never to make a big deal out of the death threat. So why don't you save a little heat and let us in? I've got a few beers in this bag and don't see why we can't have a civilized conversation."

Jake replied, "You're fucking wasting my time." He then paused for a few seconds, thinking while eyeing Leo's bag. "OK, OK, It wouldn't hurt to talk. I've got nothing to hide, and I just don't need any more trouble in my life right now."

Jake opened the door. Adele and Leo settled in to two ragged, unmatched living room chairs. Leo passed around three beers.

The room, with its grimy, dark colors and stale, smoky air, set the right tone for Jake's story. A lever-action deer rifle hung on the wall above the chair next to the TV, surrounded by the splendor of the peeling green wallpaper.

Adele prompted Jake, who was now seated underneath the rifle, "So tell us about how you knew Klarissa, why you threatened her . . . yeah, and what was the favor you mentioned?"

"OK, OK. I told my wife, Chantal, not to call that fuckin' mental health agency. That's where all the trouble started," grumbled Jake in a deep voice. "They talked her into going to Colebrook for help. Chantal had some bruises, and some jerk there wanted to make a federal case out of it. So pretty soon, the cops were talking to me about abuse and threatened to arrest me. I was really getting pissed off. I figured what went on in the privacy of my home was my business. I made Chantal tell me who she called for help. It turned out to be the Wilcox bitch right here in the village, so I made a point of finding out what she looked like.

"A few weeks later I was on a toot. Shit! Donald Houle and I started drinking about eight on a Saturday morning. We promised to help his fucked-up cousin Adrian move to Albany, Vermont, in a U-Haul truck. Adrian is a pisshead, so I'm not sure how we got into this. He promised us all the beer we could drink. Hell…I remember we started by washing the bug crap off the windshield with beer. We were half-looped by the time we got the truck loaded in Beecher Falls. Donald and I drove the truck while Adrian went ahead in his junker. We hooted and sang all the way. We must have pissed ten times and never stopped driving. I remember once Donald drove from the passenger side while I hung off the running board, pissing. I almost got flipped off when we hit the frost heaves around Norton Pond. I tell you, mister man, we was in a good mood when we reached Albany. Cousin Adrian complained that we broke some of his shit, but what the fuck do you want from free labor. We drank all the way back with the empty truck. Fuckin' Donald was driving on the way home. That crazy Frenchman lost his license years ago. Well, he drove right up to the tailpipe of this old geezer's car on the curvy road just outside of Island Pond. Then he laid on the horn and almost scared the guy off the road. It—"

"Jake," Adele interrupted in frustration, "what the hell does this have to do with Klarissa?" She was excited to hear the introduction of Donald Houle's name but wanted to get the story back to Klarissa.

Jake, who was getting wound up enjoying his own story, just shrugged and continued. "I was just getting to that. When we got to town, Houle dropped his beer on the floor of the cab and ran us off the road when he tried to grab it. We were stuck in the muddy corn-field across the street from the house where the Wilcox bitch had a first-floor apartment. I didn't know she lived there. So there I was, knocking on the door to ask for a hand. She came to the door, and I almost shit a brick. I could see some woman sitting behind her at the kitchen table. When I recognized Klarissa, my blood boiled. But, by the Jesus, I might have mouthed-off at her, but I never touched her.

"Well, we managed to haul the truck backward out of the mud with a borrowed tractor. We knew that next day we'd fucked up. The geezer took our plate number, and Donald could look forward to another DWI. I knew that Klarissa would come back to bite my ass. So I decided to make nice with her. I knew she wouldn't believe me, so I had Chantal call her and tell her what a good boy I'd been lately. She did a really good job, 'cause when I went to the bitch's place and apologized, she didn't even make a fuss. I said I was sorry, blamed old Donald, and told her to let me know if I could help her out in any way. Soon after that, Chantal got a long call from her asking if she could trust me to help her. I didn't hear about that at the time, but it must have worked. Anyway, I did her a favor, and until now, figured she forgot all about me."

"What was the favor?" asked Leo.

"A few days after I apologized, Klarissa shows up at the door. She said she wants to take me up on my offer. When she told me about it, I decided, what the hell? I always wanted to visit that com-mune."

"Jake, I'm not following this," said Adele. "What does the com-mune have to do with this?"

"It was funny. She wanted me for my muscles. She said that Father Xavier told her about this lady . . . Paula . . . something who lives in the Averill commune who was a punching bag for the bum she was shacked-up with. I remember…Dickson was her last name. The boyfriend was a big mean SOB, so she asked me if I'd come along as her escort. Escort, my ass! She wanted a bodyguard. I said OK. I didn't give a shit about her, but I thought it might put me on her good side after I had cursed her out. Besides, I had only been in the commune once and didn't mind poking around there some more just for fun."

"When was this?" asked Adele.

"I don't know. When did bitch-lady leave town?"

"Klarissa? She left Canaan a year ago last August."

"Then it was that same spring. I think it was probably late April or early May. It was still muddy."

Adele knew the Averill Wildflower Commune had been active in the late 1960s. In the '70s it had declined. All that remained now was a cluster of shacks for a few indigenous hardy souls and a varying band of transients who were as free of proper legal identities as they were of roots. Occasionally, some violence would occur necessitating a visit by the local or state police, but most of the time, they lived by their own laws, which were more Darwinian in nature. Residents were seldom seen unless walking or hitching Route 114.

"We cruised up there on a Sunday afternoon," Jake continued. "Klarissa decided to wait in the car while I talked with this old lady who lives alone in cabin at the end of the first branch off the main trail. That's Bessie. I'd heard about her before. She seems to know the history of the place and all the coming and goings. Klarissa told me to ask where we could find a woman named Paula. The lady didn't ask for a last name but knew it was Dickson. She told me where Paula and this guy Brad lived deep in the park. She was curious why I wanted to see her. The lady seemed to think that it was unlikely that anyone would come to visit them and if they did, it would only be Brad doing the inviting. She said that Brad was kind of scary and a real asshole when drinking. Paula would stop by her cabin once in a while when Brad would let her, but Paula usually didn't look very 'healthy.' I think the lady figured I was cutting out Paula to take her away and Brad and me would have a big rumble. I let her think that. I was laughing about that when I went back to the car to get Klarissa.

"It's was a long walk down the main trail, and then another branch trail to the left. We found the cabin and knocked. The grubby SOB came to the door looking surprised. He sized me up and decided to play nice. We went in. Paula was over by the sink, cleaning up her hands before sitting down.

"Klarissa introduced herself. Paula looked kind of pale and glanced a couple of times at Brad. Klarissa told Brad that she wanted to talk with Paula alone on a private matter. This Brad guy looked kind of upset and maybe just a little bit scared. I hadn't expected that. I thought he'd blow up and try to throw us out. I wasn't worried; he was my size, but heavier. I was still pretty sure I could take him. Might have been fun. Anyway, he agreed. The women stayed in the cabin. We weren't to come back for fifteen minutes. So we left for a while."

"Did you talk with Brad?"

"Na, I didn't want anything to do with that bastard. We went our separate ways. I walked to the far end of the commune. It's their junkyard back there."

"What did Paula look like?" Adele asked, wondering if she had ever met the woman in town or at the hospital.

"Oh, about your height or maybe a little shorter, light build, nice tits, long blond hair. Probably looked nice sometime."

"What happened when you went back to the cabin?"

"That was funny. We all sat down. Klarissa told Brad that she had noticed bruises on Paula's arms and face and it looked to her like Paula was being beaten. She told him Paula said she had fallen gathering wood and that Brad never touched her. Klarissa said she wasn't going to do anything but that she would visit her again to check on Paula. That asshole Brad was fuming, but he showed us out and slammed the cabin door behind us. It was quiet back in the cabin, at least as long as we could hear. Klarissa wouldn't tell me anything else, but back in the car, I saw that she carried that camera, and I'm sure those bruises got recorded. After that, Klarissa dropped me off right here, and that's it . . . end of story"

"Have you seen Paula since then?" asked Adele.

"No, but I saw the asshole she lives with just last night. As ugly as ever, he was nosing around the Riverbend. Funny thing . . . you know, he was asking about the Wilcox woman too."

Adele sat up in surprise and asked. "What was he trying to find out?"

Leo leaned forward and slipped Jake a second beer.

"Hell, I don't know. I didn't talk with him. I had other things on my mind, but you couldn't help hearing them. He was mostly talking with Ike Blanchard, but I think he talked with a couple of the other guys before Donald Houle joined them."

"Donald Houle!" Adele exclaimed with increasing interest.

"Oh yeah, Donald was there. I remember now. I think the three of them were ranting about Bostwick's daughter as well as the dead bitch. I don't know what that was about . . . probably nothing. Everyone's been blabbing about that murder. Funny though," Jake said with a faint but ugly smile, "I haven't seen anyone weeping."

"We heard that Donald Houle also threatened Klarissa. What do you know about that?"

"That's an old story. Houle was just roaring drunk again and got thrown in jail for the night. He must have threatened dozens of others, but they're all still alive, as far as I know."

Adele suddenly felt ready to move on. She needed to hear what Ike Blanchard could tell them. Leo got the nod from her and stood up abruptly while saying, "Well, Jake, we do appreciate the help. Here. Keep the rest of the six-pack."

Leo's car warmed as they talked, parked next to the town commons.

"Goddamn it!" said Adele. "I don't like all our suspects nosing around, asking about Amy. Also, it's too crazy to find Jake, Donald Houle, and this Brad character all at the same place."

"Hey, let's wait to see what Ike can tell us. You know, finding those three bums together may look strange to you, but in a town this size, there are nothing but coincidences. Shit ... everyone crosses paths here.

"But I still can't get over finding Jake, Brad, and Houle in the same bar!"

"Well, from my point of view, the odds are about the same as that of finding three similar flies stuck to the same rancid piece of flypaper."

"Leo, you always seem to have a different way of looking at things, but coincidence or not, we need to have a powwow with Ike."

"Agreed. Next stop: Ike and Sal's."

"You know," said Adele with a lilt in her voice, "I feel guilty misleading Jake like that. He's such a dummy. He bought our line of bullcrap despite the fact that the police will still find out that he threatened Klarissa when they question Reilly."

"Don't worry about it. He'll be pissed at us . . . then we deal with it, but for now, just use the Golden Rule in reverse."

"Now, Leo, do I dare ask what that means?"

"My rule for handling scum bags is simple and easy. I just do unto them what they would willingly do unto me."

"Well, in that case, I don't know whether to say bullshit or amen."

Ike and Sally Blanchard lived in a diminutive apartment downstream from the village center. Their drafty kitchen was nippy on their guests' ankles as they ate an improvised dinner around the worn oak table. Ike and Sal listened attentively while Adele and Leo tag-teamed their story about Jake. Ike was astonished that he had been with all three of Adele's suspects the night before and was getting progressively more upset that he might have endangered Amy. As Sal stacked plates, Adele and Leo got to specifics with Ike.

"What about Houle?" Leo asked.

"Well, he talked about Klarissa a bit . . . didn't like her, but then he went rambling on about a bunch of other people he didn't like, and why he can't find work. Donald is always trying to get you to shed a tear for him. He probably gets beers that way. I don't think he's especially interested in Klarissa, although he was smiling, happy she was dead. But Houle arrived to a conversation that was already happening. It was Mungeon who seemed focused on Amy and the murder."

"Tell us what happened," prompted Adele.

"I arrive around nine and sat at Brad's table. He was surprisingly pleased to see me. Everyone had been talking about the murder, and Mungeon was eager to pump me for what I knew."

"Did Houle know this Mungeon character?" asked Leo.

"I didn't think so when they met, but when I came back from the can, the two had their heads together like old buddies. After that they both seemed even more interested in what I had to tell them. Brad started asking about Amy again. He almost jumped out of his seat when I told him that Amy left with Sal on Friday night. Now I know I screwed up. After Klarissa's murder, I shouldn't have said anything about Amy. I didn't find out until today that the gang was hiding her. Damn!"

"Don't worry," said Adele, "if anything, you got Mungeon to look in the wrong place. What exactly did you tell him?"

"I think I told him that Sal had taken Amy to Reilly's mom in Richmond on Friday and hadn't brought her back when she returned Sunday. Come to think of it, Mungeon left right after I told him that Amy was probably still in Richmond."

"Crap!" said Leo. "We've got to tell the police! This may be the link between the murder and kidnap attempt. It could also explain how Mungeon learned Klarissa was coming here."

"Right!" said Adele. "I want you to tell Paul Marshall what we've learned. But don't get too excited. All we know is that Mungeon is a badass who disliked Klarissa and is curious about Amy. He might have known Klarissa was coming to Vermont, but that doesn't mean he murdered her. Why put the body on display . . . the elaborate trap for Reilly? What was to be gained by kidnapping Amy? We still don't know that much. I agree we want the police to investigate Mungeon and Houle. Our new information will catch their interest. And be sure to tell them Brad may have gone to Richmond looking for Amy at Elaine Bostwick's house. Now I think we're making progress. At least I'll have lots of questions to ask tomorrow. You know . . . as much as all this frightens me, it does offer some hope for Reilly."

Leo started pulling on his jacket as he turned to Adele. "I'm off to find Paul Marshall. Where are you going next?"

"Suzanne is expecting me. Let me know if you learn anything new. When you tell Marshall what we learned about Brad and the commune, it wouldn't hurt to mention that Jake Paulson was helpful to us."

Adele stood and began putting on her parka while Leo waited in the doorway. She turned to Ike, who was still seated at the table. "By the way, do you know what kind of a vehicle Brad drives?"

"That's funny. I've seen him driving around the village several times this last week, and some of the time he looked all dressed up with his hair combed. He's normally such a grub. You know . . . now that I think of it, I couldn't get any eye contact from him when he was all dressed up."

"So what was he driving?" Adele persisted.

"It's a large black pickup truck."

Leo and Adele shared a startled glance, then headed out the door with new sense of urgency.

18.

Clandestine

Richmond, Vermont

Monty wasn't amused. His shoulders were square to the back door, with the knocking inches from his right ear. His pistol's silencer lightly touched the stained hardwood. In the faint light, his pale latex gloves almost glowed, while his black ski mask, sweatshirt, and pants blended into the shadows. He took a slow, deep breath and flexed his muscles, ready for action.

When he had told the old man that Bostwick had sent the girl to Richmond, Monty was ordered to snatch her there. The old man had said that Richmond was well suited for the abduction, but Monty should have read a warning in the old man's voice. He had sounded nervous. That was a first. The old coot had meticulously researched Canaan but hadn't had time to do the same here. The sly perfectionist had been forced to act quickly without crucial information, and now the risk was Monty's. His scouting after dark had started well, and he had broken into the house easily but soon realized that their plan had been blown. No one was home. The room air was fifty-five degrees, and the light he had seen in the living room was controlled by a timer. He took the notepad next to the phone, then went upstairs and pocketed a few trinkets while searching the bedrooms. His hunt for treasure and clues ended abruptly when he descended the stairs near the back door. Suddenly, all thoughts focused on escape.

The voice wavered a tremolo of fear. "Who's there? Whoever you are, we've called the police. And my son and his dog are at the front door, so don't plan on going anywhere!"

Damn it! Fuckin' vigilante, Monty said to himself. *I thought this operation looked too easy.* Unknown to the old man, Ellen Bostwick's village home was always watched by neighbors whenever her blue Chevy Nova was away for more than a day. That section of Richmond village had seen little transience in the last twenty years, and in that time, many informal conventions had arisen. As the crime rate had increased in the '70s, everyone had started locking windows as well as doors and had begun letting neighbors know when they were away. Two recent break-ins that winter had neighbors on high alert.

Monty knew any escape would be a matter of timing. This guy must have see his flashlight beam and called the cops. Now, before the cops arrived, he needed to confront two yokels and a dog. His truck was behind the house in a parking lot shared by a bank and restaurant. He knew the local backroads only well enough to want to avoid them where possible. Getting to his truck might be no more difficult than shooting the guy on the other side of the door. It was the step after that that worried him. He decided quickly on another approach. He went to the living room to check out front. A stout young man and a mean-looking dog were coming up the front walkway and approaching the stairs to the porch and the front door. Monty acted with practiced speed. He stepped to the middle of the living room to have the man and dog in sight. He took aim at the dog and fired rapidly three times. The first bullet blew out the window and made way for two accurate shots that dropped the dog. Monty shot the man in his left leg as he turned toward his dog. As the man screamed in pain and then called desperately for help, Monty opened the back door and made a dash for the parking lot. His diversion had worked, and no one had seen him exit.

He ran past his own truck to a young couple about to get into an old Ford Fairlaine. The girl was carrying a pizza. With a clawing motion, Monty knocked the box to the ground. He grabbed her around the neck with his left arm, held the gun to her head, and told them to shut up. As he held her, he ripped off one rubber glove, then the other, and tossed them on the snow.

He told the boyfriend. "Get in the car and wait."

The boyfriend obeyed and then watched in shock as Monty maneuvered the girl to the far door, which he opened briskly. He pushed the girl violently across the front seat into the boy. By the time both had recovered, Monty was low in the back seat, with the pistol barrel against the girl's neck.

"Start up nice and slow. Then drive down by the round church and make everything look normal, or you won't have a girlfriend any-more."

Monty slumped lower while keeping the gun aimed at the girl. They drove out of the parking lot, took a left across the railroad tracks, and then crossed the old iron bridge over the Winooski River. Monty gruffly told the boy to take a left after the landmark church. This led to a road that paralleled the river heading east. A few miles later, he had them turn right.

About four miles south, he forced them out into the snowy dirt road with no houses in sight. They were scantily dressed for the weather, and he left them surrounded by tall snowbanks as he spun around northward and drove back to Richmond. At the bridge, he stopped and pulled off his ski mask. After wiping the prints off the pistol, he heaved mask and gun downstream into an open section of cold water. He quickly removed his sweatshirt and pants, revealing a blue button-down cotton dress shirt and a neat pair of chinos. More clothes were absorbed into the cold water below.

He calmly parked in the bank lot next to his truck. He could see flashing blue lights reflected off the sides to the houses. He pulled out a new red ski parka from behind the seat. As he slipped behind the wheel, he could hear the siren of an accelerating ambulance that he imagined was heading to Burlington.

He carefully and slowly took a right from the bank lot toward the town's main crossroad. A cop was directing traffic there. He could see to his right that all of Richmond's police force was at the scene.

He turned left onto Route 2 and, just as he had expected, encountered the state police roadblock just before the interstate highway entrance.

Well, here's another chance to try the old man's paperwork.

Monty was the perfect gentleman with the cop. He answered all questions fully. A radio check confirmed his conviction-free background and the legitimacy of his truck registration. After his smooth and unrushed answers, he was allowed to pass.

With this crisis under control, Monty decided to crash in Burlington for the night. He found a cheap hotel near the rotary at the base of Ledge Road and picked up a six of beer from a mom-and-pop shop. Before going to his room, he removed his spare Beretta pistol under the truck seat. No point getting caught short.

He figured the old man would be pissed again, but he didn't give a shit this time. The grab in Richmond had been his idea. This was getting awful chancy, but now there could be no retreat.

Pittsburg, New Hampshire

The frigid Pittsburg, New Hampshire, night was shrouded in northern lights. Adele's dark-green Subaru bumped slowly over the snowy ruts up Suzanne's long driveway. Trotsky and D'Ory were alert in the back seat. The temperature was falling sharply downward like a deflected ax. Her car heater was barely able to clear the window frost. Adele was running on emotional fumes when she pulled into the high-banked yard late that Monday evening. After turning off her lights and letting her eyes adjust to starlight, she gasped as a dark-gray, shaggy, pony-size apparition charged her car. Both dogs barked protectively right behind her head, and a spike of fear shot through her. She wondered if her mind was altogether too tired to function. Soon, she shrugged off her panic and laughed at herself in relief when she realized that it was only Aggie, or more formally, Agrona, the Fosters' enormous Irish wolfhound. As the shock subsided and the golden retrievers in the back seat relaxed, Adele remembered that this was indeed a gentle beast, although Aggie was big enough to gobble small poodles as snacks. She found her flashlight in the glove compartment and left the pups in the car. Aggie greeted her and trotted merrily to the woodshed as Adele followed the steep-walled snow path to the back to the door, where she knocked and entered.

Suzanne was sipping wine in an elegant crystal glass after correcting the English papers spread out on her small desk. Without a word, Suzanne got up and gave Adele a long hug. The sound of Cisco's snoring drifted gently from the loft.

"Bet you wouldn't refuse a glass of wine."

Adele nodded gratefully as she shed her outer layers. After warming up by the round oak stove, Adele took the glass of red jug wine that Suzanne had waiting and then sank into one of Cisco's giant chairs.

"Thanks, I needed that," Adele sighed as she sipped the wine then hopped to a chair nearer the stove. "Leo Richards and I just had a delightful visit with Jake. Apparently, he likes to hang around with Donald Houle."

"Well, it doesn't surprise me. They share the same bad habits. Did you learn anything interesting about Houle?"

"Yes, but not just from Jake."

Adele explained Ross's discovery about Donald and Rita and the need to learn Houle's whereabouts. Suzanna said she would ask around town in the morning.

"We did get a more urgent lead from Jake that'll take us in a completely new direction." Adele explained Jake's role linking Klarissa and Father Xavier with Brad Mungeon and his girlfriend at the commune.

Suzanne had never heard of Mungeon but agreed that he was a more credible suspect than Jake. Suzanne had taught kids from commune families and said that very few kids were now being raised there. She thought the commune rogues had pushed out the idealists who had founded the place in the mid '60s.

"A few North Country winters can sap your idealism, particularly if there are warmer places to go," said Suzanne. "I probably shouldn't talk, because we live uncomfortably close to the land, but I still can't imagine settling in that threadbare place. On the other hand, if I were a fugitive, that commune might be the last place the law would look for me."

"Oh, I forgot to mention. Ike Blanchard says this guy Brad has been trying to find out where Amy is . . . and he drives a black truck. That's why I asked Leo to alert the police."

"I hope you don't try to interview Brad Mungeon the way you did Jake. We promised Reilly to protect you, but that's not going to work if you go poking around that commune."

"Well, don't worry yet," said Adele as she took a sip and leaned closer to the stove. "I know this guy is dangerous, whether or not he killed Klarissa. I want to find more about him indirectly, and I'm certainly not going to knock on his cabin door in the deep, dark woods of Averill. After I see Reilly tomorrow, I plan to see what Father Xavier can tell me about Brad."

"Good . . . stupid and dead isn't the best combination. Speaking of which...you mentioned Klarissa. Are you sure she's dead? What do you know about the fingerprints? Mark stopped by an hour ago and passed on the new information."

"Good. I was hoping that Mark had learned something new. The word from jail this morning was that Klarissa had been tentatively identified as the victim, but Reilly and I didn't hear anything about fingerprints. What did Mark learn?"

"Well, Mark cornered Avery Clark after school and took the crusty old constable to supper at the Northland. The factory let Avery tag along with Roland Coté, who seems to be the detective on the case. Mark couldn't get Avery to tell all, but after a few beers, he got some tidbits. He heard that Klarissa had been identified by her fingerprints and a scar on her arm. He said the state police have a record of her flight to Canada but no evidence yet of her renting a car or crossing the border."

"Damn it. Poor Reilly!" Adele jumped up and quickly paced the living room. "If this is confirmed, we'll have to tell Amy that her mother is dead and that her dad is in jail. What a sad, tragic mess!"

Adele leaned on the kitchen wall as tears came to her eyes. Her face was red as she paced the floor again. "I'm still not going to tell Reilly about the fingerprints until I hear it directly from the police or

Bob Newton. This makes me so goddamned angry! I don't believe those fingerprints. I just know that Reilly didn't do it."

"Look, this is really important," Suzanne said. "Please talk with me before you tell Amy. And please tell Reilly that I have a friend, Rosemary Mayer, who lives in Colebrook. Rosy is a counselor and has experience with children and grieving. She's wise and caring. I know she can help us when Reilly makes the decision."

"Thanks, Suzanne," replied Adele, who was gradually calming down. "You're great. Reilly will appreciate everything."

"By the way, what do we know about those strange phone calls on Sunday?"

Adele slipped back into her chair, took a deep breath, and answered, "I just called Nancy Watkins. She had to make many tries before she got Mr. Wilcox. She said it wasn't the same voice. He accepted Nancy's condolences gracefully as if he believes his daughter is dead."

"Well, that means someone else made those calls and we'll still have to stay alert to a possible kidnapping. "Oh, another thing," Suzanne continued, "as you probably heard, school was a zoo today. Some of Reilly's students were really upset. Nellie Reindeau started a group to raise money for his legal defense. And there were reporters swarming around town, interviewing teachers and Reilly's neighbors. Mark heard that people were starting to speculate about Amy. This pressure will be greater tomorrow. As much as we can mislead the reporters or even Avery, it would be a very bad idea to stonewall the state police about Amy's whereabouts. We need to be ready to work with them to protect her. I think we might be able to hold out for one day more. Reilly will have to decide soon, or it may be the police telling Amy that she has lost her family."

"Oh, and I nearly forgot," she continued, "You remember asking me about Beaulieu, or Bu-lee, as the English would say? You know, I think they enjoy murdering the French language like that." Suzanne laughed as she searched around her desk and picked up a bundle of notes. Her library training and contacts had come through. "I think I found some useful information for you."

"What did you discover?"

"I didn't remember Bu-lee when you mentioned it, but once I connected it to SOE, I realized that I already knew some helpful information. Then I phoned and heard some specifics from a British friend in New York City who was an officer in World War II."

"What's SOE?" asked Adele as frustration gave way to curiosity.

"It's Special Order Executive, one of Winston Churchill's clandestine programs for fighting the Germans. It placed agents behind enemy lines to throw gravel in the gears of the Nazi war machine."

"Are you saying that SOE trained spies?"

"No, there must have been overlap in the kind of training they received, but the goal of this outfit was to cause disruption and sap German morale. This involved sabotage of military equipment, bombing factories, and cutting communications as well as blowing up bridges, setting fires . . . that sort of thing. They also spread disinformation and, in a few cases, did assassinations. They trained agents to live months, even years, behind enemy lines before performing specific missions. That's where Bu-lee came in. It was a training school, and it must have been a tough one. A lot of agents died in the field. The slightest misstep could lead to a noose or concentration camp. They trained some pretty remarkable people, but I don't know what kind of neighbors they would make in peacetime."

"How might an American have been involved in this?"

"I think there are several possibilities that could apply to Klarissa's father. First, there were a few American agents in SOE who had volunteered to fight beside the Brits before we entered the war. Like other agents, they had to be bilingual and know some part of Europe well. A major part of his training would have been at Bu-lee. Some agents after successful missions became trainers in the program, which could mean a later stay at Bu-lee for a year or more. A third possibility comes from the fact that there were some connections between our intelligence service—the Office of Strategic Services—and the SOE. Fulton Wilcox might have been attached to Bu-lee in that role. My friend says that the OSS, which later became the CIA, learned a lot from the Brits."

"If they trained him, what could he do?"

"Agents were selected through a brutal screening process. Those who passed went to an isolated training camp in Scotland. Here they were put in top physical condition and were trained in survival and hand-to-hand combat. Among other skills, they were taught to kill noiselessly without weapons. After this, they were transferred to one of the estates that SOE took over during the war. Bu-lee was probably their most important one. Here they learned trade craft, how not to be followed, and how to be cool when interrogated. They also had to learn how to flawlessly assume another identity. Other training also included intimate knowledge of weapons, use of explosives, even lock picking. You mentioned the town of Briggens. That's interesting, too. Briggens isn't a town. It is another country estate. That is where SOE had their forgery unit. Their forgers were graduates of Britain's finest prisons, and even some convicted forgers who were removed from jail to serve."

"Wow. Did you learn anything about 'fanny'? What's that about?"

"Make that F-A-N-Y," Suzanne spelled. "That's an acronym for First Aid Nursing Yeomanry. FANY Corps was formed as a women's voluntary organization before WWI. They were brave young women who worked close to the front lines, driving ambulances and running soup kitchens. In WWII, many were drivers, clerks, and such, but there was one group that worked within SOE. Some of these were drivers and clerks, but many deciphered code and kept radio contact with agents in Europe. It's possible that Klarissa's mother was a FANY, maybe where Fulton Wilcox trained or worked."

"So we don't know what Fulton Wilcox's true role was at Bu-lee, but we know he was exposed to the SOE world. From that mindset, no wonder he wasn't thrilled with Reilly's position on Viet Nam," noted Adele. "This gives us some idea of what he might be capable of, but I don't see how it fits. He could probably stage an elaborate crime, but in this case it seems that he'd have much to lose in exchange for the satisfaction of seeing Reilly in jail. Even if he were the killer, the old guy must have had assistance dragging the body up Reilly's hill. I need something more. I don't know what." Adele slowly yawned as she finished her wine, then stood and rinsed her glass with water from a pitcher near the sink.

Suzanne got up and gave Adele another long hug, saying "Tell Reilly that we're all pulling for him and that we think you're making excellent progress. Good luck tomorrow."

Adele said goodbye, zipped up her outer jacket, pulled her wool tuke over her ears, and turned to face the painful cold. Her exhausted eyelids were drooping, but she knew that with chores ahead, relief was at least a couple of hours away. At least she knew sleep would come fast and anesthetize her against the lonesome resonance of her home with her daughter away and her love in jail.

Paul Marshall, dressed only in boxer shorts and socks, had a toothbrush in his mouth when the phone rang. He rushed to answer, hoping Francine and the baby would stay asleep. The intercept after one ring was successful, but his conversation started with a mouth full of toothpaste.

"Listen," Coté began, "your information from that nurse and teacher just caught up with me. It's all damn interesting. Bostwick's friends are obviously protecting him . . . but they're right. We need to investigate Houle and Mungeon. I'm starting to think I've been wrong about Bostwick acting alone. . . . Besides, I've got another puzzle. Motor Vehicles says there's no license or registration in Mungeon's name. Andy Huff and I plan a little talk with him tomorrow at the commune.

"We also need to find Donald Houle," Coté continued. That'll be your job. I want him questioned about his activities last week, particularly Wednesday. Border Patrol says Houle was in Canada several hours that afternoon and evening."

"Wait," Paul replied, "didn't Klarissa Wilcox arrive at Mirabel Wednesday?

"Exactly. . . . Let me find my notes."

Paul heard papers shuffling on the other end.

"I connected the two events a few minutes ago but haven't had a chance to check the timing. Here's what I know: Houle crossed into Canada around two-fifteen PM with a guy named Holman Sage. They returned at around eleven o'clock. . . . Their car wasn't searched . . . and here. . . . Klarissa Wilcox's flight arrived at four-ten PM."

"Well, I've made that same trip from Canaan. Mirabel is an hour northwest of Montreal. It might be three hours from Norton. They could have arrived just as Klarissa Wilcox cleared customs. Add a leisurely dinner in Montreal, and they could be back by eleven."

"That might be, but it brings up another problem. Why in hell would she hop in a car with Donald Houle, who once threatened to kill her?

"Right . . . but what if she knew Sage and trusted him to smuggle her into the States? Putting up with Houle was just part of the deal.

"Look," said Coté, "the woman was alive until Friday. . . . I still believe that Bostwick killed her, but he may have had help. It could be that someone delivered her to Bostwick. Maybe there was a double-cross."

"You're thinking that could be Houle's revenge?"

"Possibly, but let's not get carried away. It's worth questioning Holman Sage as well as Houle . . . but look for other possibilities. Their trip north could have just been to smuggle cigarettes or get smashed at the Auberge in Quaticook."

The call ended with Paul heading back to the bathroom. He would meet Coté the following afternoon. Ten minutes later, Evenrude followed Paul into the dark bedroom. As Paul slipped into bed, the cat leaped onto the ironing board in irritating silence.

19.

Dog Physics

The morning sky had a pinkish glow a half hour before the sun appeared. Adele rose quickly in the dark and dressed in black pants and white shirt as Bob Newton's paralegal. After a quick breakfast, she drove the five-mile trip to Pittsburg to check on the girls. She spoke with Reilly's mother while they played. Amy and Lottie were curious about their time off from school but seemed to want it to continue and apparently had not yet been disturbed by the body language of the adults around them. This would be good news for Reilly. In her heart, Adele knew that this was the critical day. She was about to lose easy access to Reilly, and it was her last day as his full-time detective. She knew that despite her interesting leads, the chance of solving Reilly's dilemma in one day was minuscule to none. Worse yet, she'd have precious little time to continue her investigation in the days ahead as she caught up on her nursing job and all the mundane aspects of daily life she had been postponing. She was clearly worried but was determined to uncover something important in the hours ahead. Failure was a lousy option.

The drive to Newport became another time for fond remembrance. As she drove past Norton Pond, Adele remembered the fun she had had the previous summer with Reilly. After Amy had gone to England, Reilly became a regular guest at Adele's home. Lottie would compete for Reilly's attentions, but he always seemed to have enough love to go around. The threesome set out on some major adventure each weekend, hiking, boating, fishing, or carousing with the summer remnants of Reilly's gang. Reilly took his two girls, as he called them, to Quebec City. Adele and Lottie had been delighted to dance a jig to Québécois accordion and fiddle on the boardwalk beside the towering Frontenac Hotel. Lottie jumped around to the music with abandon, totally delighted with herself. A few weeks later, they rambled through Old Montreal, where Reilly insisted that they have escargot. Lottie was a good sport and ate one snail knowingly. Adele and Reilly willingly finished Lottie's portion and secretly smiled at her when she said she could still taste that darn garlic two days later. Reilly appreciated Lottie's spunk and sense of adventure. He loved her free spirit yet held back not to intrude too much on the mother-daughter bond. In these summer diversions, they were quite the team. Adele remembered that dreamy time.

At the end of that summer, Reilly learned that Amy had been abducted in England. Adele had done what she could to help him face Klarissa in the London court, but like all of Reilly's friends, she could only wait helplessly at a distance. After five breathless days of silence, she was overjoyed when Reilly's mother had called her with the news that he and Amy were on a plane heading to Boston.

Reilly had returned emotionally and physically spent but had had to immediately accelerate to school speed and reintroducing Amy to her American life. These had been tough times for Adele and Reilly. Now that they were close, the pressure of both their jobs made it difficult to find private time together, yet the desire had never been stronger. It had been a few months before their lives had regained intimacy and balance. And now, despite being wrenched apart, their love had taken on a new intensity born of crisis.

Adele arrived at the jail mid-morning and continued in her role as lawyer's assistant. This time, Reilly was led from his cell by a guard. They went to a small conference room down the hall, where Adele scribbled on Reilly's yellow notepad. Adele and Reilly assumed their formal demeanor until the guard returned to his post.

The room they were in was long and cold, with windows that might have almost looked normal if they had had curtains. The sunlight slanted in, and the view beyond was a relief to Reilly's eyes. He could see a parking lot with cars moving along snowy streets. There were all the signs that life outside still existed and continued without his presence. At the near end of the room was a small table with two folding chairs. They sat on opposite sides, with Adele facing the door.

"You're looking tired, my love. Are you OK?" asked Reilly.

"I'm hanging in there. I've got a lot to tell you. Leo Richards and I visited Jake last night. We learned that Donald Houle is still in town. I plan to follow up on him later."

"So, what do we have?" inquired Reilly.

Adele wanted Reilly to feel encouraged by their progress and didn't want to upset him further about Amy's safety. She decided not to mention Mungeon's interest in Amy at the Riverbend or Ike's slip about Richmond. She continued in an upbeat tone, telling Reilly how she and Leo had tricked Jake into talking. "Well, Jake is quite the boy, strong enough to lift corpses, but probably not smart enough to deal with complicated murder plots. We do, however, have another, more likely, character that didn't care for Klarissa. He's big and surly. His name is Brad Mungeon."

"How do you like that?" she bragged with a wide smile.

"OK, OK, you're brilliant as well as beautiful. Go on."

Adele told him Jake's story of the visit to the commune and how Father Xavier had told Klarissa about the woman, Paula Dickson, who lived there. "I did more snooping on the way here. I visited with the owner of the store in Averill and talked with the postmistress in Norton. Their stories matched. Now get this!" Adele said excitedly. "We know that Mungeon drives a black truck and has a snowmobile. In fact, he might be the only guy currently in the commune who has a vehicle.

"The guy's elusive. No one seems to know anything about his past. He's been involved in a couple of bar fights in Island Pond. He becomes invisible when Border Patrol or state police are around, doesn't say hi to the natives, and other sins of that kind. I'm told this isn't uncommon for commune residents. Suzanne says there are as many fugitives in there as there are back-to-the-land types."

"So, you're saying Jake is a lowlife but a sweetheart compared to Brad the Scumbag."

"That's how I'd call it. I don't see Jake as a murderer, but if first impressions count, Brad is pretty vile. That's why Leo and I decided to tell the police everything we had learned about him. He could be a fugitive and afraid of any contact with the law. That could be why he was more scared than angry when Klarissa visited. If he's a fugitive, his girlfriend Paula's abuse complaint became a threat because his past crimes might be discovered. Maybe Klarissa crossed him some other time or had the power to expose him. I don't know."

"Someone wanted Klarissa dead and me to take the blame," said Reilly. "The murder investigation would lead to me while the murderer walked. It has to be someone clever enough to set me up. If I'm out of the scene, then someone else must benefit. Right?"

"Fulton J. Wilcox comes to mind. He's the one guy I know who would celebrate when he hears you're in jail. And he's the one guy smart enough to arrange it."

"But don't you think his daughter's death might blunt that celebration?"

"Yes, but consider this," Adele continued, "Mr. Ski Mask's visit to my house Friday points to an abduction attempt. We don't know if this is directly related to Klarissa's murder, so let's look at the kidnapping separately. What if Fulton is trying to kidnap Amy for Klarissa? Maybe that's why she came here. Then Klarissa got murdered by some local and it's just bad luck for Wilcox."

Reilly considered this for a moment. "If that were the case . . . the kidnapping effort would have been called off. The truck sightings Saturday night and phone calls Sunday suggest that someone is still looking for Amy. If this killing is the revenge by a local, it's strange that he or she would go to such efforts to set me up. Also, when you think about it, this murder had to involve extremely complicated planning."

"Which reminds me," said Adele, "Suzanne researched the connection between Fulton Wilcox and Bu-lee." She went on to explain what she had learned about SOE, Briggens, FANY, and OSS.

"That explains a lot about dear, sweet Fulton," said Reilly as he looked up at the wall and paused. "Smart enough for intricate plots and ruthless enough to carry them out. He might be capable of kidnapping or murder. We know he has the brainpower and experience for covert operations, but I don't understand what the heck he has to gain."

"I don't know that yet, but I still have suspects to investigate. My next interview is with Father Xavier, who knew Klarissa and has met this guy Brad."

Just then, they heard footsteps in the hall. They looked up as a guard came into view. Reilly sat up stiff and straight to the table.

"Ms. Clayton, I have a note for you from Mr. Newton," the guard said.

Adele waited for him to depart the room before opening and reading the folded paper. Her frown immediately told Reilly that it wasn't good news.

"Well, apparently, Wilcox provided the medical examiner with Klarissa's fingerprints and blood type, and that'll confirm her identification. The gun, primer marks, shot size, and gunpowder all match, too."

Reilly slumped, with his head on the table and groaned, "I guess the time has come to tell Amy her mother is dead."

Adele took his hand and pleaded, "No . . . let's wait one more day. Even if we have to tell her, we need to prepare."

She told Reilly about her conversation with Suzanne and the professional help that was available to comfort Amy. He agreed to wait but asked Adele to contact the counselor.

Adele stood and said, "I'm off to talk with the good father. I don't know what I'll be doing this evening. It depends on what I find. I probably won't be back today. I have to work tomorrow, but I'll come to visit afterwards. Don't be too glum. I have a feeling that the opposition is on a short timeline, too, and might make a mistake that'll help us. Just remember, if I can't get you out of here, Ross, Conner, and Leo will probably stop by with hacksaws and ladders."

"I wouldn't doubt it. Good . . . so, my love, please be careful and always remember how much I love you. Keep the gang working. The news is discouraging, but I think you're making progress."

When Reilly arrived at his cell, he realized that it was Tuesday morning, just as his Physics class was starting. The sub would be Mildred Kelley, who, at sixty-eight, knew about as much about physics as Trotsky the Dog. He suspected that his prize students, Nellie and Vivian, were teaching the lesson to Mildred.

20.

Last November?

Burlington, Vermont

Early that same morning, the faint tint of red in the eastern sky matched the color in Monty's eyes as he barged his car into Burlington's early rush-hour traffic. The twenty-degree air seemed refreshing. The forecast warned of an evening blizzard spreading from the Lake Champlain region toward the northeast corner of the state. He headed back to Canaan knowing he'd be ahead of the storm. Nonetheless, he was in a foul mood. His trip had shredded time he couldn't afford to waste. He was also worried that he may have been a bit sloppy. The description of him on the morning TV report of the break–in, shooting, and kidnapping was practically worthless, but he knew he had left fingerprints in that couple's car. He could hope that soon wouldn't matter. It was time to concentrate on the road again.

He checked his watch and reminded himself that the next contact would be a call to his apartment on the commons at 12:30 PM.

It was 11:15 AM when Monty's black truck crept past the park in Canaan. He drove slowly around the village and then circled several backroads before heading to Pittsburg. He had decided to reconnoiter all the residences he had identified for the teachers that Bostwick hung around with. He was guessing that the girl would be staying at one of these houses. He had no luck in Canaan, but when he arrived in Pittsburg, there was enough smoke coming from Conner Murphy's house that he guessed the stove had recently been loaded. There was also a blue car in the yard, and when he checked more closely, he could see lots of small bootprints in the yard. The house was too much in the open to approach at this time of day, so he resolved to investigate more closely after dark, and returned to the apartment for the check-in call.

Canaan

Monty sat in his turret perch, his eagle gaze scanning the commons and pathways below. He had finished his lunch by the time the call came at precisely 12:30. He brought the old man up to date on his searches and gave him the phone number, which, by this time, Monty had figured out belonged to the Clayton woman. He had the feeling that this name was popping up far too often. Just as he had this thought, he focused intently on an approaching station wagon. He stifled a curse as a familiar green Subaru drove past Fletcher Park.

"Boss, the Clayton woman just drove up. . . . She's parking next to this place. . . . She's right below me, getting out and going across to the diner. You know, this bitch makes me nervous."

"That may be, but you need to steady. This woman can be useful to us," the calm voice reassured Monty. "Remember . . . she's the one to watch if we're going to find the girl. Now listen carefully. I've got things for you to do. I want you to make two more calls to the apartment in Springfield. My man is down there minding the place. Talk for a few minutes for each call to leave the phone records we want. I'll continue to call from pay phones here. I'll probably drive up to Averill today. That way I'll be able to get in place quickly if you find the girl. I'll make up my mind in the next hour or so. I don't want to get caught in the worst of the storm. If you need to contact me before I leave, call Springfield, and my man will call me from a pay phone there. Remember, this is our last chance."

Around one o'clock, Adele left the diner and returned to her car for the yellow notepad. She walked westward, beyond the town commons to the houses beyond. "What's she up to now?" he questioned. After watching another minute, he muttered, "Damn it!" when she turned and knocked on the door of the parish house. Of all the people in the village, this was the one person he didn't want her prying for information. "What does that bitch know?" Monty, getting increasingly edgy, suddenly had a completely different interest. A familiar blue car was coming south from Beecher Falls. It stopped at the sign, then crossed Route 114 and continued straight across the intersection, driving cautiously. Monty got up and changed his view to a south-facing window. The car pulled into Sam's yard next to the apartment house. Monty had identified this as one of the places the teachers had gone after their party Saturday night. And just as Monty felt sure this was the same car he had seen in Pittsburg that morning, two little girls led an older lady up to the porch of the downstairs apartment. Now Monty was really agitated as he grabbed the phone and dialed the Springfield apartment. Ten minutes later, Monty's phone rang just once. He described what he had just seen.

"You need to make certain that the girl is Amy before we do anything. As soon as we finish talking, I'll drive to Averill. When you're certain one of the girls is Amy, come to the commune to meet me. No . . . wait! . . . Your first task is to find out which way the Clayton woman goes next. If she heads west toward Averill, we need to know if she goes to the commune. Unfortunately, her talk with the priest might lead her there. If that happens, she's learned far too much. Your first task is still to confirm the girl's identity, but as soon as you do, drive to the commune. If the Clayton woman is there, it's time for her to disappear until at least spring thaw. Take care of it your own way, but make sure there's no evidence outside the commune. However things turn out, sit still until I arrive."

When Adele walked up to the parish house door, she heard noise within as though someone were waiting on the other side. After three knocks, the door opened fully, and Father Xavier filled the entranceway of the cozy reception room as he greeted Adele. He had a large, round face with a kindly expression and neatly trimmed black hair that was combed back and held in place by some fragrant and expensive grease. When he looked down at Adele, he appeared somewhat puzzled but immediately invited her inside. From his movements, it was obvious that the good father was energetic, and he moved so gracefully that it was easy to forget his bulk. Adele had been curious to meet him. She had started hearing about this legend even before she had met Reilly the year before. His name surfaced in a wide variety of contexts.

Father Xavier was a man of the cloth: actually, lots of cloth. He was more than six feet tall, weighed upward of three hundred pounds, and was in every way a commanding presence. He exuded confidence and was never at a loss for an opinion. He was a highly cultured church intellectual and a brilliant musician. Somehow, within a year of his arrival in Canaan, he had insinuated himself into the nooks and crannies of the town's secrets. He knew his village. And in return, the village imbibed rumors of his colorful dealings. He was said to be using church funds to make money by trading American and Canadian currency as exchange rates fluctuated. After losing some of his flock to the Jehovah's Witnesses, he had made a scathing denouncement of their kind to the full gathering of his parishioners. The gossip that he was attracted to altar boys was the lowest denomination of Father X rumors.

Whereas most people arrived in Canaan voluntarily, Father Xavier's arrival had an air of mystery. He was too cultured and had too fine an intellect for the church to spend him on so small and remote a village. It was as if he were in exile. These thoughts crossed Adele's mind as she took off her black parka and snowy boots.

Adele asked if she could have some of his time to talk about a sensitive matter. They went into the plush living room with red deep-pile carpet and original art on the walls. It appeared that the good father was especially fond of cherubs. From where she was sitting on the soft sofa, she could see the grand piano and vintage harpsichord in the next, equally elegant, room.

"What brings you here this afternoon, my dear? I don't believe I know you. Do I?"

"No, we have never met, although I have heard a lot about you. I'm Adele Clayton, a friend of Reilly Bostwick. I'm sure you have heard about his ex-wife's murder."

"Yes, I was absolutely shocked. I knew Klarissa. We weren't close, but we consulted informally at times when members of my parish had family problems."

"Well, that's what I want to talk about. Reilly has been arrested. His friends are looking for the real murderer. We believe someone is setting Reilly up so perfectly that the police won't look beyond him. We're investigating other people who may have wanted Klarissa dead."

"So what does this have to do with me? I only know Reilly superficially and certainly don't know any of Klarissa's enemies."

"Maybe you do. Listen. I just learned that you told Klarissa about a woman who lives in the Averill Wildflower Commune named Paula Dickson. You told Klarissa that this woman's cabin mate . . . a guy named Brad . . . was beating her."

"That's right . . . but how do you know this?"

"Jake Paulson told me. You probably don't know that after you spoke to Klarissa, she visited the commune with Jake as her bodyguard. She documented the abuse and put Brad on warning. That's why I think Brad might have been a threat to Klarissa. Would you mind telling me about your visit and your impressions of Brad?"

"Normally this would be confidential, but you already know part of the story. I also have my own concerns for Paula. Maybe we can help each other.

"The woman you're talking about is Paula Dickson. She attended Mass one Sunday. I'd guess it was early spring last year. She was a new face at Mass, so I made a point of talking with her. I discovered that she lived at the commune, didn't have a car, and had hitchhiked from Averill. She told me she wanted to reconnect with her Catholic roots. Of course, I encouraged her. I arranged for one of my parishioners from Norton to bring her to Mass and back every week. She thanked me and said she'd see me next Sunday. The next week, the ride I had arranged stopped at the commune, but she never appeared. A few days later, I decided to search for her myself. I had always wanted to get a look inside that commune, so here was my excuse.

"This was how I met her boyfriend. His name is Brad Mungeon." Father X shifted ponderously in his chair and continued. "I drove up to the commune, stopped at the first cabin, and had a nice talk with a lady named Bessie. She told me Paula and Brad were having vicious fights and that Paula was under this man's control. I got directions from Bessie. I took the long walk to their cabin and knocked on the door. What a horrible place. They weren't caring for their home or each other. They were fighting while I was there. Brad is a big man...my size, but really hard and muscular. He tried to bully me, and I found myself getting nowhere talking with him. Finally, he told me to get out in terms I won't repeat. I could see that I wasn't helping things, so I left. That's how I met the couple. And that's the connection to Klarissa, also. I was concerned about Paula. Even in cabin light, I could see that her face and arms were bruised. The next week, I told Klarissa and warned her to approach the situation very carefully if she chose to go there. Brad had very dangerous body language.

"I knew Klarissa Wilcox was connected to the mental health agency in Colebrook. I had also learned that she was working with two women in my parish, setting up a shelter for battered women in Colebrook. That's why I mentioned Paula to her. I also considered telling the police, but when Paula showed up at Mass the next weekend looking happy, I let it slide. If fact, she came to Mass for several weeks, then stopped. She started to come again after my second visit to the commune but only came twice, so I'm quite worried for her."

"I can explain part of what happened," Adele replied. "As I said, Klarissa visited the commune after you talked with her and took Jake Paulson along for protection. Now that I think of it...that was a gutsy thing to do, but nonetheless, Jake was a strange choice of bodyguard. Klarissa was obviously working far beyond her authority. She apparently had enough effect on Brad for him to refrain from abusing Paula and let her attend Mass. But I didn't know you made a second visit to the commune. When was that?"

"That visit was in November. I went with Klarissa's father."

"That's a surprise. What does Klarissa's father have to do with this?"

"Well, last November, Klarissa's father contacted me by phone and then came here to the rectory. He—"

"Last November? You mean *a year ago last November?*" she interrupted excitedly as she emphasized the words.

"No, no, it was here in town two months ago."

Adele couldn't hide her shock. Two months ago was *after* Reilly had returned from England with Amy. She knew Fulton Wilcox had been in Canaan to clean out Klarissa's apartment more than a year earlier. Her lines of inquiry had suddenly merged but didn't yet make sense.

"But what did he want from you?" she asked. trying to catch her breath.

"Well, he said he was asking me a favor on Klarissa's behalf. He asked me to introduce him to the couple who live in the Wild-flower Commune. He said Paula Dickson was a friend of Klarissa's and he had a gift for her that he wanted to deliver personally. It didn't make much sense to me, but at that time, Paula had stopped coming to Mass. I wanted to see if she was all right."

Meanwhile, Adele's mind was leaping wildly ahead. The connection of Fulton J. and Brad had added a whole new dimension to explore. "So, what did Klarissa's father really want with them last November?"

"I never found out. That was my second visit to the commune and hopefully my last. I drove Mr. Wilcox to the entrance, and we walked down the long trail together until I could point out Brad's cabin. He rudely told me to wait outside. Apparently, his story about having a gift for Paula was a lie, or at least a deception. He really went there to see Brad, because he quickly gave Paula some little trin-ket and then sent her outside too. When she saw me, she was very relieved because she needed badly to talk. She was actually quite upset and made sure we couldn't be seen out of the cabin window. I told her that even though it had been some time ago, I was the person who had reported to Klarissa that she was being beaten. She told me while crying that she desperately wanted to escape the commune but was afraid to. She wouldn't say why. I told her to start coming to Mass again so we could talk about finding her temporary shelter."

"And that's it?"

"Almost. Wilcox and Brad must have talked for half an hour inside. It was like they knew each other. When their meeting broke up, I made a point of confronting Brad and encouraging him to let Paula come to Mass. He looked at Wilcox and calmly said 'sure.' It was strange. After that, we drove back to the village. I haven't seen Klarissa's father since then."

"Did Paula ever come to another Mass?"

"Yes, she came to Mass two more times before Christmas, but not recently. That is why I'm concerned."

"By the way, what does Paula look like?"

"About 5'6", a light build, but a nice figure. She has pretty, long blond hair."

A spark flashed in Adele's mind, but the idea it illuminated eluded her for the moment.

Monty wiped the prints off the phone with a cloth and toured the room. He picked up his rucksack and said good riddance to his turret lookout. After walking quickly to his truck in the Northland Hotel lot, he drove a few hundred yards and parked in front of the Alice Ward Library to resume his vigil across from Sam's apartment. He was soon richly rewarded as Adele walked east on the upper edge of the common and then down the far side to the apartment house on the corner opposite Monty. When the door to the ground-floor apartment opened, he could clearly see the two girls hug her on the porch. Yes, he was certain one was the Bostwick girl. He smiled as he thought that maybe his cursed luck had finally changed.

Fifteen minutes later, Monty watched the Clayton woman say goodbye to the girls and walk back to her car. Finding Amy should have been a relief for Monty, but every minute of Adele's conversation with Father X had ratcheted up his anxiety. It was another ominous development when Adele drove west out of town toward Averill, the direction from which she had come. Monty could see that it would probably take more blood on snow to salvage the old man's already-precarious plan. Monty impatiently waited five minutes and drove west as enormous flakes of snow began to fall steadily.

21.

Cold-blooded Game

Adele drove toward Newport with a new swirl of ideas. There was much to tell Reilly. As she approached the commune entrance, she saw the empty pull-off on the left. Intuition suddenly overpowered caution. Adele surprised herself by braking suddenly. She felt so close to a solution that she was almost compelled to grasp for the last clue linking Fulton Wilcox to Brad Mungeon. She knew it was time to see Paula Dickson in the flesh.

Snow was falling lightly at the commune entrance. The wooded road was tamped down by snowmobile tracks and covered with boot-prints. In the summer, this was a tractor path bordered by stately balsam firs. Now it was an uninviting path to danger. The late-afternoon light was fading quickly as the storm moved in. The path would have been completely dark but for snow covering the ground and frosting the trees. Adele walked slowly down the main trail, with the yellow notepad in hand as the darkness of the woods enveloped her. After several tense minutes, she turned left on a boot-print trail. This she expected to lead to Bessie's cabin. After a kink in the rough path, she could see a small log structure ahead. The snowy clearing was just broad enough to lend the cabin a glow like silvery moonlight. She scanned the scene cautiously, noting smoke rising from the chimney and fresh bootprints in the white powder. Adele looked up. The first rush of wind through the treetops told her the storm was rapidly intensifying. She felt a ripple of fear as she approached and knocked gently on the door.

The heavy, ill-fitting door opened slowly with a dry creaking sound. The woman opposite Adele had a heavily lined face that spoke of harsh winters and heavy smoking. Her thin brown hair was oily and straggly. Adele could smell a stale mixture of vinegar and cigarette smoke within. Bessie was dressed in a red-plaid wool coat and ragged pants with dirty knees. Adele wondered about her age. She was weathered and worn such that she could have been forty-five just as easily as sixty. Her movement was lively, but her left leg showed an obvious limp. Just before stepping across the threshold, Adele froze in place. The snowmobile's whine behind her was ominous. She turned and listened as it moved through the woods from her right near the highway, growing louder as it approached the turn to Bessie's cabin. Adele's heart was beating frantically even after she realized the snow mobile hadn't turned.

"That's only Brad," Bessie said lethargically.

Adele felt a near-overwhelming urge to run. Her car might mean enough to Brad to look for her within the commune. She didn't want to meet him any place, but particularly not here. She willed herself to be calmer. The information to save Reilly should be here. She'd stick this out. With that determination, Adele stepped inside, unzipped her jacket, and sat beside the woman on a dilapidated couch next to a small woodstove. She forced herself to focus intensely on Bessie. Then, while looking into this simple woman's face, Adele had a hunch . . . the intuitive spark returned, but this time, intense heat and light would soon follow. Before Adele began to explain the purpose of her visit, she quickly thumbed through the yellow notepad and pulled out the picture Reilly had shown her of Klarissa standing facing the camera dressed warmly for a snowy day. Without question or comment, she handed Bessie the photo.

Bessie looked at the photo briefly, started to say something, and then handed it back to Adele. Bessie stopped suddenly with a look of confusion . . . as Adele anticipated what was about to happen. Bessie took the photo back from Adele's hand and gave it a slow second look, just as the spark reignited twentyfold with sparkling magnesium brightness in Adele's mind.

"What do you see?" Adele asked, not masking her excitement.

"Wow, that was a surprise. I thought you had given me a picture of Paula Dickson, a friend of mine. She lives just up the trail here in the park. But when I handed it back to you, I knew that I had to look again because something wasn't quite right. They're a lot alike except for their faces. I'd say this lady is prettier than Paula."

Adele was jarred by a fireworks-like burst of insight. In an instance, she felt sure she knew the killers, the victim, and how Reilly had been set up. The corpse was Paula Dickson, not Klarissa. Here was the evidence to free her love . . . and, almost unbelievably, this information could spare Amy the death of her mother. Adele fought for control.

"Now that you mention her," said Adele, heart racing and with rising excitement in her voice, "Paula is just the person I came to visit. Let me guess . . . you haven't seen her recently."

"Yes. That's strange. You know, nothing ever happens here, and hardly anyone comes to visit. But this morning, two state troopers were looking for Brad Mungeon, and now you're here asking about Paula . . . and it wasn't but a few weeks ago when that fat priest and some stranger came looking for them both. Maybe . . . ."

Adele was shocked and couldn't restrain herself from interrupting. "Did the troopers find Brad?" she asked excitedly, hoping that the ominous snowmobile had a different owner.

"No, I told him if the truck wasn't here, neither was Brad."

Adele, not pleased with that answer, pressed her previous question. "But what about Paula?"

"Funny you mentioned it. You're right. I haven't seen Paula all week. She'd usually stop by to chat most every day. I believe I'd have seen her if she still lived here, but I'd be disappointed if she took off without telling me. I was beginning to wonder if she and Brad finally split. It sure would have been a good move on Paula's part. That Brad isn't worth a quart of spit! You watch out for that one!"

Adele felt an intense chill as a sudden burst of fear displaced her excitement. She now knew that Brad was hunting for her with murderous eyes. It was possible that he wouldn't recognize her or her car, but all of Fulton's plans had been meticulous. They would almost certainly know that if she came here, she was far too close to their secret. She had delivered herself to the place she could be most easily killed. Now she had to craft her fear and anger into an escape plan.

After thanking Bessie, she zipped up her long black parka and peered left and right carefully as she stepped out Bessie's door. She walked briskly down the path toward the main trail as she listened intently for the snowmobile. The woods were silent except for the hush of falling snow. As she turned onto the main path, she heard the dreaded snowmobile rev deep down the trail behind her. Adele turned and started sprinting on the packed snow toward the highway. For the moment, the snowmobile behind her was still out of sight.

As she ran, she was surprised by the sudden change in sound. The snowmobile's engine changed pitch in a yowling sound and then resumed its high-pitched roar. She stopped long enough to confirm that its direction had changed. Brad had turned onto the narrow trail toward Bessie's cabin. Adele turned back toward her car and started running again.

Bam...Bam! Adele heard the snow-muffled rifle shots above the barely audible sound of an idling snow machine, then the ascending scream of the motor. Adele could now see a lighter area ahead where the trail opened into the edge of the road. Suddenly, the snowmobile's sound changed pitch as it turned onto the main trail toward her. Adele was a few hundred feet from the road but knew she couldn't make it.

The machine wasn't yet in sight as Adele decided to bushwhack through the deep snow diagonally to the path until she reached the highway. It was so deep that she knew her progress would be slow at best. She ran along the trail and jumped into the waist-deep snow near the far side of a large spruce so that her exit point from the trail wouldn't be obvious. She used the tree to try to mask her frantic progress as she swept snow away with her arms while attempting to leap and lurch forward. She grabbed branches and pulled herself along where she could. She had only made fifty feet or so before the snow machine came into sight. She slumped suddenly into the snow, her black clothing blending well with the darkened woods. The snowmobile's engine continued to roar its movement toward the road. Adele used those precious seconds to claw, thrust, scrape, and push her way toward the snowbank ahead. She figured that she was now within a hundred feet of the highway and quite close to where she had parked.

After Adele heard the snowmobile engine die, she managed to advance halfway to the road before she again froze in place. A movement caught her eye. There, barely visible through the woods, was a large man with a rifle, walking back along the trail, looking for her bootprints. Adele made a desperate scramble toward the high snowbank just as Brad found her trail near the big spruce and saw her movements deep in the woods. Adele had just enough time to reach the snowbank and start to crawl upward on all fours. She heard a faint chunk-chunk as she crested the bank and then the sharp sound of the rifle's report as she rolled down head-first into the road. She hoped that from a distance it looked like a kill.

On an adrenaline surge, Adele struggled to her knees and surveyed the danger. Her car was just ahead, parallel to the snowbank on her left. Beyond that, she could see a black truck and snowmobile blocking the commune entrance. Keeping low, she slid into the driver's seat and locked her door as she started the car. She sat up partway and peered ahead. With no sign of movement, she abruptly put the car in gear and spun her tires, heading past the commune entrance toward Newport. Just as her peripheral vision picked up movement along the path, a bullet ripped into metal somewhere close behind her. She was gaining speed in second gear when her rear view mirror showed Brad running into the road and taking aim again. She did an intentional zigzag and recovered just as the bullet tore a ragged gash in the back gate of her station wagon. Adele must have careened through curves, frost heaves, and falling snow for twenty miles before she felt sure that she wasn't being followed.

Derby State Police Barracks

Whiteout conditions pelted the Vermont State Police with cold choices and few solutions. At Derby Station, snow was gusting outside Bud Yager's office window, while inside, Roland Coté was slowing losing momentum in a quiet argument with the station commander. At contention was how to stretch eight troopers to handle an intense storm and a rapidly expanding murder investigation. The weather was winning. Yager, who ran the show, was unwilling to dispatch anyone to the stake out the commune. Reports of two more fender benders arrived as they argued. Although Coté was animated by what he had just discovered, he conceded defeat when Paul Marshall was dispatched to a serious collision at Wenlock siding. Coté knew he couldn't persuade his boss to call Waterbury headquarters for extra help unless he had Mungeon cornered. Even then, he wasn't sure what was possible in this weather.

Coté muttered to himself as he returned to his office. There he found a wet, disheveled Adele Clayton waiting impatiently. Although they had never met, Coté was aware of her efforts on Bostwick's behalf. The implications of her harrowing story magnified the discovery about Mungeon that Coté had confirmed not twenty minutes before.

That morning, he and Trooper Huff had visited the commune. The interview with Bessie had yielded little more than a physical description of Mungeon. When he had returned to Derby, Coté had learned about the break-in in Richmond. Remembering Marshall's information about Bostwick's daughter, he had called Williston Station to find the site of the break-in. The question had been booted around, but finally, his call had been returned. When Elaine Bostwick's name popped up, Coté had reason to believe that the attempted kidnapping story was true. He was now convinced that Mungeon was armed and dangerous. This was the information he had taken to Yager. Now Adele's story of blazing guns at the commune added the urgency that would change Yager's mind. Still, he knew if they responded immediately, they would confront an intensely dangerous situation with a woefully insufficient force.

Coté was immersed in a flurry of activity as Adele left the building to bring the explosive news to Reilly. She arrived at the jail just after Bob Newton had departed.

Reilly's jail cell

"Wow, what happened to you?" Reilly asked when Adele arrived at his cell breathing heavily. Her hair was askew, her makeup smeared, and her clothes wet and crumpled, while Reilly sat on the bed smiling.

Adele ignored his question and countered, "You're not going to believe the news I've got!"

"I'll bet I've got bigger news!"

"Goddamn it, buster! This time you don't! Did you just get shot at?"

"Say what?" Reilly's jaw dropped. He knew it was listening time.

Adele explained Father X's explosive news about Klarissa's father.

Reilly was stunned by the connection between Brad and Fulton Wilcox.

"Now that I have your attention," said Adele, "I think I know who was really killed."

She explained how Bessie had reacted to the picture of Klarissa and how Jake and Father X's description of Paula also fit Klarissa.

Reilly's heart was racing as he listened to how close Adele had come to being killed. He stood and paced the cell as they both registered the meaning of the two shots at Bessy's cabin.

"This means," Reilly continued excitedly, "that Klarissa is still alive!" He looked to the window, then turned suddenly. "Wow, this is a big plus for Amy . . .except if her mother is behind this. . . . She should be in jail instead of me."

"Right! But if she's behind this, what would she gain?" said Adele.

"I don't know, but it has to be a scheme to take Amy from me. There was no legitimate way Klarissa could have regained custody after her antics in England and the trial there. She and her father must have invented another way paved by mayhem and murder. One thing is sure: This is a cold-blooded game, and Amy is the prize."

They sat in stunned silence, thinking. Then Reilly said, "Your evidence trumps mine, but I just talked to Bob Newton, and I've got some details that are suddenly starting to make a lot more sense.

"The murderer made one and a half mistakes. Bob heard on the news about the break-in at my mother's house in Richmond last night. Apparently, a local man was shot and a couple kidnapped by the intruder. Bob knew that Amy had stayed there Friday and Saturday nights and recognized this as another kidnapping attempt. He alerted the state police. They had lifted this guy's fingerprints from the couple's car. Bingo! They matched a California man wanted for two murders there! At this point, they have an identity and a picture. What do you want to bet that it looks a lot like Brad?

"What's even better, the police have a fingerprint of the murderer in Canaan. Or, I should say, part of a print . . . maybe half. It was on the zipper pull of the woman's jacket. It wasn't enough to make an identification, but bless the wizards at the crime lab! Somebody put the prints together, and the half print from Canaan matched a full print from Richmond. When Bob found this out, he started processing the paperwork to get me out of here!

"So," Reilly continued, "Brad murdered Paula execution-style, and most conveniently, Klarissa's father gets to identify the body. I'm jailed, and Paula's absence wouldn't be noticed. Your visit to the commune unnerved Brad, and he decided to kill you on the spot, but I wonder why he'd take the risk. He must have feared that you would discover the resemblance between Klarissa and Paula and uncover that Paula had disappeared. He could have created a dead end to that trail by making you disappear as well."

"So, if Brad killed me, you would be convicted of murder and Amy would end up with Klarissa, but by doing so, he'd probably be on the run with his reward from Fulton J."

"He will be on the run if those last two shots mean what I think they do."

"But there's still a piece missing," Adele interjected. "What about the kidnapping attempt?

"Maybe we can figure that out together if you can get Gene Jackman to whisk me home as soon as the paperwork clears."

"Sure, but this blizzard will make it a slow trip," Adele replied. "Also, you should know that after I talked with the state police, they decided to call headquarters for extra help arresting Mungeon. They have also started a search for Fulton J. The sooner they round up those bastards, the more secure I'll feel."

The implications of Adele's discoveries were dawning on Reilly. He stood up, hardly able to catch his breath. "Wow, I just figured out the best of everything! Amy's mother isn't dead, and soon, her father will be out of jail!" But then followed the afterthought: "Who is with Amy now?"

"She, Lottie, and your mother are at Sam and Mark's apartment in town until Shelley Roberts gets home."

"I think you should call the gang together there to update them on the good news and to place more security around the girls until the police arrive."

"I agree. I'll call from here."

"You know," Reilly said with humble sincerity, "you're incredible! . . . my genuine heroine."

"Glad you noticed," purred Adele.

"At the risk of pissing off Bob Newton," said Reilly as he took Adele in his arms and gave her a long and tender kiss. Just then, the same guard who had been surprised by Adele's snow-drenched arrival peered, aghast, into Reilly's cell. She was strangely startled by this novel form of legal entanglement.

22.

Ross, Conner, and Leo

The trip back to Canaan was dangerous even in four-wheel drive. At first, Adele was focused on the slipping and sliding cars near Newport. Soon, the roads were empty and the snowbanks were thick enough to cushion against a catastrophic wreck, but the visibility was poor. With snow everywhere, there was no contrast to define the road. Her headlight highbeams, which would have matched her speed, reflected only a wall of falling snow rather than the route ahead. Low beams were effective, but they didn't extend far enough forward to warn against the unknown. Adele knew the road well enough to anticipate when to run flat-out in third gear and when to four-wheel drift the corners.

Her benchmarks were Derby, just east of Newport, then Morgan and Lake Seymour. There, the winds started whipping loose snow sideways from the lake, forming drifts in the road. When the Subaru nosed into the junction with Route 114 west of Island Pond, four or five inches of snow already covered the road. Adele's overcorrection at the one-lane railroad underpass put the car into a skid. She plowed into a snowbank sideways but managed to back out onto the white road surface. Some relief was in sight when she at last reached Norton. A car passed her near the schoolhouse and then veered north toward Canadian Customs.

She was apprehensive as she approached the commune. She had hoped to see a line of police cruisers. Instead, the dreaded black pickup truck was there, but without any sign of the snowmobile. There was also a set of recent car tracks. Someone who had parked there from the onset of the storm had recently headed out toward Norton, perhaps the car she had just passed. She drove on with a shiver of fear. Near the Averill store, she thought she spied a faint flicker of light in her rearview mirror and thought about the black truck. She studied the rearview intently as she continued past Wallace Pond. Now there was no sign of anyone following. After descending the long, curvy hills to the plain west of Canaan village, she was comforted by the sight of occupied houses with smoke rising from the chimneys all bedded down for the storm. As she relaxed a bit and slowed her pace, she again thought she could see a brief flash of light through the dense snow behind her. She downshifted into third gear and increased her speed. By the time she crossed Leach Stream at the edge of the village, she was sure there was someone there. She looked at her watch. With the intense snow, it was completely dark, and only 4:30, about the time she had expected to meet Leo Richards, Ross, and Conner at Samantha's house.

Adele swung the right turn at the town commons and pulled into the snowy parking space next to Sam's old Plymouth Valiant. Adele was so excited with her news and happy to be with the girls that she didn't look back. Meanwhile, the black pickup truck with its lights off turned onto the lane on the opposite side of the commons and coasted to a stop in front of the library. Adele climbed the three steps onto Sam's front porch and greeted the girls, who had just opened the door, with exaggerated hugs that the girls appreciated but didn't understand. "Sam, I've got the best news! I can't wait to explain. Everything is going to be OK for Reilly," Adele exclaimed breathlessly. "You won't believe—"

Suddenly, Adele found herself in midair, heading downward toward the snowbank by the side of the porch. Brad had quietly approached, leaped the porch steps, and, in a single swinging motion, swept Adele into the air and over the railing with his powerful left arm. He then pushed Samantha over the porch rail on the opposite side. Both young girls were screaming and kicking Brad's legs as he reached down and grabbed Amy by the waist and carried her away, kicking and yelling. Adele, even with her head in the snow, knew from the sound exactly what was happening. By the time she had freed herself from the snowbank, Brad had forced Amy into his truck across the commons. The truck roared as its lights switched on and it lurched forward, kicking up snow as it headed south out of the village toward Van Dyke hill. Adele quickly helped Samantha climb out of a large snowdrift. She was OK but shaken. As Adele assisted her up the steps to where Lottie, Reilly's mother, and Sam stood, speechless, Conner's Rover skidded to a stop in front of the building. Adele quickly turned to Ellen and yelled, "Call the state police and please take good care of Lottie," before jumping down the steps just as Leo Richards, Ross, and Conner were opening their car doors.

"Stay in there!" Adele shouted as she piled into the back seat next to Leo, slamming the door behind her. "Conner, Go! Go! Go! Straight ahead!" Conner worked the old Rover up through the gears as the other doors slammed shut. "There's a truck ahead of us, and the guy has Amy." As she caught her breath, she exclaimed, "Damn it, this is one time I wish the police weren't an hour away." Adele then quickly explained what had just happened as Conner raced across Leach Stream and drove up the gradual hill south of the village.

"You say it was the same guy and the same truck?" asked Leo. "If he's got a snowmobile in the back, he'll probably be able to drive OK through this snow, but we should still be able to go faster."

"We may have an advantage," said Adele. "I don't know what's going on, but I don't believe the snowmobile was on the truck when he left town."

"That means we have a real advantage catching up with him. What does this have to do with the commune?"

Adele, was hanging on to the back of the driver's seat behind Conner's head, said, "I'll tell you about that later. I just figured out how to prove that Reilly's innocent, but nothing means anything until we save Amy."

Ross, in the passenger seat and staring deep into the Rover's headlight beams ahead, spoke up. "If he's only a few minutes ahead of us, we should be able to catch him before he gets to Lemington. I'll feel better when we're close enough to see his lights."

Lemington is a spot on the map opposite Colebrook, but on the Vermont side of the river. It's the place where someone traveling south could continue on the small road ahead or choose to cross and travel east or south in New Hampshire on faster and better-maintained routes. Conner knew it would be a lost cause if they couldn't head off this guy before these trails split.

When the Rover hit the flatlands two miles south of Canaan, Conner became concerned that they couldn't see car lights ahead, when Ross remarked excitedly, "You know, these tracks we have been following are filled in more than they would be in a few minutes."

"And they look too narrow for the tread of a truck," observed Leo.

Without hesitation, Conner downshifted into second gear and intentionally sent the Rover into a skid that left them facing north. "I think he turned off on the Canaan Hill Road. If I'm right, we still have a good chance of catching up with him."

After retracing a mile or so, Conner put the Rover into a skidding turn next to the Canaan Hill Road sign. Yes, there were fresher tire prints in the snow, and the tread was wide and truck-like.

As they picked up speed, it was apparent that the truck had left a clear path as it clipped snowbanks and busted through drifts. Conner floored the Rover on the flats and downshifted to ascend the first hill. By then, everyone knew that the truck's escape plan wasn't to the south. Canaan Hill Road formed the curvy leg of a triangle connecting the road south of Canaan with Route 114 in Averill. But no one could make any sense of what the driver was up to.

A tense four-mile ride over the twist and turns of the almost-impassable road was executed at foolish speeds, as Conner and the others weren't considering safety. There was a burning anger at this unknown man, a desire to stop him at all costs.

"I see a light ahead," called Ross over the engine's roar.

"There he is," yelled Conner as a short portion of the road straightened out. Conner wrung even more third-gear speed out of the old Rover as he started to close the gap. By the time they reached Forest Lake, they were fifty feet from the truck's bumper, but the road was only wide enough for a single vehicle. The truck would lurch, then surge forward as it exploded through snowdrifts. Conner closed in on the truck, bumper-to-bumper.

Then suddenly, everyone was thrown forward as the Rover collided with the back of the truck, which had intentionally slammed on its brakes. The snow made the truck slide ahead rather than stop quickly, so the impact wasn't severe enough to disable the Rover. Conner, who had bumped his head on the steering wheel, sat upright suddenly as he struggled to downshift into second. Just then, Ross screamed "down!" as two explosions scattered a shower of glass from two holes in the windshield. Conner, who was slightly too groggy to duck, could see the gun at the end of a long arm out the driver's side window. He immediately braked to a stop as the truck shifted into low and accelerated away. Conner wanted to back off beyond pistol range and to check if everyone was all right.

Everyone was OK but even more enraged. They soon reached Route 114 and were completely surprised to see the truck drift a sliding right-hand turn toward Wallace Pond and Canaan instead of west toward the Norton border crossing or Island Pond. The snowfall now was straight down and steady as flakes and cold air streamed through the windshield.

"What the hell?" exclaimed Leo Richards. "That doesn't make any sense."

It was then that they noticed a scraping front-end sound on the Rover. Metal bent by the impact was rubbing on the right front tire, and the noise was growing louder. Conner eased onto Route 114 and resumed as fast a speed as he dared. They were losing ground to the truck. By the time they drove by Wallace Pond, they couldn't see its lights. As they drove by the camp road east of the pond, Adele shouted, "I think I saw truck lights down near Jackson's! Conner, turn around!"

They knew that this side road headed north along Wallace Pond, toward the nearby Canadian border. "I think they're heading to Canada," yelled Ross as Conner downshifted and drifted a 180-degree turn to the clanking, scraping sound that was now ominous. Conner drove back the short distance to the pond road and did a skidding turn to the right. He misjudged a bit, and the Rover's left wheels almost slid down the drop-off toward the pond shore. As Conner jerked the wheel hard right, Ross pointed ahead to Brad's truck at Jackson's Lodge. Conner gently eased the Rover back onto the road and floored first gear, quick shifted into second, then gunned the engine again. As they approached the truck, they could see a snow-mobile track over the snowbank heading toward the snow-covered beach. He braked hard and skidded into the snowbank next to Brad's truck, which was still running with lights on and both doors open. All four doors of Conner's Rover burst open. Everyone scrambled up onto the snowmobile trail and down toward the beach.

Brad was already on the snowmobile at the edge of the snow-covered ice a few hundred yards from Canada on the lake's northern shore. The snow was thick in the air. Amy was flailing her arms at him and trying to wriggle off the seat in front of him, where he had to use one arm to keep hold. Her struggling had slowed him down. He had barely managed to get the machine started and keep Amy in place securely enough to start moving.

That was Brad's last memory of snowmobiling. Ross cleaned him off the seat and into the snow on the other side with a bone-crunching tackle. Acting without hesitation, Adele snatched Amy from the seat and ran over the snowbank as the sound of the fighting became more frantic. She quickly checked Amy to see she wasn't hurt and then helped her into the idling black truck and told her to lock the doors and wait there. Adele climbed back over the snow-bank in time to hear two gunshots.

By this time, Brad had pulled his pistol and fired it twice as Ross sat on him and Conner struggled to keep the muzzle pointed away from everybody. Leo Richards had had enough of Brad. He moved in closer and stomped his foot down on Brad's head, deep into the snow, and held it there hard. And as he pressed down, Brad gave up the gun and the fight. Leo then grabbed the gun and dragged Brad away from the snow machine while cracking him smartly across the head with the pistol barrel.

When the guys looked up from the battle, Adele reassured them that Amy was safe in the truck.

Conner questioned Ross as he breathed heavily. "Where was he going with Amy?"

They looked over the snowy pond to the camps on the nearby Canadian shore as they caught their breath.

"Maybe the question is Where in Canada was he going," answered Ross.

Conner focused on one point on the shore to his right. "You know," he said, "the real question is Who was he taking her to?"

Ross's eyes also were attracted to the same sparkling spots on the far shore near one of the larger camps. They could see a flickering, faint set of headlights pointing across the pond.

"Well," exclaimed Ross, smiling at Conner. "I feel that a trip to Canada is in order. What do you say?"

"I think that would be a grand idea," replied Conner. "If you don't mind the extra weight, I'll bring my deer rifle from the back of the Rover."

Conner cranked the snowmobile and headed in a screaming straight line toward the faint lights. They ducked low in the seat, and Conner held the Winchester 94 tightly against their legs. When they arrived about fifty feet from shore, Fulton J. Wilcox, already anxious from the sound of unexpected gunshots, discovered that he was going to get a large dose of Ross and Conner. Although he did not know whom he was dealing with, he knew they weren't going to stop when they reached him. He turned quickly and started to run awkwardly through the deep snow as Conner slowed enough for Ross to tackle him on the way by. Fulton's struggle was surprisingly violent. He had hurt Ross's right arm and shoulder by the time Conner firmly pressed the rifle barrel hard under his chin and suggested that Fulton might want to consider giving up.

Ross lost the coin toss and was walking in the track far behind the snowmobile. Conner got to bring the bad guy back like a hood ornament sprawled across the snowmobile seat in front of him neatly hog-tied with their belts. Conner showed all the signs of triumph, waving and whooping all the way across.

Adele waited until she could see that Conner and Ross had returned safely. She then took Brad's truck and drove Amy back to the village and called the state police. She was pleased to learn that Trooper Marshall, Detective Coté, and five other troopers were already on their way to Averill.

Meanwhile, Conner soon remembered a six-pack of home brew in the Rover. The boys had a fine time poking and kicking Fulton and Brad when they started to get too frisky. The main point of speculation while they sipped their brew was how many state, provincial, dominion, and federal laws they had enjoyed violating in the name of justice.

Troopers Paul Marshall and Andy Huff took the pragmatic stance that possession is nine-tenths of the law. They scooped up Fulton and Brad while ignoring all tracks north to Canada. With the fugitives secured in the back seat, they were ready to give them the long, slow, bumpy ride to Newport, where they would be very much wanted.

23.

Tangle

Revelations tumbled out over the next weeks, with many surprises. Adele and Reilly heard snips of information as the courts lost interest in Reilly and gained interest in Brad and Fulton. The investigation started as a tangle tighter than one of Adele's fly-fishing knots, and it was at least two weeks before the seemingly contradictory information started to tease out, unravel, and make sense.

Reilly, who had been released from jail the evening of Fulton's and Brad's capture, traveled home, blissfully unaware of the kidnapping, chase, and capture. He was overjoyed as he opened Sam's front door and Amy gave him a long hug. He was overwhelmed by the frantic tales she, Conner, Ross, Adele, and Leo competed to tell.

The kidnapping had traumatized Amy, but the gang praised her fighting spirit. While Adele and Lottie tended Amy, Ross told her she had participated in a great adventure that the good guys had won. This was tempered by a promise from Conner and Leo that her dad would soon explain the secrets of the last few days. All were careful not to tell about the capture of her grandfather. Reilly sat with Amy on the old couch in Sam's front bay window with his arm around her to chat about ordinary things. They talked about Trotsky, her time with her grandmother, and her squabbles with Lottie.

Then Reilly explained where he had been and why she and Lottie had been given an extra vacation. He had already resolved to have her counseled in the weeks ahead. He didn't know the scope of Fulton's crimes, so he told her most of what he knew but did not mention Klarissa's involvement. That would wait until he knew more.

Amy was frightened to hear about the murdered woman and how the police had incorrectly thought it was her mother. She was surprised that her dad had been in jail, but fascinated that Adele had solved the case. Reilly told her that the murder was linked to her kidnapping, but he didn't know how. Then he paused and explained that her grandfather Fulton was somehow involved. This distressed Amy, but for the moment, she seemed to accept the news. It was clear to Reilly that Amy would need extra love and attention while she dealt with the developments that would follow. But this special evening, she was caught up in the spirit of celebration that grew as most of the gang gathered at Sam's and Mark's apartment.

When pictures of Brad Mungeon were shown around the village, his apartment perch and new persona were discovered. Fulton had cleaned up Brad and created Monty. Brad's fingerprints matched those from Richmond and the zipper pull. They also matched Raymond Gifford, a fugitive murderer from California. The police investigation of his roost soon led to the apartment in Springfield, where they found a ransom plot, or at least, so they thought at first. They uncovered a head-scratching conundrum. There were pictures of Amy and several ransom notes, but they didn't make sense. The notes were addressed *to* Fulton Wilcox. At first, the police were confused. The person they had caught kidnapping his own granddaughter had, for some reason, planned to send ransom notes to himself. In Gifford/Mungeon's coat pocket, they found an almost perfectly forged passport for Montgomery Mitchell and a one-way plane ticket to Costa Rica. Gradually, these contradictions resolved.

The strangest twist occurred the day after Wilcox had been arrested. Reilly learned about it later. It began with a phone call. Klarissa had dialed her mother from Canada to ask about Amy. Diane Wilcox had been devastated by her husband's arrest and completely blindsided by his machinations. When the phone rang she had been working up her courage to call Klarissa in England to tell her the awful news. Diane had had no idea that Klarissa was in

Canada and had known nothing about her expected visit with Amy. The stories they exchanged left them both aghast.

Klarissa told Diane that Fulton had promised to bring Amy to visit her in Canada. He had told her not to call Burlington, but she had had no choice. There had been no contact since Fulton's last call, and her return flight to England was that evening. When Diane realized that Klarissa didn't know her father had been arrested, she interrupted hysterically. She exclaimed that Fulton had been charged with a murder in Canaan. Klarissa's disbelief became fright when she had learned that Amy had been abducted then recovered. Diane struggled to control herself and tell the one piece of good news: Diane had spoken with Amy that morning. The girl was unharmed and talkative, but confused.

After this call, Klarissa decided to postpone returning to England and to travel to Burlington. In the meantime, the police learned that Klarissa was in Canada, waiting to receive the kidnapped girl. Just as they were expediting the paperwork to detain and question her, Klarissa stepped into the state police barracks in Williston, Vermont, inquiring about her father. The police were further surprised by her willingness to speak freely without a lawyer. This turned to astonishment when their investigation verified her story. They could find no evidence that she had broken the law.

During this time, Klarissa and her mother learned the extent of Fulton's infamy. They were mortified. Where they once had had the certainty of answers, they now had the insecurity of questions. How would their lives change without Fulton's contact and support? How could he have been so cold and distant? Was he really a calculating, heartless murderer? They spent hours wondering how they could have known so little about this man. He had always been arrogant and secretive, but the vicious side of his nature had been well hidden. Even while they were horrified by his actions, they started to look beyond themselves to Amy.

Meanwhile Adele and Reilly were spinning theories about how Klarissa must have been the mastermind to this sordid enterprise. It was in the middle of one of these conversations that the phone rang in Reilly's kitchen.

"Hello, Reilly." The monotone was familiar yet unexpected. "This is Klarissa." Reilly nearly dropped the phone. He had thought that she'd be in jail. All his theories about the murder and kidnapping were upended when he learned that she hadn't been accused of any crime.

This contact started a series of phone calls that helped them both assemble the fragments of information about Fulton and his wily activities. Reilly's dislike of Klarissa ran deep, but he needed to know the whole story behind her father's plan, and Klarissa desperately wanted news of Amy. There was a note of contrition in her voice that was new to Reilly. She wasn't as self-assured. To his surprise, she started to admit mistakes and slowly begin to take some responsibility for the harm she had caused Amy. Her remorse seemed sincere to Reilly, but he hesitated because of her history. When Adele heard about this change, she didn't buy one syllable.

After one of Reilly's longer talks with Klarissa, Adele spoke her mind. "Reilly, don't get taken in by that demented woman. It was her choice to step out of Amy's life right after the divorce. She left the next day after the court's custody judgment. She didn't try to postpone her exit for Amy's sake. How in hell can you believe anyone like that? And in England, she declared war to steal Amy from you. That's what you got from trusting her!"

"Right, and I still don't, but I can't hold her father's crime against her. I won't take risks, but I sense the possibility of change for Amy's sake."

Over several conversations, Reilly arranged some limited contact between Amy and her mother. Although he remained deeply distrustful, he recalled that even after London, he hadn't had the heart to sever all contacts. The Essex County court order was still in effect, giving Reilly full custody, and it now appeared that the state of Vermont had no interest in prosecuting Klarissa for having once violated it.

A bump in the road to reconciliation was Rita Webster. Reilly soon discovered that she and Donald Houle had had nothing to do with murder or kidnapping but that Rita had been spying on Reilly for a year and a half. She had called Klarissa to report a few days before the murder and found her missing. That is why Rita had thought the body might be Klarissa's. Reilly's disappointment with Rita was nothing new. What was different was Klarissa's admission of her interference and her apologies for it. This was new territory for Klarissa, who seldom admitted mistakes.

Three weeks after Reilly's release, he and Adele had figured out Fulton's plans. In the meantime, Reilly was pestered by all his friends for the details. He and Adele decided to invite their pals to a meal and explain the sordid tale. They planned the celebratory feast for the following Saturday evening at Reilly's home. When they heard, Cisco and Suzanne volunteered some champagne. Reilly had a case of brew that had just reached six weeks of aging, plus he planned to purchase a few bottles of Barolo. The week before the gathering, all Reilly's friends at school were in good cheer, anticipating the party.

Adele and Reilly agreed that Amy and Lottie should miss the long, convoluted explanation of the crime but join the gang for the festive meal. They made arrangements with Nellie Reindeau to tend the girls at her farmstead home up the road from Reilly's house and then return them to the celebration when Reilly called.

24.
Krug

It was an unusually warm early March afternoon. The above-freezing air and steady sunlight combined to compact the deep snow in Reilly's yard. Dripping icicles decorated the eaves outside his large picture window. He had recently delivered the girls up the road to chat with Nellie and play in their enormous cow barn. Lottie and Amy liked to chase the chickens, and Lottie wanted to place name tags on strings around the necks of the ducks. They loved to jump from the high rafters into the hayloft.

Soon, Reilly's driveway looked like a worse-for-wear used car lot. All his close friends crowded into the cozy living room, which overlooked wavy pastures with a thick winter crop of snow. Reilly and Adele had baked a feast, and a glorious blend of the aromas from roasting fowl, baking rice, potatoes, and steaming apple pies wafted from the kitchen.

Reilly took the floor and stood by the woodstove. The gang was arrayed on the sofa opposite and a cluster of mismatched chairs set around the large, warm room.

"Ladies and gentlemen . . . and Ross," he said.

Ross burped loudly. As everyone looked at him, he held up his mug and said, "Thank you. Thank you."

Adele stood on the other side of the stove and continued, "Ladies and gentlemen, we have gathered to help you solve a dastardly crime. Reilly and I think we finally have the scoop on what happened."

"That's right, and we want to do this as an old-fashioned guessing game," said Reilly. "We'll tell you what we know, and you'll tell us what it means. We'll toast the correct answers and razz the lame guesses. Along the way, we also will want to salute the heroes and heroines of our adventure. First, it's my honor to introduce to you our chief detective to fill in some background for you. Please welcome Adele Clayton!"

The crowd hooted, clapped, and whistled as Adele, in her shapely blue jeans and tight, red-plaid flannel shirt started in her largest voice. "We know about the spectacular end of the chase, but a few things happened before Ross, Conner, and Leo so manfully captured those two scumbags on Wallace Pond. Conner, Leo, Ross, please take a bow."

Conner, Leo, and Ross jumped to their feet and gave two exaggerated bows to the applause of all.

"As I was saying, there are a few things you need to know to play our game. First, as some of you may know, Reilly knew that Jake Paulson had a grudge against Klarissa. So as Reilly's A-number-one detective, I decided to check out Jake, the little charmer. Giving credit where it's due, I want to ask Leo Richards to take a bow for being my thug and bodyguard for the Jake interview. Leo, please take a bow; better yet, let's toast him." Adele raised her mug of home brew and said, "Here's to Leo Richards, consummate rent-a-thug."

"To Leo Richards, consummate rent-a-thug," the gang yelled back, clanking glasses and drinking brew.

"Thank you so much," said Leo, smiling broadly. "A puny kid from the Bronx has finally achieved his lifelong goal."

As the laughter subsided, Adele continued, "Well, we discovered that Klarissa had extracted a favor from gentle Jake. She took him with her for protection when she went to the Wildflower commune in Averill to investigate a woman who she heard was being abused. So this is where Brad and Paula come into the picture. Klarissa went there to investigate Brad, you remember, Bad Brad?" Adele questioned. The crowd booed and hissed.

She continued as the noise subsided. "She was trying to learn if Brad was beating up Paula, which . . . big surprise . . . he was. Well, anyway, she took pictures of Paula, replete with bruises, and she managed to sneak one of Mr. Brad."

"Wait! You're saying that Paula was living with the guy who murdered her?" Nancy exclaimed. "Wow, I get it . . . Klarissa saw that Paula resembled her and that Brad was the potential murdering-type of badass!"

"Wrong, Nancy, but nice try," said Reilly as a few boos were heard in the background. "That's what we thought when the jail door first closed on Klarissa's dear old dad, Fulton J. Wilcox, and his buddy Brad, but it wasn't true. Klarissa didn't make any such connection. She was just trying to protect Paula from the wild animal she lived with."

"But I don't get it," complained Joanie. "I don't see how Jake was involved. How did you figure this out?"

Adele, realizing that she was ahead of her audience said, "We know of three visits to the commune that connect all our characters. I'll tell you about them in the order they occurred. The first happened after the lady named Paula Dickson came to Mass one day at Father Xavier's church. This happened the spring before Klarissa left town. Father Xavier found out that Paula lived at the commune and wanted to attend Mass regularly. When she didn't appear at church, the good father traveled to the commune alone and found her living with Brad. He could see that she was being abused by him and reported this to Klarissa. This is why Klarissa wanted to go to the commune."

Adele paused, then continued, "Jake Paulson now comes into the picture, but he turns out to be an unimportant character in this plot, which, based on what you told me about him, seems appropriate. When Leo and I talked with Jake, we found out about the second crucial visit. This was when Klarissa used Jake as her bodyguard so she could go as a posse of two to the commune and investigate the abuse. It must have happened a few weeks after Father X reported that Brad was beating on Paula. Klarissa took those pictures that confirmed the abuse, but we guess that Paula refused to press charges. Klarissa kept the records of her talks with Father X and her visit to the commune. This is important because Fulton Wilcox later found these notes and pictures among Klarissa's belongings. We think he discovered the resemblance between Paula and Klarissa from the photos. There was also a sneak picture of Brad that turned out to be important because it probably allowed Fulton to figure out his identity.

"When I found out about the third commune visit, I had the key to the case. It happened last November. Fulton Wilcox induced Father X to take him to the commune to introduce him to Brad and Paula. Wilcox soon confirmed what he knew already by then: that Brad could be a murderer for hire and that Paula was a Klarissa look-alike. They lived in the same household and didn't care much for one another. That's an understatement, because Brad was a fugitive mur-derer, and Paula's interest in escape threatened his cover. She had become disposable. So Fulton J's brain and Brad's violence were cre-atively combined.

"This last piece fell in place when I discovered the resemblance between Paula and Klarissa. Then almost everything made sense."

"So the plan was her father's, not Klarissa's. I should say her wealthy father," interjected Suzanne.

"Thank you, Suzanne, brilliant as always," praised Reilly. Suzanne smiled beatifically to her grinning admirers.

"But, "continued Adele, "you might also have had some insider knowledge about the old fox. Please tell the folks about Bu-lee and Briggens."

All eyes turned to Suzanne sitting in the middle of the sofa as she started to speak. "Reilly remembered that Klarissa's old man was stationed in England during WWII and he worked in some branch of intelligence. He let slip that he was at an estate called Bu-lee and fre-quently visited a town called Briggens. It turns out that Bu-lee was a training site for the Special Operations Executive, or SOE, which sent agents into Europe to undermine German operations from behind their lines. This involved counterintelligence, bombing, even assassination. It turns out that Briggens was where the SOE created their forged documents."

"Could someone trained by this outfit mount an operation like Fulton J. did?" asked Big Frank.

"Well," replied Suzanne, "I forgot to mention that when we started up the CIA, this British agency was their model. They were used for large-scale, complicated operations. Their agents helped plan missions in which they might live unnoticed in a German-occupied town for more than a year before activating their assignment. They were under constant pressure. The Germans had equipment to locate their radio broadcasts. The simplest mistake could be their downfall. One agent who was subsequently tortured and hung was noticed walking on the left side of a sidewalk, English style. Agents could never relax while just trying to blend in with the locals. When they started destroying things, they were even more vulnerable. They had to be very cool and very smart. I can't imagine anyone doing what Fulton J. did without that kind of training."

"Wow, talk about a tough training school," mused Frank.

Reilly then turned to the group and spoke up. "And we know who to thank for this information. I give a toast to Suzanne, our lady of official secrets."

"To Suzanne, our lady of official secrets!" the crowd cheered.

As the glasses stopped clinking, Adele picked up the story again. "The police search of Klarissa's father's workshop at home revealed many items of interest. He had several sets of forged Vermont license plates which still had the shipping envelope from a small village in Belgium."

"That explains why several of us thought we were followed by the same truck but the plates were always different," said Conner.

"Right," said Adele, "but he was much sneakier than that. He had matching Vermont registration papers from some small town in Italy. The alternate sets of truck and car plates and corresponding paperwork matched actual Vermont vehicles. So Brad's black Ford pickup could masquerade as several different Vermont trucks. There were two other sets of plates that were complete phonies. There was no such vehicle registered in Vermont."

"That explains why Trooper Marshall couldn't trace the plate number I gave him," added Ross.

"But here's where things get really interesting," said Reilly. "They also found the forged paperwork most crucial to his black-magic plan. He had a complete set of phony identity papers for Klarissa and Amy with near-perfect Australian passports. They were the best forgeries the Vermont detectives had seen. He also had real plane tickets for two from Canada to Australia."

"So Klarissa, now deceased, is resurrected as a new person free to live a new life with her actual daughter," noted Nancy.

"I still don't get it," admitted Leo Richards. "Wasn't this Klarissa's idea?"

"Hold on for a minute and you'll see," said Reilly. "Where was I? Oh, yeah. I don't know if you remember how Klarissa stormed out of town a year ago last August. She didn't pack up her apartment. I knew her parents had come to town more than once, hauling stuff away to their house. We now know this included her winter clothing and her work journal, with its tales of Jake, Father X, Paula, and Brad. It also contained several pictures of Paula showing the bruises from where she had been beaten. Interestingly, as I mentioned, there was the sneak shot of Brad coming toward the cabin door. Klarissa's notes on Brad and his possible psychotic nature were there, as well as her speculation that they were both fugitives. Paula had mentioned California to her. Klarissa's father must have had a burst of insight when he noticed the resemblance between Klarissa and Paula."

"So how did the old man discover that Brad was the murdering type?" asked Joanie.

"Excellent question, Joanie," said Adele. "It looks like Fulton was pretty secretive and cautious. He used his law-enforcement connections and the photograph of Brad to investigate him. He may also have secretly lifted Brad's fingerprints when he visited the commune. When he narrowed the search to California, he discovered that Brad was wanted for two murders there. So Brad was a fugitive, and Fulton J. had that leverage on him. That was the stick. The carrot was big and, in this case, green. He offered Brad money and a new identity. Fulton had apparently stayed in touch over the years with the best technology that forgers had to offer. Brad was to have a complete new identity and a plane ticket to Costa Rica to relax in the sun and make his money last. The scheme hinged on Paula's resemblance to Klarissa and Fulton J.'s ability to fool the medical examiner. Then in Brad, he had discovered the ideal guy to kill Paula and frame Reilly. No one would miss Paula, so she'd be the perfect substitute. Oh, I didn't mention, Paula was just someone Brad had picked up driving across the country, and she's still a bit of a mystery. Her fingerprints aren't on file anywhere."

"Reilly, why didn't Fulton just kill you to get custody of Amy?" asked Joanie.

"We think two motivations fired Fulton's madness," replied Reilly. "He was moved by his deep hatred for me and his desire to return Amy to Klarissa, not to have custody himself. This was a guy who didn't want me to marry his daughter and didn't really warm to me even when his granddaughter was born. He was the bastard who looked at me across the courtroom with hateful glances both when I won custody in Guildhall and also at our rematch in London. We believe he financed and masterminded both fights and was in a cold fury because he lost. So, as he perceived it, I had beat him, and that really boiled his liver. And because of the abduction and my mistrust, I had been restricting their opportunities to visit Amy since last fall. This made him smolder all the more. We believe his masterstroke had two edges: He planned both to restore Amy to her mother and to put me into a special kind of hell—more satisfying from his point of view than just killing me. I'd be in prison for the rest of my life knowing that my daughter had disappeared and that I'd never see her again. It's just as brilliant as it is sick."

"I got it. I got it!" exclaimed Cisco, who had been thinking about another nuance. "I've figured out the body identification."

"OK, Cisco, show your stuff," laughed Adele.

"I think that the fingerprint set Klarissa's father provided to identify the body was forged. That is, the official-looking paper was forged, and the fingerprints were lifted from Paula, probably after they killed her. And the scar he identified was one he knew Paula had."

"Give Cisco a round of applause," continued Adele. There was applause and the clanking of mugs. "Yes, almost exactly. In fact, it was even a little slicker than that. He provided police with forged medical records and a lock of Paula's hair but gave them the actual paperwork accompanying a set of Klarissa's prints from a police station in England. Fulton had had prints done when she was a teenager. They apparently fingerprint children there as a courtesy to parents for making identifications in emergencies. In this case, the fingerprint document was real and the medical examiner actually called and checked their authenticity, but Klarissa's prints had been replaced by those lifted off Paula. And as Cisco said, Fulton also knew about a scar on Paula's arm. He told the medical examiner about the scar before viewing the body, and like magic, there it was. He was damn clever. That's also why the hair, footprints in the cellar, and the blood type all matched. It was simple; Paula simply matched herself while father finessed her misidentification. The medical examiner could have gone to dental records, but the first shotgun blast mid-scream pretty well scrambled her teeth . . . probably intentionally, so I guess they went with what must have seemed obvious."

"But how did Fulton J. arrange to meet Brad?" asked Ross. "Wouldn't it be kind of dangerous to go to the commune and say, 'Hi, Brad, I understand you have deep roots in California'?"

"We don't know how he did that, but we do know he risked having Father X show him to the commune. Maybe he thought that safer than going by himself."

Shelley piped up excitedly, "So, I can see how the murder eliminates Reilly. Klarissa grabs Amy and leaves the country, but how could she possibly escape after snatching Amy? I have never heard of a kidnapping in Vermont, and we scarcely have a dozen murders a year, so the press would have linked the kidnapping to the murder. I don't think his plan had a chance"

"And I can't imagine how Klarissa would agree to leave the country with Amy if she hadn't been part of the whole nasty plan," protested Shelley.

"Well, she wasn't in this country, but I'm getting ahead of myself," Reilly answered. "Klarissa's father is not one to underestimate. We now know he had Brad in his Monty persona rent an apartment in Springfield, Mass. After kidnapping and depositing Amy in Canada with Fulton, Brad was to drive to the Springfield apartment briefly and mail a ransom demand. Then he was to be off to a southern airport and sunny Costa Rica with lots of Fulton's money to spend. There were phone records and intentional clues left in Brad's Canaan apartment to the address in Springfield. They left other ransom notes and photos of Amy there for the police to find."

"Not ransom notes to Reilly, I should hope," said Cisco with a big grin. "He hasn't got a pot to piss in, and he still owes me fifteen bucks!"

As the laughter died down, Adele continued, "That was a big surprise. The ransom notes were addressed to Amy's poor, distressed grandfather, Fulton J., who had tragically just lost his daughter to murder. The tricky old fox made it look like the kidnapping was to tap his own wealth while he threw the police completely off the trail. We can assume all those documents were fingerprint free and nicely forged, or maybe they had Jack the Ripper's prints on them. I wouldn't put much past him. You remember how Brad appeared to flee south when he snatched Amy? That was part of his scheme, too. He wanted to be *seen* heading south, not doubling back to the border."

"Yeah, but that still leaves Klarissa," exclaimed Nancy. "Are you really sure she wasn't behind all this?"

"That was our biggest surprise," continued Adele. "Fulton arranged for Klarissa to come to Canada two days before the murder. He paid her way to fly there and drove up to meet her. He left her at a resort in the Laurentian Mountains northwest of Montreal, where she waited. He promised to bring Amy to visit her for a few days. Klarissa was between jobs again and agreed immediately. So while things were exploding here, Klarissa was waiting impatiently in Canada, not knowing anything about her father's bigger, badder plan."

"We now are pretty certain that Fulton was going to deliver Amy to Klarissa, not for a visit, but to present her with a deal she couldn't refuse. He would hand her the money and forged identities to live full-time with Amy in Australia. The only price in return would be her absolute silence, which would really be her complicity from that point on. If she were to refuse, her father would probably go to jail for murder. After Amy had been delivered to her in Canada, Klarissa would surely face kidnapping charges herself and lose Amy altogether. So, to expose her father's crimes, she'd lose both her daughter and her father and maybe have to go to jail besides."

"Wasn't Fulton even vaguely concerned about screwing up Amy? How did he expect her to play this new role?" asked Shelley.

"Well, he didn't care as you and I would," continued Adele. "We think he was blind to other people's emotions. Over the years, he learned to tune out the feelings of others. And for his intelligence training, he needed to be as cold as stone and seemed to expect the same from others. However, it does look as if he staged things initially so the body wouldn't be discovered while Amy was home."

"How do you know that?"

Reilly took over with the story. "We think they scouted my house thoroughly before the murder. He was a stickler for tight plans. We know Amy's invitation to Lottie's pajama party lay on Amy's desk that week the murder occurred. Plus, she commonly stayed with Adele and Lottie on Friday evenings, sometimes with me there and sometimes with a babysitter. We think the murder took place Friday morning and the body was set up to be found that Saturday morning. They probably had some backup plan to show the police my cellar. Adele thinks they would have called the fire department, maybe to report a fire in my cellar. Or there might have been an anonymous call from an alleged neighbor saying he had seen me drag a body up my back hill. Anyway, Amy was supposed to be out of the house when it happened. If they had succeeded in snatching her Friday night, they might have sprung the trap on me right away to eliminate me from the picture. Amy would be traumatized by the abduction, but she'd soon be heading north in Canada with her grandfather to the safety of her mom. She wouldn't know anything of the murder and mayhem left behind."

"That obviously didn't work, so what was his plan B?" asked Shelley.

"He had a problem because he didn't know where Amy was staying," said Adele. "He had Brad, alias Monty, looking for her. That was the phantom truck several of you saw as well as the reason for his break-in in Richmond. We think Brad saw me visit Father X on that Tuesday and somehow figured out that Amy was at Sam and Mark's place. Sam's apartment entrance is visible from Brad's high apartment on the corner. Anyway, that's when all hell broke loose. Brad thought that my visit to Father X meant that I was close to figuring out their plan. He followed me to the commune and tried to kill me. If he could eliminate me, he would buy time for the kidnapping. He planned to vanish, anyway, so what was another body? We don't know why Brad killed old Bessie, but he may have thought her an inconvenient witness to my murder."

"I think that you and that old lady would be frozen in storage out behind Brad's cabin if you hadn't escaped. That would have kept a lid on things for a while," Reilly added.

"Thanks, honey," Adele continued. "The snatch he made was probably his last chance. He had to make sure where Amy was located and then alert Fulton J., who could then drive through Norton Customs to the Canadian side of Wallace Pond. Those pieces were finally in place Tuesday afternoon, a few hours after he shot at me. When I drove through Norton in that snowstorm, I think I passed Fulton's car heading for the border crossing. After he grabbed Amy, Bad Brad headed south to throw us off the trail. Then he doubled back to Lake Wallace. If Conner hadn't figured out that he had turned onto Canaan Hill Road, their plot might have succeeded. Police would have found the truck, and the ransom note probably wouldn't have been mailed, so Brad and Dad would have had plenty to worry about. So, as I was saying, we owe Conner a debt of gratitude. Conner, please stand."

Conner grabbed the back of Frank's chair and stood to a wild round of clapping and hooting. "Thank you, thank you."

"Hey, it was the rest of us who told him to turn around," yelled Leo and Ross. The crowd grumbled and bantered good-naturedly.

"Well, I can tell you that I really like your whole story, but you know . . . I'd really prefer to eat." The crowd laughed while Cisco stood and continued, "But just before we do, I propose a champagne toast."

As Cisco was talking, Suzanne handed out Champagne flutes to everyone, and Nancy pulled two bottles of Champagne from a cooler around the corner. Cisco explained a bit about the Krug, saying it was the Frenchie stuff, not the California stuff. Cisco popped the corks dramatically to the cheers of all, and Nancy and Suzanne served the bubbly.

When everyone had a full glass, Cisco rose and said, "I propose a toast to the woman who saved Reilly and Amy. To the best-looking and smartest do-it-yourself detective in the North Country. To Adele Clayton."

All raised their voice,s "To Adele Clayton," and sipped what they found to be, despite Cisco's understatement, the finest champagne any of them had ever tasted.

Suzanne proposed a toast to Reilly, and the good cheer continued. In the meantime, Adele slipped over to the phone and invited the girls back from the neighbor's farm to share the feast.

Then Conner stood and raised his right arm, index finger pointing skyward, waiting for the noise to hush. In town-meeting style, he continued, "I make the motion that we eat! Is there a second?"

Hands went up around the room to the roar of laughter. "The motion has been seconded by Ross. All those in favor should try to beat me to the dinner table," Conner called out as he lurched for a chair in the nearby dining room. "Let's eat!"

Amy and Lottie arrived just after everyone else was seated. They returned exuberant after having named and petted every animal on Nellie's farm. The feast was a grand success, and there was hardly a bite of food left, although someone managed to salvage some fine table scraps for D'Ory and Trotsky. Everyone took a turn at entertaining the kids in their favorite way as the party went on until late evening. Folks scrubbed and straightened up before they left.

Ross insisted on being the last to leave so he got to read a bedtime story to two very sleepy girls. "Once upon and around a time . . ."

Adele and Reilly stood in the picture window watching last cars pull out of the snowy driveway to wend their way back toward the village. There had seldom been a better day.

25.
Woofus

Midsummer 1985

"He bit my finger!" cried Lottie as she squirmed in the back seat of Adele's car.

Reilly and Adele ignored the bumping and scrambling . . . then . . . "Hey, he's sucking on my ear," came Amy's giggling voice.

The little golden furball jumped down on the floor and started untying Lottie's shoelaces while his lamp-brush tail swished against Amy's leg.

"Hey, that tickles!"

Both girls were held back by their seat belts as they tried to reach the pup on the floor. Suddenly, the pup jumped up between them, and Lottie gave a squeaky half-scream.

"Girls, if you don't want to look after him, you can always hand him up front," laughed Reilly from the passenger seat.

"No way! No way!" chimed both girls.

Soon, the puppy was spinning on the back seat between the girls as each in succession tweaked his tail. When the pup turned on his tormentor, the other girl would tweak again, and the process would continue.

The giggling stopped, then the girls were strangely quiet and whispering for a few seconds.

Adele and Reilly knew they were up to their mischief.

"*Are we there yet?*" they belted out in unison.

Reilly caught Adele's eye and whispered, "Are you ready?" to which she nodded.

"*NO!*" they said even louder with a shared smile.

The girls turned their attention back to the puppy while Adele and Reilly enjoyed the brief diversion. Unlike the girls, they were in no rush to reach Bethel, Vermont, which was now less than twenty miles distant. Their apprehensions were building as they considered the same question: *What would it be like to meet Klarissa and Diane Wilcox face to face?*

Sometimes childhood scars heal invisibly. Occasionally, they add character at the cost of flexibility. Too often, whether in scar tissue or behavior, they extend the pain that caused them. Held secret, they can shape a life. This had been the course of Reilly's worry as he had cared for Amy after the kidnapping. Time, counseling, and a father's love had helped the healing. Although one element was missing, Reilly felt hopeful that Amy would heal unblemished.

Reilly and Adele's half families had merged in the summer after the kidnapping. They shared their lives in Reilly's rambling house. At first it had been the home of daily adjustments. Each girl would squabble and use the loyalty of her parent to leverage dissension that rippled the general harmony. Reilly soon negotiated a peace treaty by ceding his study to Lottie for her own bedroom. By fall, Adele's varying hours and Reilly's teaching obligations had framed a normal, but somewhat harried, home landscape. Reilly and Adele soon had found complementary ways to care for the girls. Life became easier, and their love remained intensely warm. Even on the bad days, all four knew from firsthand experience that life could be a whole lot worse.

As months passed, the combined household had bloomed with growing affection tempered by the confounding complexities of step-parenting. Lottie had started to bond with Reilly, and Amy had begun to feel the love of a mother and a home. Amy had gradually moved back on track at school, and each girl had found an instant sister who, despite adjustment problems, remained a good friend. Most of the time, the new family experience was welcome, and now with six puppies living on the back porch, the house bubbled with excitement and promise.

Two months before today's trip, Reilly had been perplexed by a blast of unwelcome news: Klarissa was returning to Vermont. Immediately after the kidnapping, he had banned all of Amy's contact with Klarissa and her mother but had relented a month later when he had fully understood Fulton's rogue behavior. Then for two years, the Atlantic Ocean had provided a convenient natural restraint that helped Amy focus on her improving life at home while allowing phone contact with her mother. Meanwhile, Reilly had arranged short visits with her grandmother in Burlington. Now he worried how Amy's renewed visitations with Klarissa would affect her adjustment at home.

Diane Wilcox's Burlington home had collected memory ghosts she needed to flee. Klarissa's arrival was timed to help her move to Bethel. They had been unpacking one morning when Reilly's call had started a pained and brittle conversation to arrange Amy's first visit.

Diane and Klarissa had been cordial when he and Amy arrived, but little had been exchanged in that emotional moment. Reilly had been so uneasy that he had chosen to observe Diane's house from a nearby hill all that afternoon. Subsequent visits had proved progressively less worrisome. In fact, over six weeks, Reilly had sensed a change in Klarissa's tone and attitude, which was reflected in Amy's cheerfulness following each visit.

While in England, Klarissa had struggled to accept any share of responsibility for her family's tragedy. In Bethel, she learned a new perspective on Reilly and Amy's home life. Then, Amy's first hug released a flood of tears and one key insight.

Reilly's dread of renewed contact had gradually resolved. He was relieved by Amy's progress but had had no idea what further sign of healing would make longer visits possible. Perhaps something would be revealed today.

This visit was the first to include Adele and Lottie. Klarissa and her mother had welcomed the idea. Reilly's family had planned a vacation in Maine, and the side trip to Bethel had been Amy's request. Adele had had no desire to meet Klarissa or her mother but reckoned that she could put up with almost anyone for an hour or so. She had only agreed to the plan after both girls had begged shamelessly.

The puppy gift was both girls' idea. Reilly consulted Klarissa secretly to make sure she and her mom were ready for a puppy whirlwind. She had been delighted by the gesture. Klarissa said that now that she had a steady job nearby and was well settled with her mother, a puppy would please them. The girls thought it would be wonderful to see one of D'Ory's and Trotsky's pups grow up there. Somehow, they intuitively knew that this was a way of sharing something more important than the gift itself.

That late-July morning, the sky had recently cleared after a shower, and the warm air was fragrant with the moist smell of freshly cut hay. Buttercups and Indian paintbrushes decorated the roadside as they turned into the drive of a large yellow Victorian house set against the White River and the lush green valley beyond. Amy shouted greetings while Adele pulled into the long driveway. Then Amy was running across the lawn with the pup and Lottie at her heels as Reilly and Adele walked casually behind.

After giving her mom and grandma hugs, Amy excitedly introduced Lottie. Klarissa and her mother told Lottie how happy they were to meet her. Amy then said, "Lottie and I have a present for you. We promised Trotsky and D'Ory that you would take very good care of their little pup. He doesn't have a real name, but Dad calls him Woofus. Maybe we can help you name him."

Lottie picked up the pup and handed him gently to Klarissa, who exclaimed, "What a handsome pup." Klarissa held the pup in her arms while Diane pet him to his unashamed delight.

As Adele and Reilly slowly climbed the stairs to the porch, Klarissa turned to look at them, and Reilly introduced Adele. In turn, Klarissa introduced her mother.

"I'm overwhelmed," said Klarissa. "Adele, thank you for coming. I've heard much about you from Amy." She turned to the girls and continued, "Thank you for this wonderful gift. He's the color of champagne, and I'm sure he will bring sparkle to our lives."

"Oh, I almost forgot," said Adele a little stiffly as she handed Diane a jar of clover-blossom honey from the Reindeau farm in Canaan, "we thought you might enjoy this in your tea."

"Why, thank you," Diane said graciously as she invited them up to sit on the large wooden chairs and wide swing on the porch.

By this time, the girls were playing a puppy-adapted game of keep-away using a ragged old tennis ball. Adele and Reilly sat on the porch with Klarissa and began to relax a little as her mother served them tea in bone china cups. The girls were served tall glasses of milk with long spoons and chocolate syrup. Soon, the girls went back to play on the lawn.

The adult conversation underwent a shift that surprised Adele and Reilly. At first, everyone was awkward and gently avoided difficult subjects. Remarks favored the puppy and the girls, who were now out of earshot. Then they began talking in a more ordinary way, still careful but a little less guarded. They spoke to the beauty of the season and then started to superficially catch up on each other's lives.

That accomplished, Klarissa paused and said in a gentle voice words Reilly would think about for years. "We have given a lot of thought to what happened two years ago. This is hard for me to say." She paused and shifted in her seat to look directly at Reilly. "Many things can't be undone. If I could undo the damage, I would. I can't change the past, but maybe in some small way, I can change the future."

Klarissa leaned back and looked up to the distant hills, then turned to Reilly and continued, "Season after season, I've hated and blamed you for what happened. I realize now that my anger hasn't let me see the truth about my father . . . and probably about you. More importantly, I know that my feelings toward you haven't helped Amy."

Her mother continued, "We know that you have reason to doubt us and we need to earn your trust for Amy's sake. We want to move beyond words . . . maybe after events like these, only action holds meaning. So we have promised ourselves to be steady for Amy and to support her emotionally, and we now make this same promise to you."

Diane paused and looked over to Adele, assuring her that she was addressing them both. "Klarissa has convinced me that we need to support both Amy and Lottie. Although we know it might not be much, we have also started saving to help you send both your girls to college. We hope that as we earn your trust, Amy can stay with us again. In fact, when you are ready, we would be thrilled to have both girls. We also hope you might invite us to the girls' school events."

Reilly and Adele were speechless in surprise. They had had modest hopes for a fresh start if all remembered civility and their common love of Amy. But this was especially touching. Their talk tapered into a calm silence as girls and puppy reappeared from the back yard.

A few hours later, their car crossed the eastern New Hampshire border into Maine. The girls were napping in the back seat while their parents talked quietly. Both Reilly and Adele, despite some discomfort at finally meeting together with Klarissa and her mother, felt they were bearing witness to a most improbable change in Klarissa and Diane, which had arisen from their despair. As they drove toward the Maine coast, Adele remarked to Reilly that she had been surprised by the meeting and felt that it held promise. In some strange way, it reminded her of the most meaningful of Quaker meetings, where there was a thread of inspiration in the ideas expressed spun from the best of heart and mind. Maybe it was the common trauma they had all endured and survived together. She didn't know, and preferred not to guess, but she felt something very unusual and special begin that bespoke the better side of human nature. She reached across and took Reilly's hand as he drove. A simple touch of the hand spoke the truth they felt and carried with them.

Epilogue

Sunset, early fall, 1984

Reilly's eyes sketched in red, blue, orange, green, and yellow . . . mostly yellow. His mind's canvas framed the western shoreline's horizontal symmetry with hillside forests in autumnal flames reflected in a rippling watercolor forest below. The complementary patterns of form and color melded as these cold flames were enlightened by the late-afternoon star. This was nature's grand exultation of shade and hue. The sky, too, mirrored horizontal, yellow-streaked clouds above its aquatic doublet. He looked high overhead to the glowing full-moon portent of the coming frost. As he again gazed over Big Averill, a pair of mallard ducks flew across the sunset sky. They were on flickering wings, which they then cupped rigidly still, floating thistle-down-like to the flat water. They created intersecting and expanding concentric rings on the almost-still surface. The sun's tangential light flattered the pair's plumage in, which Reilly sensed another unity and contrast. As he looked up to the approaching sunset, he thought of how the beauty of this quintessential fall day was perfect and unique. The sensations expanded his joy with the taste of spruce gum, the smell of venison stew, and the chatter of friends. With Amy and Lottie playing by the shore and Adele on the camp porch laughing, his world was complete.

After a delightful string of crystal summer days, a late August frost proclaimed the end of another Canaan green-tomato summer. Now, a month later, the tamaracks and hardwoods displayed their soon-to-be-sacrificed leaves with flamboyance. It was almost that fine scattering time when yellow, orange, and red leaves animate the air and define the fall breezes. A season's weight of leaves would soon brighten forest trails with their final yellow glow. Then they would fade to brittle brown in their submission to decay. They would be invested in the soil for future trees long after their brown hues had combined with residual grays of land and sky to speak of approaching winter. But not yet.

Reilly's hammer sent out staccato echoes that faded as his last pine boards completed a new toolshed between woods and water beside Adele's cabin on Big Averill. Reilly suddenly remembered that he had volunteered to stir the venison stew on the camp's kitchen stove. It was Ross's contribution to the feast from last fall's harvest, and Reilly was in charge of not burning it. He quickly cast his tools in the shed and jogged down the short path parallel to the lake shore, bounded up the steps, passing Adele, Cisco, and Suzanne on the porch before disappearing into the kitchen at the back of the large log cabin.

As he passed them, Reilly heard Adele telling Cisco for the second time the toast she intended to give, but he still enjoyed acting puzzled.

"Wait, wait, wait," insisted Cisco. "Let me understand this toast," he said, smiling. "So . . . you want to do a special toast. I can understand that . . . and I knew your uncle and would drink to Josh anytime . . . but what are these important things you want us to toast?" Cisco was sipping a glass of Reilly's best Riojan red. Adele had just told him about her promise to her uncle and how she had requested that all gather again at sundown when she'd invite everyone to join her in a toast.

Cisco and Suzanne were sitting in weathered Adirondack chairs, and Adele was standing on the top step, leaning on a front-porch rail of the rustic cabin on the eastern shore of Big Averill: the camp Adele had recently inherited. It was the last Saturday of September. It was a time when the descending sun, vivid fall colors, and the still water they viewed to the west could make an Impressionist painter tipsy. Reilly appeared out of the kitchen and stopped to listen.

Most of Reilly's and Adele's close friends were nearby. They had all gathered for a potluck dinner by the lake. Some of the gang were playing volleyball on the side lawn. Others were out in canoes, paddling toward camp. Adele and Lottie were playing by the edge of the water with occasional adult incitement. Leo Richards was throwing a stick out in the water for the two golden retrievers to fetch.

Conner had just challenged Lottie and Amy to see who could make a flat stone skip on water the most times. After practice and repeated tries, Lottie managed eight skips on her best throw. Amy reached seven when Conner, on his last try, skidded a round, flat piece of basalt for ten skips and was about to crow as champion. But then Nancy Watkins sneaked up behind Conner and gave him a push with her hip that almost knocked him off a flat rock and into the lake. Nancy then went close to the water's edge and prepared to throw a beautifully smooth rounded, thin piece of shale. She swung her shapely hips to one side and made a perfectly smooth sidearm throw that sent the stone forth level for one, two, three, another, another, again, and again, and, as both girls counted aloud, faster than the numbers would come forth, for fourteen skips as shouted by Amy and fifteen as cheered by Lottie. Nancy, who stood with both hands in the air, acknowledging the girls' cheers, turned defiantly to Conner and yelled, "There!" Just then, Trotsky shook off about a gallon of water right behind Nancy. Conner near doubled up laughing.

At Ross's suggestion, the girls decided to make boats out of walnut shells using bubblegum wads to support toothpick masts with impaled paper sails. They were about to launch their boats for a race. Ross, who had planned ahead, provided the materials and coached the boat building while reluctantly foregoing an entry of his own. He also personally volunteered to provide the wind power to "motorvate" the boats, as he called it. Katie had agreed to provide floating sticks for the start and finish lines and to judge the contest. Adele and Reilly enjoyed watching this develop, wondering how Ross could be the big wind and not get soaked.

The ostensible occasion for the gathering was the first day of partridge season, which Reilly considered the most important, yet unrecognized, Vermont holiday. It always came on the last Saturday in September. He and Trotsky had hunted most of the day and had two partridges in his game bag. His tradition was to have a fine game feast and wine that day. For Adele, the gathering was the perfect confluence of place, time, people, and beauty. She felt a wonderful rush of excitement as sunset approached. It was the peak of Vermont's colors viewed from an incomparable location. Distracted momentarily by nostalgia and beauty, Adele remembered Cisco's question about her toast and turned back to reply.

"Cisco," she said while thinking about the best way to illustrate her idea about important things. She paused for several seconds before saying in a stately manner, "It's like this." She slowly pointed from one side of the extraordinary scene to the other. Cisco stopped to think about Adele's comment and stared across the water.

By now, Lake Averill's waters and the clouds above had assumed bright peach-skin hues. The hills were still radiant in late-afternoon light. Around the shore and far back onto the rounded hills, the woods appeared a splashy pallet of color-wild maples, birch, and beech interspersed with stately green pine, spruce, and a few odd yellowing tamaracks. A few hardwoods were yet to take their turn to yellow. Some of those now-dominant yellows were progressing to sunny orange. Fewer yet of the orange hues had gone fire-red. This was nothing less than nature's total protest to dullness: a display of color extraordinarily rare in time and place.

To their left, two canoes were approaching. Conner and Karen were in the lead, Gene and Shelley in their wake. The late sun defined the curved lines of the canoe gunnels, and the paddlers' shadows on the water illustrated their grace of movement. The total effect made it seem as if beauty could stop the memory of time.

"You mean," replied Cisco, "like this . . . meaning places so beautiful that you have to gawk at them?"

"This is a scene so beautiful that it almost makes me cry, but gawk or cry, this moves us all. To me, it's a kind of experience we should celebrate and discuss."

"So is seeing it the important thing, or is talking about it?" queried Cisco slyly.

"Well, I don't know . . . but you can't talk about it if you don't notice it. I'm using an idea my dad and Uncle Josh would sometimes talk about." Adele laughed and continued as she swept her hand around toward the sky, "I'm sure Dad and Uncle Josh would think anyone a dolt who didn't respond to this. But they would say that people often don't talk about deeply meaningful experiences, so in this case, the failure to mention this view would be to miss a superb opportunity."

"Then if I follow the flow of this conversation, I think we qualify because we have acknowledged one of the most wondrous sights of the year," Suzanne said with a smile. Adele nodded yes.

Cisco, knowing Adele well, said, "What makes me think that the phrase could mean other things or ideas besides?"

"I've never tried to explain this before, but I'm game to try. Look around again and search for something notable that is not visual beauty," suggested Adele.

"I see a group of great friends having fun together. They're making this a special time for Reilly and the girls, particularly on his own personal bird-hunting holiday," mused Suzanne.

"Right," said Adele. "Our gathering and friendship are crucial to us. And by recognizing this time as special, I think that qualifies, too. If you look at the girls, what do you see?"

Suzanne gazed at the shore, where both girls had their jeans rolled up and were ankle deep in the water, cheering wildly. Ross was on wet knees by the water's edge, blowing himself dizzy as the sails of two wildly gyrating miniature sailboats skittered toward Katie's finish line.

"I see kids using their imagination to play. That's important. I teach some kids who can't do that anymore," remarked Suzanne.

"Right," said Adele, who then explained to Cisco and Suzanne her dad's experience of Quaker meetings, where he had found that people expressed thoughts and experiences they didn't elsewhere. How he had listened to these statements and puzzled why people didn't more commonly talk about such things.

"So, that's my toast. I think you get the idea," added Adele. "It's just an invitation. You are the one who will choose your own meaning, but it amazes me how often people speaking from the heart agree on what really matters."

Reilly, who had been listening from the back of the porch, returned inside the cabin to prepare for the toast. Meanwhile,

Conner, Karen, Ross, and Shelley dragged the canoes up on shore and joined the others on the porch who were listening to the conversation.

"So, if I hear you right, you also mean discussing birth and death and why we believe something is moral or immoral, or maybe even the meaning of life?" questioned Suzanne.

"Hey!" said Cisco with a mischievous smile. "But what if you already know these things . . . say, like the meaning of life?"

"Then we'll all appreciate when you explain it to the whole group over dinner," joked Adele.

"Yeah, Cisco, we can't wait," ribbed Leo and Ross to smiles and laughs all around.

Adele then looked far to the west, where the sun was gently nested on the edge of the most distant hills. From the cabin came the quiet sound of liquids pouring and the tinkle of glasses.

"OK," announced Adele with joyful eyes, "it's approaching sunset, and although this place is now mine, it will always truly be Uncle Josh's camp. I promised him to toast him from this porch whenever I was here at sunset. There just couldn't be a finer day for doing it than this one. And there couldn't be a better set of friends to join me."

Reilly carried a tray from within the camp and handed out mugs of root beer for Lottie and Amy and glasses of the fine Spanish red for everyone else. Reilly sat and gestured for Amy to squeeze next to him on the chair. Adele moved back to the top step, beckoning Lottie to her side and putting one arm over her daughter's shoulder. When everyone was ready, Adele stood and casually turned to the group with her glass in hand. "I was going to do this toast to Uncle Josh, but I'm sure he wouldn't mind me being more inclusive."

She raised her glass to the lake and woods and then to the girls and, finally, to the motley crew of friends who cohered famously. "To love, family, friends, and important things."

The girls looked up to Adele and raised their heavy mugs. Reilly winked to Adele as he raised his glass. Cisco and Suzanne held their glasses high in admiration. The rest of their friends lifted and clinked their glasses as they all repeated, "To love, family, friends, and important things."

As the earth turned, the rich smell of dinner lured everyone inside to the long table in the cabin's front room. Table topics, with both girls assertively involved, ranged from frogs to dragons to pruning perfect Christmas trees. Conner rose to tell some outrageous stories, and Cisco lovingly kidded Adele about defining important things. Reilly then stood and requested a vote on an unusual motion. He made a strong argument that the group declare that September day the start of a new year. He said it was a worthy and wondrous benchmark by virtue of its outstanding quality, and besides, who had any reason to think January first was a better choice. Members of the group were surprised and skeptical at first, but no one could come up with a good reason to defend the status quo. Reilly pointed out forcefully that January first was neither the shortest nor longest day of the year, nor the time when the earth was closest or furthest from the sun. Cisco agreed and declared traditional New Year's Day once and for all astronomically irrelevant. A few alternative days, including birthdays of group members, were tossed around, but the present moment seemed especially magical, so Reilly's proposal was soon brought to a vote. The measure carried unanimously, to the cheers of all.

And why not? This was every much the start of a year as any day and, for the same reasons, just as appropriate an end. And who should dare say where the earth starts or finishes its revolution around our star? For change is paradoxically constant, and there and then, in a small cabin on a North Country lake, the fire of love flared most brightly, providing heat for the soul and light for the year ahead.

Shadow on Cant-dog Hill

A Tale of Love, Mystery, and Redemption in
Vermont's Northeast Kingdom

By John H. Vibber

First published by Dog Ear Publishing
4010 W. 86th Street, Ste H
Indianapolis, IN 46268
www.dogearpublishing.net

ISBN:978-160844-108-2

This book is printed on acid-free paper.

Printed in the United States of America